MUSTANG

BLACK OPS MMA BOOK 5

D.M. DAVIS

MUSTANG
Black Ops MMA Series by D.M. DAVIS

Published by D.M. DAVIS

ISBN – 979-8-9869509-6-9

www.dmckdavis.com
Cover Design by D.M. DAVIS
Cover Photo by Michelle Lancaster
Cover Model: David Tomasic
Editing by Tamara Mataya
Proofreading by Mountains Wanted Publishing & Indie Author Services
Formatting by Champagne Book Design

This book is a work of fiction. Names, characters, places, and incidents are either the product of the author's imagination or are used fictitiously.

The octagonal competition mat and fenced-in design are registered trademarks and/or trade dress of Zuffa, LLC.

This story contains mature themes, strong language, and sexual situations. It is intended for adult readers. Some scenes may have triggers.

ABOUT THE BOOK

**My mangled heart beats for *her*, but hers beats for
him… And maybe *me*.**

I've never been one for norms. I fight *and* bake for a living.
Why should I expect my sex-life to be any different?
And I don't mean *love*-life. I don't do *love*.
I've been there. Done that. My heart is mangled for a reason.
My best friend, Walker, and I like to share… As in *together*.
I'm a transactional, one-time only kinda guy.

Then we met *her*.

She set off a seismic tremor that threatened to crumble
the wall around my heart.
She haunts my thoughts, sinking under my skin like a demon.
Unrelenting.
Remorseless.
I hate how easily thoughts of her sway my body and mind.
It's a constant battle of wills between what I *want* and what I can *have*.

She's not meant for *me*. I'm not *her* forever, regardless of Walker or my
treacherous heart trying to convince me otherwise.

I'm her *right now*—that's all I can ever be.

D.M. Davis' **MUSTANG** is an angsty, heart clenching, why-choose,
contemporary sports romance that has Jess fighting his desires, Walker
praying he won't be forgotten, and Berklyn willing to lose them both
because she *won't* choose one over the other.

MUSTANG is Book Five and the last in the *Black Ops MMA* series.

NOTE TO READER

Dear Reader,

First off, thank you for picking **MUSTANG** as your next read. I'm deeply grateful and appreciative, and for that reason, I want to advise:

For maximum enjoyment, I suggest the *Black Ops MMA* Series be read in order to fully experience the world and the yummy alphas (and their amazing women) who inhabit it. Though each book is a standalone—MUSTANG more than the others—they are integrated with subplots that carry through Books 1-4.

Please start with NO MERCY, ROWDY, CAPTAIN, and COWBOY before diving into **MUSTANG**. I promise you won't be disappointed with all their yummy angsty goodness.

Content Note: MUSTANG is a *why-choose* love story with multiple partners and an HEA.

XOXO,
Dana
(D.M. DAVIS)

PLAYLIST

Savin' Me by Nickelback
Desire by Ryan Adams
Turn me On by Nora Jones
Violin by Amos Lee
Daydream by Lily Meola
Crazy (I Remember When) by Anthony Gargiula
Wrap Your Arms Around Me by Gareth Dunlop
Love in the Dark by Adele
Before You Go by Lewis Capaldi
Wasted On You by Morgan Wallen
I See Red by Everybody Loves an Outlaw
Just Say I'm Sorry by P!nk, Chris Stapleton
If I Need You by Lyle Lovett
Lost on You by Lewis Capaldi
Every Little Thing She Does by Sleeping at Last
Kiss Me by Dermot Kennedy
Breakeven by The Script
Lost Cause by P!nk
Dive by Ed Sheeran
Have a Little Faith In Me by John Hiatt
Hurt Somebody by The Dirt Drifters
Wild Love by James Bay
Crashing Down by Elyse Myers
Pointless by Lewis Capaldi
Lift Me Up by Rihanna
No Ordinary by Labrinth
Turning Page by Sleeping at Last

Fight Entrance Song:
Follow You Home by Nickelback

DEDICATION

For those of us who are intrinsically everyday normal, yet on a deeper level, there is something special that drives us to *be* different—to *have* different.

MUSTANG

BLACK OPS MMA BOOK 5

CHAPTER 1

BERKLYN

BREATHE IN. BREATHE OUT. I'M MAKING LEMONADE.

It's all good. I don't smell like puke.

I don't smell like puke.

I'm making lemonade.

It's all good.

I definitely don't smell—

"You smell like puke. Here." Nadine sets a change of clothes on the bench behind me and heads for a bathroom stall. "They're my back-up-backup scrubs. Return them when you can."

I eye her offering and sigh. "Thanks. I really appreciate it." It's my third change of clothes today. I usually prepare well enough to make it through my shifts, but today has been especially… Messy.

Some days I make it all day without a spill or changing clothes. Other days, like today, it's a madhouse where I seem to be a magnet for bodily fluids, spilled coffee, or whatever I ate for lunch.

"Is it a full moon? It has to be, right?" I aimlessly scrub my neck, chest, and stomach for the umpteenth time, cursing myself for not packing an extra bra. This one is drenched. I'm going to be freezing later.

Cold nips for the win.

Nadine chuckles from the other side of the stall wall. "No. Seems like, though." She flushes and comes to stand beside me, washing her hands. "It's slowed down. Thank God." She eyes my chest as I use paper towels to squeeze the cups of my bra, hoping to suck up enough moisture to not seep through the scrubs. She motions to her locker. "Hair dryer will help."

"Oh, yeah, that'll work." Or will it lock in the puke smell? So gross. I shudder. Blood, I'm good with. Puke, not so much. "Thanks. Again."

I'm not a first-year. This is not my first rodeo.

I'm making lemonade. It's all good.

"Oh, Berklyn," she stops at the door, looking over her shoulder, "your guys are back. They asked for you."

I freeze. *My guys?* Butterflies erupt in my tummy. *My. Guys.* I don't ask who she's referring to. I know. "They're not my guys," I grumble. I kinda wish they were. They've been coming in for months, one or both of them injured. Since the first time I rushed to Jess to staunch the flow of blood from a head laceration, they've been asking for me. I dread their visits nearly as much as I crave them.

What's wrong with me? I can't like *both* men. Walker is a sweetheart. What's not to love? As for Jess, well, he's a bit of an a-hole. Besides, I'm not sure he can even stand me. Yet, there's something… "Where?"

"Bay six." Her smile is sympathetic at my state of dress—or more like, my undress. "I'll let them know you'll be a minute."

Yeah, a minute or thirty. I toss the paper towels and stand straight, scrutinizing my reflection in my black bra and panties, curves everywhere, even in places I wish they weren't.

Deep breath. In. Out.

I swipe at the smeared mascara under my eyes, finger tendrils of coppery hair back into my messy bun, and punch out my flushed cheeks on an exhale. It's nearly the end of my shift—and it shows.

I'm making lemonade, I chant after doing my best to dry my bra with the hair dryer and wrangle my body into the borrowed, too small scrubs, exasperated I ate a hamburger and fries for lunch instead of a salad. A very small one. These scrubs only accommodate salad eaters, apparently.

Sweat beading on my forehead and over my top lip, I suck in a breath and think thin as I tug the top down and over my waist and hips, unable to avoid a glimpse in the mirror. They're indecently tight. At least they're purple—one of my favorite colors.

Wish they were black.

It's all good.

It's all good.

I dab at my face and wash my hands one more time before clipping my badge on and sniffing my arms and shirt. "Do I smell like puke?"

I don't know if the smell is in my nose, stuck in my brain, or if I have to burn this bra. I don't have time for a shower despite the desire to smell good—or at least not offensive. I shrug again, catching my reflection as I pack my stuff away in my locker to deal with later. I look like a pug in purple spandex. They won't want to get close enough to smell me.

JESS

I nearly swallow my tongue when five and a half feet of luscious curves tightly covered in purple scrubs pulls back the ER curtain, her green eyes locking on me before landing on Walker, smiling like he's just won the lottery.

When it comes to the Doc, I suppose he has.

I tamp down the jealous bone that threatens to beat him over the head. He's already bleeding... Can't hit a man when he's down.

"Hey, Doc." Walker waves like an idiot. I want to smack him all over again.

He's supposed to be playing it cool, not acting like some teenager who's drooling over his first set of titties. Though, damn, said titties are looking like they need to be set free. Just one slice of a scalpel right down the center of her top should do it.

Berklyn's brow puckers as she takes in Walker's bloody shirt and blood-soaked bandage above his right eye. "I'd like to say it's good to see you gentlemen, but I'd be lying."

Gentlemen. I don't know why that gets my engine revving. We're far from gentlemen.

"Oh, don't say that, Dr. Berk—"

"Fortier—" she interjects, fighting a smile. Walker will never call her that.

"—you love us. No one takes better care of us than you, Doc." Walker practically pants, begging for a treat like the dog he is. He doesn't even care he's injured.

When Gabriel's hit landed and the blood started dripping, Walker grabbed me and practically ran out of the gym, spouting, "It's been too long since we've seen Doc."

It hasn't been that long. Maybe a month. I met her nearly six months ago, busted my head in a car accident. Walker came to drive me home, but when he saw Berklyn, he fell in love. All I felt was the deep desire to own every inch of her body inside and out. It was—is—lust, pure and simple, for me.

Berklyn's narrowing eyes meet mine. "You do this?"

My stupid heart pings at the heat in her tone and accusatory brow.

I step closer, leaning in, breathing in her floral shampoo, and considering her attire. "You just come out of the dryer, Dr. Fortier?"

Walker might not call her by her formal title, but I have no qualms giving her the respect she deserves. It's just that *Doc* seems too mundane for a looker like her with brains to boot.

My roommate frowns, punching my biceps. "Be nice," he mumbles.

"I, uh…" Berklyn's blush lures me in closer. She's embarrassed, and it only feeds the beast in me.

I can't help pushing till she pushes back. "Let me know if you need me to cut you out of your scrubs later. Might need the jaws of life."

"Shit." Walker balks as her eyes fill with hurt. I ignore him. The looker in front of me has my undivided attention.

Her eyes narrow as she finds her mettle, remembering she doesn't take flack off me or anyone else.

Tell me off, Berklyn. Give it to me. I salivate in anticipation.

"Since lunch, I've been covered in blood, urine, and puke. I've run out of clothes." She crosses her arms over her chest, which only accentuates the state of her tight-in-all-the-right-places attire. "I'm sorry I'm not up to your standards, Mr. *Mustang* Riley." She spits out my name like I'm dirt on her tongue, the bones of her oppressors she's had to defeat and step over to get to where she is.

"Damn, Berk. So fucking hot," I practically growl in her face, wanting to devour her right here—wanting to kiss the sneer from her lips—

What the fuck? I don't do that. I don't kiss. Not her. Not anyone.

At least not on the mouth.

She opens said mouth and closes it just as fast, turning to Walker but mumbling over her shoulder, "It's Doctor Fortier."

"I know. Hot as fuck." The bite in my tone is not for her but for my wayward thoughts. I lose my mind around her. She makes me forget, makes me want things I have no business wanting.

Her blush is back. So beautiful. I can practically smell the flush on her skin, like sunshine and lilies.

She's not a toy.

Not a plaything.

Though, I'd sure love to play with her for as long as she'd let me. Let *us*.

Walker glares death at me. "Forgive him. He was born without manners."

"You sure he was *born* and not *forged?*" Her lips curve just a smidge as she fights a smile.

There's my Spitfire.

Walker laughs. "Naw, Doc, he just doesn't know how to deal with all this sexual energy buzzing around us." He nudges her hand. "Stitch me up, then come have drinks with us. I promise he'll be good."

"Good?" She eyes me as I hold my breath, waiting on her answer now he's gone and formally put our interest out there. "Do you know the meaning? Do you need a dictionary?"

I lean down and whisper in her ear, across her neck, "I think maybe you could inspire all kinds of *good* out of me, *Dr. Fortier.*"

"Please give my patient and me privacy."

It's no rejection—her eyes twinkle for me as she says it.

"Yes, ma'am." I step back to give them space.

I could play this game all day, but Walker really does need stiches.

CHAPTER 2

BERKLYN

H E'S SWEET. ALWAYS HAS BEEN. WITH WALKER,
what you see is what you get. And what you see is hot, athletic
perfection, dark blond hair, and golden eyes that shimmer with life
and a touch of uncertainty that makes him almost seem attainable. His
smile is easy, his compliments easier, with a ready laugh and a teasing
smirk.

He's the polar opposite of Jess with his dark hair and even darker demeanor. The only thing light about Jess is the hue of his iridescent green
eyes. He's temptingly hot, radiating sex like an underwear billboard on
steroids. Walker swears Jess is not always an ass—I haven't seen his al-
leged sweetness other than his panty-melting flirtations, which are more
dirty than sweet.

Jess Mustang Riley makes my blood hot and my temper boil.

"He doesn't mean it, Doc," Walker whispers after Jess steps out of the
bay to call Gabriel, who I've met a time or two with his own injuries. He's

the one who did damage to Walker's face today. The thought of Walker getting hurt doesn't sit well with me. The unexpected need to protect him and his handsome face is unsettling, and I almost feel bad for assuming Jess is the one who hurt Walker.

Without Jess in my space stealing all the air from my lungs, it's easy to focus on my patient again. He's so good at blending into the background when Jess and I interact, it occurs to me that he may be sort of… Wingmanning for Jess while flirting with me too.

Does that mean they're actually both interested in me?

I'm not sure how you shamelessly start dating two men, but these two combined could tempt a saint.

Standing between Walker's spread legs, closer than is appropriate or needed, my gaze slides to his as I slowly peel off the bandage above his right eye. "You don't need to defend him. Or me."

"I feel like I do." The worry in his eyes suggests he's the peacemaker.

His tenderness has me smiling despite the topic. "I'm a big girl. I can take care of myself."

"Yeah." His hand I've been trying to ignore since traveling from my thigh to my hips, squeezes and sends a shiver down my spine. "I know. He respects you. He just likes to push your buttons. It's hot when you push back."

I arch a brow. "You two—"

"Are sexy as fuck and you wanna have that drink with us? Or food. We'd be happy to feed you too." So much hope resides in his eyes.

I want to say yes. I *always* want to say yes. But it's complicated. They've been my patients. They're overwhelming with their attention and focus. I'm not sure I'd survive an evening with either one of them, much less both. Walker's earnest desire to please balanced against Jess' desire to antagonize a reaction out of me is intense. I'm not sure I'm equipped to deal with what saying yes would entail.

"That's not—"

"Say yes, Doc. You won't be sorry." He squeezes my hip again, sending more tingles along my skin, settling between my thighs.

For a moment, I forget about my too-tight scrubs and the *extra* that lies beneath. "How do you see this playing out? I go out with you both. We have a great time getting to know each other. Then what? Choose one of you at the end of the night like a bad reality television show?"

His smile brightens the ER bay as he scans my face before locking me in his heated gaze. "Why choose, Berklyn, when you can have us both?"

I freeze, everything stills except my racing heart. "What?" I whisper, finding air hard to come by even with Jess out of sight. "Are you serious?"

"Look. I know it seems like I'm the easygoing one and he's the ass. But he's not always like that, and I'm not always easy. We're never just one thing. We both want you. I won't fight him over you, nor will he—"

"Bros before hoes and all that, right?" My flippant reply is laced with inexplicable hurt over this unexpected and entirely too personal discussion they've obviously already had without me.

The corners of his mouth turn down as he tips my chin, keeping my gaze on him. "*I* didn't say that. You're not a ho." His vehemence takes me by surprise. He did say he's not always the easygoing one. I try to step back, but his hold stops me. "We enjoy sharing, and we want to share you."

"*Share* me?!"

WALKER

I'm screwing this up. Jess is the closer. *Where the fuck is he?* This is his area. I woo with kindness and intrigue. Jess closes with the broodiness and sultry promises. It's not an act. It's who we are. We know our strengths, and right now, I'm fucking this up, jumping the gun. I can't help it. My patience is undone in her presence. The idea of going another month or two before we're bleeding and get another chance to lock her in has me pushing forward without my wingman.

But shock and awe are all that greet me after I tell Berklyn we want to *share her*. While I've never been so brazen in the presentation before, it's a compliment, right? What woman wouldn't want two guys taking care of her, seeing to her needs, making her come so many times her brain melts?

Her hands don't shake, but I swear she's trembling as she stitches me up. A stupid cut I never should have gotten if I'd seen it coming.

Yet, I'm not sorry. It's landed me here with her focus on me. Her hands on me. And her delicious floral scent coating every inhale of life-affirming air, despite the undertones of puke and whatever other fluids have been thrust upon her. Her natural scent is etched in my brain. No work-related disaster will ever change that.

I've never seen her out of scrubs, but I have no doubt she'll be hot in anything—especially nothing at all. She's curvy in the best places, enough to hold on to and not feel like she might break if taken too hard. Also the best to cuddle after a great fuck or on a lazy night watching TV.

So what? I jumped the gun. I'm not sorry one bit. I can do this. I can close the deal.

"I didn't mean to freak you out," I break the silence as she knots the last suture on a deep exhale as if she was working extra hard to stay focused.

"No?" She avoids making eye contact. That won't do. I need her eyes on mine, if only fleetingly.

"No." I bite the reflex to flinch as she cleans up my wound and the blood on my face. Her focus on my lips has my heart pounding and my grip on both hips now tightening. "You don't need to clean me up, Doc. I can do it when I get home."

Her green eyes finally land on mine. "You're probably an expert at cleaning up your injuries, huh?"

"Yeah, comes with the job. I don't mind. I'm not squeamish."

She laughs, shaking her head. "That why you declined Novocain?"

"Nah, I declined so you'd know how tough I am," I say it teasingly, but it's no lie. She sees me as a softie. I want her to know I'm more than that.

"Declining drugs is *stupid*, not tough." Her scolding only makes me want her more, does things to my insides.

Put me in my place, Doc. Show me you care. "Hey, at least I let you stitch me up this time."

She crosses her arms, popping her hip. "Doesn't your fight club have its own cutman?"

I bark out a laugh. "It's not a *club*, Doc. I'm a professional fighter. It's not a hobby. And, yes, we do, but you do a better job. Plus, how else am I supposed to ask you out? You won't give me your phone number."

Her eyes narrow. "Tell me you didn't get hurt just so you could see me."

Naw, never do that. "I'm not gonna lie. The thought has crossed my mind. But no," I motion to my eye, "this was earned the old-fashioned way. An elbow to the face." *I didn't see coming.* I scrub the thought from my brain. I can't do anything about it. It's a consequence of the job I signed up for.

"Jess really didn't do this to you?"

"No. I was sparring with Gabriel, getting ready for a match." I tug on the hem of her scrub top. "You should come see me fight, then help me recover afterwards."

She releases the smile she's been fighting. "You never give up, do you?"

I rarely give up on something I want. "Come have drinks with us on Friday." I hold out my hand. "Give me your phone. I'll put in our numbers, and you can think about it."

Neither of us breathes as she hesitates, considering. "Just drinks?"

"Drinks. Dinner. Whatever you want." A house. Kids. Truly. *Whatever* she wants. I don't mention the *sharing* stuff again. She's leaning into the idea, and I don't want to shove her in the wrong direction by saying something stupid.

Her smile is addicting. "I'll think about it." She hands over her unlocked phone. "No promises."

"Good. In the meantime, you need anything, I mean *anything*, you call, text, send smoke signals, I'm there—*we're* there."

"You're intense." She backs up, making notes on her tablet.

Yeah, like a fox. I add both Jess and my numbers to her contacts. I favorite them and text myself before she can even catch what I'm doing. "All set." I return her phone.

She eyes me. "I don't suppose you'll accept a prescription for pain meds this time?"

"Nope." Acetaminophen and occasional ibuprofen are about as medicated as I get.

"Watch out for infection. I know you know the signs. Come back," she trails off, eyeing her phone, "or, I guess, call me if you think you need an antibiotic."

There it is. My way in. She cares. She'd take my call just to be sure I'm doing okay. "Or you could check me out yourself over dinner and drinks on Friday," I suggest in case she forgot. *Not likely.*

"Or maybe that. I'll let you know." She turns to leave but stops. "It's good to see you, Walker." Her gaze feels like a warm caress as she checks out her handiwork but frowns at the blood on my shirt. "Try not to get hit in the face till that heals."

"Yes, ma'am. Doctor's orders." I give her a smile when all I really want to do is pull her closer and give her a kiss—give her everything, *anything* she wants.

CHAPTER 3

JESS

THE WEIGHTS CAN'T BE THIS DAMN HEAVY. I CHECK the barbell, count the discs and catch Jonah's arched brow as I struggle through my set.

"You okay?" He's smirking, and all I want is to knock it off his smug face.

"Yeah, peachy." No. No, I'm not. I barely slept last night, checking on Walker to be sure he didn't have a concussion. He slept like a baby until I woke him up every few hours just to be sure he wasn't choking on his own vomit and could count my fingers and knew what day it was. Though, to be fair, even I'm a little vague on the day of the week at three in the morning. "Just tired."

"And grumpy," Gabriel chimes in.

Yeah. That. "It's your fault," I grumble, going for five more presses before giving in to the sluggishness keeping my strength captive, and accepting Jonah's help to secure the bar on the J hooks.

"I thought he'd deflect the blow." Gabriel stands before my bench as I sit up, swiping the sweat from my face and arms.

That's what we all say when we land an unexpected kick, punch, or, in his case, an elbow to the face while sparring. "It's fine. *He's* fine."

We're all good.

Except I feel undone and not myself.

Berklyn. She haunts my thoughts, sinking under my skin like a demon. Unrelenting. Remorseless. Damning. And… completely unaware.

She has no clue the effect she has on me, except I turn into a complete and total asshole in her presence. It's unintentional, not an attitude.

Not my problem.

It's *her.*

And it's me.

The idea of an *us*, even if only for a few sweet hours of hedonistic, sweaty bliss shared with Walker, makes me itchy and unhinged.

I don't do unhinged. I'm *the guy* others go to for help. You need me, I'm there. You need a laugh, a shoulder to cry on, a ride, a drink, a good fuck—I'm your man. Shit, I'll even babysit and bake you the best damn bread you've ever tasted.

But if you're Dr. Berklyn Fortier, I'm a total cocky asshole. Zero subtlety.

I don't know why. I scrub my face, considering… Maybe I do.

"Earth to Jess." Rowdy throws a towel at my face. "You listening?"

Obviously not. "What?" I toss the towel back.

Gabriel growls and heads to the locker room, throwing over his shoulder, "I'm in. Invite Walker."

"Invite him where?" I shoot to Rowdy as I stand and chug the rest of my water.

"We're going out Friday night. Everyone. The girls too."

My brow tightens. "Everyone?"

He looks at me like I'm an idiot. "We have babysitters lined up."

I shake my head in disbelief. It was only a few years ago that none of these guys were married with kids. Now they're wifed up and spitting out babies like it's a competition. If it is, Cap is winning, considering Rowdy and Taylor are his grown kids and he has the twins Cade, Wade and sweet baby Iris with Cher. Gabriel and Frankie are catching up with two kids and another on the way. Rowdy and Reese have one kid and are knocked up too. Landry and Taylor are trying but not *really* trying.

As for the rest of us, we're happily single. Well, I am. I can't really speak for Jonah and Walker. Both seem to want to settle down more than the rest of us holdouts.

Me? No, thank you.

I'm not cut from the cloth that makes for good husbands. I'm made out of the worn, stained leather meant for hot sticky sex and cab fare home. I'm the emotionless encounters that have you praising my name as you come but thankful you can forget me the moment the door closes behind me. I come in hot and leave just as fast. I'm not built for forever. My father made sure of that.

"You in?" Rowdy prompts with Jonah eyeing me over his shoulder as if my response drives whether he'll come or not. Maybe it does. No one likes to be the odd man out among the married crew.

"Yeah, sure." Why not?

Walker won't be happy. That's the night he's hoping Berklyn will finally agree to meet us for drinks. As I think on it, her number is burning a hole in my phone. Walker has never given my number out or made sure I added her as a contact in case she says yes, but more importantly, in case she calls and needs something. Apparently, he signed me up for Mr. Chivalry duty.

He's convinced I need to branch out, give the woman a chance to prove she's not the same as the woman who hurt me and closed my heart like a clenched fist. He thinks Berklyn is just that woman. She probably could be—to someone. Not me. She could be that for him, I've no doubt.

I humor him, let him push to make me a better version of myself. But I'm fine the way I am. I don't need love. I don't need forever. I have my fighting and the bakery. I don't need a gooey heart or moldable emotions to share a good woman between us. He can be the functional, touchy-feely. I'll be raw, hard cock that drives it home. It's the perfect arrangement. His soft center to my hard exterior.

I have her number, which I'll never use, and she has my mine.

Walker is delusional, though, 'cause there's no way she'll call me instead of him.

And there's no way I'd dump everything—or anything—to help her out.

That's the line I'm sticking to.

I'm not her savior. I'm not *her* hero.

WALKER

The pounding in my head won't give it a rest. I finally broke down and took two acetaminophen, which haven't kicked in. So, I'm lying on the couch staring at the ceiling with *Sports Center* on the TV, counting down the seconds since I last checked my phone to see if Doc called or texted.

She didn't, of course.

I really thought she might—must've been hit harder than I realized to read the signals so wrong. She gave me her number—finally. I thought this time might be different. It's been months of ER visits, not really on purpose, but enough for her to get to know me and Jess.

Jess. I don't know what's crawled up his ass when it comes to Doc. She's sweet and sexy as fuck. He's never like that with the women we share—and we've shared a lot over the years. It used to be only occasionally. Now, it's more sharing than not.

I'm not complaining.

Except, maybe I am. I want Doc for us—for me.

There are two side to Jess. The good guy who's a great friend to me and to our Black Ops family. He'd never treat Taylor, Frankie, Reese like he does the women we fuck. He draws the line with his dick. If you're in the no-dick zone, Jess is all smiles and a supportive give-you-the-shirt-off-my-back kinda guy. If you're in the dating pool, then it's the cooler-hearted Jess. There's no in-between. Yet with Doc, I don't miss the glances, the yearning. He's never looked at a conquest like he does her. He wants more. He *needs* more. I just have to get him out of his own damn way.

Damn, my head hurts too damn much to think on this right now. Maybe I should have taken Doc up on those pain meds. At least I could have slept through this painful waiting period of "will she or won't she call."

Jingling keys in the door draw my attention. Peering over the arm of the couch, I catch Jess as he drops his wallet and keys in the bowl on the bar.

"Hey." He eyes the muted TV, my cereal bowl on the coffee table and me. "You feeling okay?"

I shrug. "Yeah."

He frowns and dips down to snatch my bowl and empty cup. "That's all you've eaten today?"

"Yeah."

His brow twists. "I'm fixin' dinner. Anything you don't feel like eating?"

"Nope." I'll eat anything he makes. He makes magic in the kitchen as well as the bedroom. One I've tasted. The other, I've *watched*.

He nods and slips into the kitchen, rinsing my bowl and putting it in the dishwasher. I should've done that when I got up earlier.

"Here." Jess hands me water and an ice pack. "Drink it all. You need to hydrate. It'll help with the headache."

"How'd you know?" The ice cubes clink as I rise up on my elbow and drain the glass before handing it back. "Thanks."

"TV's on mute, you've barely eaten, you're giving quiet one-word answers, and you're clenching your jaw. All signs your head hurts." He takes my glass. "I'll get you more." He touches my head and cheek. "No fever." He checks my eyes and the bandage. "You sleep at all today?"

"Not really."

He nods and hands me a kitchen towel. "Put that on your head and rest while I make dinner. A good meal and a bath will help you relax and sleep."

I wrap the towel around the cold pack and lay it over the bridge of my nose and forehead. "You're a good wife."

He chuckles. "*You're* the wife."

"You're the one nursing me and cooking," I tease, glad he's home.

"Lucky for you I put out too."

"Yeah, but you're a dick."

"No, I *have* a dick. Not the same, *wife*."

I roll a little toward the back of the couch. "Too bad I'm not gay. You really would make a good wife."

"You mean, *we're* not gay. And *you'd* be the wife."

"That's what I said." Totally not what I said.

"Shut it and sleep already."

I smile to myself and sink into the couch as sounds and smells of him home and taking care of me ease the tension. I start to drift off with thoughts of Berklyn being with us, cuddling with me on the couch, running her fingers through my hair, telling me how handsome, sexy, and sweet I am while also teasing Jess about what a good wife he'd make us.

CHAPTER 4

STARE AT MY PHONE IN DISBELIEF. MID-SHIFT, I received a text from Jess. I never in a million years thought it would be Jess texting me first. I would have bet my life on Walker. Good thing I don't bet. I would've lost big time.

> **Jess:** *Hey, just wanted you to know Walker's doing good. He's on the mend. A bunch of our friends and wives are going to Mel's on Friday. We'd like you to join us. Happy to pick you up or meet you there. Let me know.*

That has to be the friendliest he's ever been. It must have hurt. Maybe it's not him.

> **Me:** *Who is this? How'd you get Jess' phone?*
>
> **Jess:** *Funny. It's me.*
>
> **Me:** *Prove it.*

Can't be too sure. Even if it is him, I can't fall for his trickery. When someone shows you who they are, you should believe them. And I have zero reason to believe Jess can tolerate me, never mind *wants* me, despite what Walker says.

My phone vibrates with his reply, only it's not a text. It's a selfie. He's standing in front of a mirror, droplets of water all along his impressively defined chest and, dear God, an eight-pack to define all eight-packs and his—

Holy. I can't even. I glance around, clutch my phone to my chest, my pulse thumping in my ears. He's naked. Naked, except for the scrap of towel he's holding over his...

Jesus on a cracker. I fan my face.

Jess: *Proof enough?*

I can't even. I turn my screen off, needing a minute. Thankfully, I'm on my lunch break. I ignore the vibration in my pocket as I order a grilled chicken Caesar salad with a side of fries. My stress requires fries. Doctor's orders.

Sequestered in my favorite corner booth, I fork a bite of salad and unlock my phone to a stream of texts from Mr. Give Me A Heart Attack himself. I nearly jump out of my skin when it vibrates again with an incoming phone call.

"Hello?"

"You're not answering your texts. Did I scare you off?" The gruff in Jess' voice does complicated things to my pride and warring girlie parts.

"I'm at work. You can't send pics like that. What if I wasn't alone?"

"Then they'd get an eyeful." He's all too amused.

"I suppose you're just fine with that." Why am I being bitey? He's being nice. Why am I resisting something I want so much? His laughter has me sighing and relaxing into my seat. "Now you're laughing at me?"

"No, Berks. Never. You sound territorial, and I like it."

Berks? Territorial? He likes it? "Am not."

Another chuckle. "Say yes."

"Yes to what?" I need specifics.

"To coming out with me and Walker... And our friends." The new warmth in his voice is like a comfy blanket around my soul, smoothing the edges that don't trust easily.

"It won't be weird, you bringing a stranger?"

"No, and you're not a stranger. You've worked on Gabriel." His response is quick and simple, but doesn't ease my worry.

I prefer small gatherings with people I know. I work on strangers all day, so I like my socializing more intimate. "I'll think on it."

"Don't think. Just say yes. I know you want to."

"Conceited much?"

"Confident. There's a difference." He releases a long breath. "It would mean a lot to Walker..."

Sweet Walker—somehow, we already feel more connected, yet Jess is the one on the phone making a date. I touch my lips with the tip of my finger, pushing more than I should. "Just Walker?"

The silence that passes is heavy, weighted with expectations and vulnerability. Do I want him to want me too, or just be here wingmanning for Walker?

"No. Not just him."

I wait.

And wait.

"Do you need to hear it?" he finally replies.

"Yes," I whisper, toying with a fry in ketchup... Waiting.

"It would mean a lot to me too."

"Really?" My heart skips, making me take a shaky breath.

"Really, Berks. Say yes."

"Yes." I hang up before I scream like a school girl with a crush, or he ruins the lightness I feel in this moment by saying something crass. I want to think he wants more than just sex. Though, really hot sex could be just what the doctor ordered.

I guess I'm going on a date with Walker... And Jess.

Lord, help me.

JESS

She said yes. My stupid smile won't ease. I grab a couple of non-alcoholic beers from the fridge, pop the tops, and hand one to Walker. "Berklyn is coming on Friday."

I didn't tell him I was reaching out to her. He didn't say if he had or not. I'm leaning on the *not* side of things based on the surprise riding his face. "What? Wait. You talked to her?"

As I sit in my recliner, I take a long pull and relish the cool liquid that hits the spot. "Yeah, we texted and talked."

"Wow. I hoped but never really thought she'd agree. The Closer strikes again."

That nickname suddenly rubs me the wrong way. No idea why. I focus on the action flick he started before I jumped in the shower. My dick was so hard at the mere thought of texting her, it required immediate attention. Afterwards, the idea of not actually reaching out to her seemed stupid, cowardly. I'm not afraid of her.

I'm not.

"Don't get invested. It's just a date." It doesn't mean anything. *She* can't mean anything. At least not to me.

"I know." He doesn't have a clue. He's already invested. He has been since he laid eyes on her all those months ago. I actually saw her first, but he doesn't need the reminder.

Doesn't matter anyway. She's just shared company. That's all. Will never be more.

There is no *more* with me. I'd never want to hurt her or take the chance of her getting further under my skin and finishing off what's left of my mangled heart.

"Were you nice?"

I want to be affronted, but he has good reason to doubt. "The nicest." I drain my fake beer and go for another. "You feeling okay?"

"Yep. Couldn't be better." His smile backs up his words. If he were a dog, his tail would be wagging.

"It's just a date," I reiterate.

"Uh huh. I know." He nods, his eyes on the screen, but his mind is somewhere else. On Doc, I've no doubt.

She's for us.

She's just not for *me*.

CHAPTER 5

WALKER

JESS IS LEAVING FOR THE BAKERY JUST AS I'M walking out of my room on a yawn. "Morning."

He pauses, keys in hand, cocked eyebrow trained on me. "You're up early. Everything alright?"

I rub my chest on another yawn. "All good. I've got some computer stuff to do. Update needs to be done before my client opens for business." I've put off working since ordered to take it easy. I've lazed around long enough.

"I'll be back for lunch before heading to the gym if you want to go with me."

His offer surprises me. I thought for sure he'd push me to pass on working out for a few more days. "Sure." I lift the coffee, thankful he made a full pot. "You need one to go?"

"No. I've had my allotment. It's all yours." He turns for the door. "You want anything from Sugarplums?"

Damn. He had to go and tempt me. He's been working at Cher's bakery for years, helping out with the baking and whatever else needed. The things he makes at work are next-level with their industrial equipment and fancier ingredients than he spends on himself at home. He still makes the best damn bread and cinnamon buns I've ever tasted. Don't tell Cher or Gabriel—they think theirs are the best. "Yeah, anything. Everything."

His laughter trails him to the door. "One of everything coming right up. See ya later."

"Yep." I scratch my head, fighting another yawn. "Definitely need more coffee." Maybe some cereal too. I can eat and type one-handed. Besides, once I get logged in and start the upload, I just watch it run.

I boot up my laptop, refill my coffee, and pour a bowl of Jess' cereal mix. Some of it's homemade, like the granola and roasted almonds, and some of it's from different store-bought cereals all thrown together to make it healthier and delicious-er. My power meal will be with Jess before we work out. Greens and protein, protein, protein. I'm lucky to live with him. He's a great cook and eats clean. I help where I can, but my superpower lies in clean up and laundry. Oh, and computers.

I log onto my client's server. A few keystrokes and a spoonful of cereal, and my security update is running. I check app settings behind the scenes that won't interfere with the upload, then settle in to watch the screen and finish off breakfast.

As the program continues to run without errors, I take a quick shower and examine the state of my eye—or more like the cut above my right eye. It's looking purplish-yellow, which is a good sign it's healing. Of course, that makes me think of Doc. What is she doing? Is she working? Still asleep? Is she thinking about Jess and me and our date on Friday? Is she nervous? Excited?

I don't for a minute believe she's indifferent. I've made our desires known. She said yes—to Jess. Never saw that coming: him reaching out and her agreeing to him. It's a good sign. A *really* good sign.

He acts like he's not affected by her—he's anything but. His crabbiness is directly related to how she makes him feel. And *feel* is the key word. He feels too much, and it scares him. His past is messing with his head. He doesn't trust love. Sex, he's good with, but starting to care for a woman who could be more than just a good time scares the ever-living crap out of him.

I know he's capable of more. He moves further away from his past with each passing day. He knows how to love. He's completely capable of it. He loves our friends, our family. He loves me. He shows me every day in his actions. He's just afraid, and I want to help him move past that.

I want the future he once wanted—a family of his own. I just hope I can be a part of it, best friends for life. I want Doc to be our future too. But I worry she could care for him more than me. He's the tough guy she'll want to conquer. I'm the nice guy anyone can get.

My fear is not the same as his.

He fears she'll want more from him.

I fear she *won't* want more from me.

JESS

I take a deep breath and let it out slowly as I knead the dough, folding it into itself, pressing down, turning, folding, pressing. Deep breath. This my Zen place, my go-to when I'm stressed or just can't get out of my own head.

As the dough gives to my manhandling it, coming together to form a smooth skin, I slap it on the counter, fold, knead, slap. My grandmother taught me everything I know. The slap is her signature move. Waking up to the sound of that slap was home to me. I knew what was coming. The mouthwatering smells had me jumping out of bed, getting dressed, and doing my chores so I could have a bite of warm, buttered goodness.

I might have learned a few tricks from Cher over the years, but most of what I know, I learned when I was a kid from the only person who ever loved me.

My Gran.

I enjoy baking. In fact, I might enjoy it more than fighting. But fighting serves a purpose, and I won't always be able to do it. So, I'm eating it up while I can, but I know somewhere down the line, I'll be doing this full-time. Cher's already hinted to the fact she doesn't want to lose me. I have no intention of leaving. I've tossed around the idea of opening up a second Sugarplums, but to be honest, I'm good with my level of commitment here. Plus, I get to work with Cher. She's not my gran, but her love of baking is similar. It's her escape—or it was before Cap won her heart. Now her family is her escape, not that she needs one.

The door chime brings me out of my baking fog. A moment or two later, a smiling Cher stands in front of me, eyeing my batch of Honey My Buns wheat bread. "You make it look easy."

A barked laugh rips from my throat before I can stop it. "You're one to talk. You live, eat, breathe this stuff." My tone softens. "I wouldn't be here if it weren't for you."

She frowns, tilting her head, considering. "Maybe, but you would have been baking regardless of me giving you a home for your talent."

"I don't know about talent. It's an escape, a sense memory." My smile grows. "Gran loved your pumpkin spice cake you sent. Did she tell you?"

"Oh, yeah. She called, gushing over it. Said her pinochle group devoured it. Asked that I send two next time. One to share and one to keep."

Another uninhibited laugh escapes. "I bet she did." I grow thoughtful. "Gran would have loved to own a shop like this. If she'd been a few years younger, she would have been here helping you out when you were pregnant." I shake my sadness away for the missed opportunity. "Her hands…"

Cher waves me off. "Someday arthritis will probably get me too. I've been doing it for so long." She stares as her hands. They're so small but surprisingly strong, just like her. Her sympathetic gaze lands on me. "Are you happy here?"

"I—" My words fall away as concern takes root. "Are you firing me?"

"What?!" She rears back. "No. Definitely not. The opposite, actually."

The opposite of firing? I already work here nearly forty hours a week…

Her eyes soften as she comes to stand next to me, brushing her hand over my shoulder, leaning in. "I'm wondering if you want to become a partner. Maybe thirty-seventy initially, then more once you're sure it's what you want. I'm partial to the place. Cap's gift to me. I can't image giving it up completely. It'll always feel like home. But—"

"The restaurant?" Gabriel and his sister Reese have been talking about opening a restaurant with her for some time now. Maybe it's moving into the planning stages.

"Gabriel and Cap found a space. It's not something I was considering doing now with the kids still so young. But the place, the offer, it seems right. If we do it, I'd need more help running Sugarplums—which you already do so much. You basically kept us afloat after the twins and Iris were born. It only seems right to offer you a part of the business on top of your salary. If you're interested."

I won't lie and say I haven't thought about it. "Yes. I'm interested." Gran would be so excited and proud to see her tutelage leading to me owning—partially—a bakery.

"I know you're still fighting, so I'm not expecting you to give that up, but I'd need help managing the place, handling payroll, more ownership-type stuff. I think your baking hours could stay the same, unless you want to hire a replacement—I'm okay with that too." She returns to her stool across from me. "Again. It's all up in the air. I just wanted to get a feel for what you want. Where you see yourself in five years."

My heart pounds. "This feels like a job interview."

Her laugh is soothing. "Jess, you already have the job. It's just a matter of *if* you want more and when. Will it make you happy?" She leans in. "I *want* you to be happy."

My brow puckers as I wipe my hands, considering her statement. "Am I not?"

"Sometimes I'm not sure you are, at least not fully. But only you can truly answer that. I don't want to add to your plate unless it's what you want." Her hand grips mine. "There's more to life than working. Sometimes, I think you boys forget that."

"Boys?"

With a roll of her eyes, she stands. "You know what I mean. Gabriel, Rowdy, and my Cap have settled down—found their happiness. You, Walker, and Jonah need to do the same. Life is more than a paycheck and bigger than the octagon."

"Not everyone gets what you and Cap have." What Gabriel and Rowdy have found too. Not all of us are lovable.

She pats my cheek—reminding me of my Gran, even though she's far younger—before she steps way. "We all deserve love. Cap taught me that. If I'm worthy of love, so are you."

So are you.

The itchiness is back.

I promise to think about Cher's offer before wrapping up for the day.

I've got lunch with Walker and a date with whoever's willing to spar with me once we get to the Black Ops Gym.

If baking is my Zen, fighting is my salvation.

I couldn't give it up if I tried.

CHAPTER 6

BERKLYN

I SNAP THE FLAT SHEET AND NEARLY DROP THE phone nestled between my shoulder and ear, making a grab for it as the sheet floats through the air and settles over my mattress.

"What are you doing?" Mom asks.

"Making my bed." I change it every few days, religiously. If I had a maid, I'd have it done daily. I love the smell of freshly laundered sheets and blankets. But daily is overkill, especially since it's only me in the bed, and it's seen little action since I started my residency—which is entirely too long.

I don't really want to think about my abysmal sex life while talking to Mom. Though, she, of all people, would be entirely too open to discuss it—in painstaking detail. *Gross.*

That's what happens when your mom is a sex therapist.

"Does that mean you've finally had a man—or woman—in your bed? Maybe both?"

She doesn't have to sound so hopeful.

"Mom, we're not discussing my love life." I'm hoping she'll take the "lesbians are fabulous lovers" path of encouragement instead of reiterating the sad fact that there hasn't been *anyone* in my bed.

Her sigh could dust my room if she were here in person and I hadn't already dusted the entire house. "It's too bad, really. Woman make amazing lovers. No one knows your body like another woman."

Yep, I've heard this sales pitch my whole life. I think she's disappointed I'm not gay, which in and of itself is telling, considering she's never dated a woman as far as I know. Because God knows she'd tell me all about it. Does she wish she had? How would my dads feel about that?

"You're twenty-six, Berklyn. It's time to get serious about finding a life partner." She doesn't say husband. She wouldn't want to box me in with stereotypical gender roles. Sometimes I wish she would, because her openness to exposing herself to other people's life experiences is exhausting. Not because they're bad, but because I feel like I *have to* want to experience them and then share with her. And I don't.

I'm not as open and free-spirited as my mother. Apparently, I received most of my looks from her but not her free-loving gene. I'm sadly disappointing. Her acceptance of all walks of life is wasted on me, her straitlaced daughter who hasn't had sex in three years.

God, has it been that long? I count back, thinking of the last... No, it's been longer.

Dang it. It's. Been. Longer.

"Birdie?" She pulls me back from my self-loathing internal rant.

"I've been busy being a doctor, Mom. I mean, doesn't that count for something?" Maybe even get me somewhere on *her* scale of success in life—even if I'm not a lesbian doctor or a bisexual doctor? Or a reverse-harem doctor. *God, she'd love that.*

31

My success in life shouldn't be measured against her bloated expectations of what my sexual prowess should be.

"Of course, being a doctor is important. I'm proud even. But—"

"There's more to life than a degree? I know." *I know.* She's told me enough times, it's tattooed across my forehead in ink that's only visible to her scrutinizing stare. "Maybe Rider will turn out non-cis-hetero. There's still hope. Don't fret." My younger brother is sixteen. I'm sure he'd know by now if he were into the D. After all, he's had his hand on his own enough to know how it works and if he'd want to cross beams with a dude.

"Berklyn! Is that what you really think? I don't care if you or Rider are heterosexual, homosexual, bisexual, or any orientation known to man— or woman. I just want you happy and *fulfilled.*"

The way she emphasizes *fulfilled* makes me think she's going to send me a care package of vibrators, butt plugs, and how-to videos on self-pleasure and freeing my inner goddess.

I don't need a package because… "I have a date on Friday," I blurt before my brain can stop those inciting words from forming.

No. No. God, no. Why'd I say that?

"Yes! Tell me everything." Her excitement is cringy and adorable all at the same time.

"Um…" *Don't do it! Don't. I beg you.* But I'm kind of weirdly proud to have something to share. "It's actually two guys." Gah, I did it. I squeeze my eyes closed, silently banging my head against my mattress. Two guys. *I couldn't just let it slide, a lie of omission?*

"From the hospital?"

"They're professional MMA fighters."

The line is quiet so long, I move the phone to see if the line dropped just in time to hear her shriek, "TOM! Well, isn't that something? I bet they have amazing bodies, muscles for days and energy to burn."

Eww. Stop. Please, stop.

"Who has amazing bodies?" I hear one of my dads in the background.

"It's Berklyn, Tom. She has a date with *two* MMA fighters—"

"Give me the phone, Scar. Let me talk to our daughter."

A muffled conversation ensues before Dad comes on the line with, "Birdie, what's this about you dating two guys?"

"It's…real."

"What?"

"It's just drinks, Daddy. Maybe food too." *It's not really a date date.*

"*Maybe* food?" Uh-oh, I know that tone. He's angry. "No no-good *men* are taking my daughter out and not buying her dinner too. Why I… Give me their—"

"Daddy, it's casual. We're going out with a group of their friends. I'll eat. I promise." *Calm the F down.*

"How'd you meet these guys? Are you safe with them? They're fighters."

"They're *professional* fighters, not street brawlers. I'm safe. They won't hurt me. I've known them for a while, and they've been respectfully asking me out for months. I just finally gave in and said yes to going out with them."

"Two of em, huh? I'm not sure how I feel about that."

Me either. "Honestly, I'm not sure either." I'm crazy to agree to seeing them. Their expectations alone are enough to scare me into canceling. *What was I thinking?*

My uncertainty dissipates his anger. "It'll be fine, Birdie. Maybe trying it your mother's way for a change will lead to something different in a good way. Even just to go out for the night and have a good time in a social setting would be great for you. Just be yourself, and they'll fall right in line, tripping all over themselves to make you happy. Probably be in love with you by dessert."

Love? Hardly. And Daddy's idea of dessert probably doesn't equal what Jess and Walker consider dessert—potentially *me.*

Long after I hang up with my parents and a follow-up phone call with my other Dad, Everett, I sink into the tub, turning on the massage jets. I take a few deep breaths as the water froths and beats against my tense muscles and frayed nerves.

Everything will be okay.

I have this. It's just drinks.

It's just drinks, and *maybe* dinner with their friends.

If I had any friends outside of the hospital, I'd invite them so I wouldn't feel uncomfortable and completely awkward. I'm not even sure I know how to have a normal conversation that doesn't include medical jargon. What do normal people talk about? They're MMA fighters. Do they just talk about that? Gah, I'm so out of my comfort zone here. Even so, I'm not about to invite coworkers on my double date where I'm the only girl in a hottie sandwich. I mean, that's fantastic gossip.

It's outlandish for me to think I could possibly handle two guys. I haven't had sex in three years. *Over* three years. I'm a doctor, I know where things go. How A fits into B. But physically, I'm rusty, and there are two A's in this scenario—well, more like two D's, but who's counting? Oh, yeah, I am. What the heck do I do with two D's?

Wait, am I seriously considering their offer to *share* me?

If it were only Walker *or* Jess, would I even be thinking about sex at this point in our haven't-even-had-a-first-date-relationship status?

Am I a booty call?

Can it be categorized as a booty call if we haven't had sex yet *and* it's planned? It's not a booty call. It's… Drinks. I only agreed to drinks and maybe food.

Drinks and food—that I can do. With Jess and Walker, *and* their friends.

It's just drinks and dinner.

I haven't agreed to be the filling in their meat sandwich.

Wait. Aren't they the meat?

Would I? Could I? They're over-the-top hot on their own. Add them together and it's sensation overload. Has to be. What would it feel like to have their hands, mouths, D's on me—in me. Could I handle it? Do I even want to find out?

My inner goddess screams, "Yes," from the recesses of my mind. My mom put her up to it, I'm sure.

Lord, I need French fries. Doctor's orders.

CHAPTER 7

WALKER

I'M SUCH A CHICK, BUT AS I STARE AT DOC'S WORDS on my phone, I can't muster the testosterone to give a flying fuck. I let my smile free along with a *whoop* and a fist pump. She texted me. Finally!

> **Dr. Berklyn Fortier:** *Good morning. Hope I'm not waking you. How is your eye? Can you confirm where and when I'm meeting you and Jess tonight?*

Then...

> **Dr. Berklyn Fortier:** *I'm nervous. How silly is that?*

It's not silly. I stare at her full name on my phone and contemplate changing her contact to just *Doc*, but that almost feels like it would be negating her full name, her accomplishment, and the respect she deserves. She's more than a nickname—even though I love calling her Doc, like I did something to earn that right. She deserves her whole name on my phone. I need to find out her middle name, make it officially her entire name.

Considering her words, I want to reach through the phone and give her a hug, not because she shouldn't be nervous, but because she is, which means she cares. I need her to care. I want her to be as off-kilter as I am when I think of her, when I see her, when she graces me with a smile, her attention.

> **Me:** *Good morning. Nervous? Is that what's going on in my stomach? I thought maybe I swallowed a butterfly or something. Good thing I've got a date with a doctor just to be sure I'm alright.*

> **Me:** *My eye is good, btw.*

It's a great morning. It couldn't be better unless she was waking up between Jess and me. Now, *that* would be a spectacular morning.

> **Me:** *And it's not silly. I'm counting down. Maybe we could play hooky and start our date early. As in NOW.*

> **Dr. Berklyn Fortier:** *As tempting as that is, I'm afraid I can't. People are counting on me to Adult today.*

> **Me:** *Adulting? I've heard of it but can't place it.*

> **Dr. Berklyn Fortier:** 😂 😂 😂

I made her laugh, even if only through text. My world is complete. I send her the address to Mel's along with the time, but reiterate:

> **Me:** *We're happy to pick you up. But we understand if you want to have your own car.*

> **Dr. Berklyn Fortier:** *I'll Uber there.*

> **Me:** *You feel safer getting into a car with a stranger than us?*

I'm sure that's not her intent, but it feels like a slap to the face to not allow us to pick her up after all this time. I was open to the idea of her driving her own car so she felt in control. But I don't understand her giving it up to a stranger to drive her there.

The three dots dance as she types her reply...

Three dots...

Three dots...

Still waiting...

Finally, my phone pings.

> **Dr. Berklyn Fortier:** *I honestly hadn't considered that. Now it's all I can think about. Thanks for putting that doubt in my head.* 😟
>
> **Me:** *I can ease your doubt really easily. Let me come get you.*
>
> **Dr. Berklyn Fortier:** *Okay.*

She sends her address, and I confirm the pick-up time. I'm about to jump out of my skin with excitement when I realize I have to tell Jess I'm picking her up. *Only me.* She didn't specifically request that, but I felt the intent. I promised I'd make her feel safe, and if that means Jess has to wait for us at Mel's, then so be it. Her comfort is all that matters right now.

> **Me:** *Have a great day. I'm going to try that Adulting thing myself and get to work rather than show up and steal you away for a day of debauchery. See you tonight.*
>
> **Dr. Berklyn Fortier:** *I want to ask what kind of debauchery but feel that won't aid either of us in our Adulting endeavor. See you soon.* 😊

I want to follow the decadent path she seems open to but decide to take the win and not push my luck.

Me: *I knew you were smart. Raincheck on the day of debauchery then?*

Dr. Berklyn Fortier: *Raincheck and I'm not always smart.*

Raincheck. Is tonight too soon to call it in?

Me: *You agreed to go out with us. I'd say you're a genius.*

Some would argue the complete opposite. We have nothing but good intentions, though they might be of the dirty and incredibly sexual variety, but delicious nonetheless. Jess and I are a team, not just team-mates. When it comes to the bedroom, we're serious about giving more than taking. In the end, the woman's pleasure is ours too. We've had no complaints other than we don't do repeats—or rarely. I wouldn't mind, but Jess has no interest in double-dipping. Once they've had both of us, I'm not comfortable going solo. Expectations are too high.

She gives my last text a heart. It's getting late. I'm sure she's at work and knee-deep in patients. I contemplate the best way to tell Jess about me picking up Doc without him. I could text him or wait until he gets home later. With my stomach looking for sustenance and my work caught up, I decide for the direct in-person approach and not to delay. I head to Cher's bakery.

JESS

It's not unusual to hear the door chime at Sugarplums, but it is unusual for Jam's raucous laughter and Walker's deep chuckle to follow. I close the ovens and set timers on the sourdough loaves and the chocolate cakes that will turn into Death by Chocolate seven-layer cakes.

As I turn, I catch Walker on this side of the door that divides the back from the front of the bakery. He's hugging Cher, but his eyes are on me. Something in them has me stepping back to wash my already clean hands, giving him my back while I prepare for whatever he's here to tell me.

It's been a long while since he's come to the bakery. In the early days, he was here working on the Sugarplums app and computer system. But now all that is running smoothly, he doesn't stop by socially. Plus, I bring whatever sweets he wants home, so this is an unexpected—and possibly unwanted—visit.

I grab my coffee and take a long pull, eyeing him as he nears.

"Hey." He gives me a chin nod as he sinks his hands in his pocket, looking about as uncomfortable as I feel.

"Hey." I scan the empty kitchen, noting Cher stepped out front, and land back on him. "You hungry?"

His shoulders fall on an exhale. "Starved."

"I was just about to make a breakfast croissant. You want one?" I don't know why I ask. He never turns down food. I swear he'd live off frozen pizza and cereal if I didn't feed him healthier alternatives.

His eyes light up. "Yeah, that'd be great."

I motion to the employee coffeemaker. "Make yourself a cup or grab a water, then we can sit out back if you want."

"You want anything?"

"I'll take a water."

I start assembling the sandwiches with the already fried eggs, bacon, ham, and a thin slice of cheddar as Walker steps out back. Cher has a shaded patio for employees just off the side patio for customers. I place sandwiches under the salamander and grab plates as I wait the few seconds it'll take to melt the cheese and toast the croissants.

Once on the patio, we eat in silence. Since it's closer to lunch than breakfast, I made two sandwiches each with a side of sliced tomato and avocado salad, and a cinnamon roll chaser for Walker. I try to avoid sugar as much as possible. It makes me sluggish afterwards. Same with alcohol, so I abstain. It's what's best for training and for my body.

I won't deny I enjoy watching other people appreciate my sweets. I'm not sure who enjoys them more, Walker or Rowdy. Maybe Rowdy since he tries to abstain as well. But Walker's moaning and finger-licking make me think about Berk and how we'll be making her feel later tonight if all goes as planned.

"You nervous?" I know him enjoying all this food is not just because he's hungry. His twitchy knee conveys his anxiety over tonight, or something else is bothering him.

"A little." He sucks cinnamon and frosting off his thumb and middle finger before wiping his hands on his napkin. "Doc is nervous. She texted me earlier."

"Is she backing out?" My heart dips at the thought. Is that why he's edgy?

"Naw. She was just sharing. It's cute. Told her I was nervous too." He finishes his coffee, setting down his mug. "I don't want to fuck this up."

"You won't." It's not him I'm worried about.

"I was thinking," he pauses, biting his lip and glancing away before meeting my eyes. "If things go where we want them to, I think we need to take it slow. Make tonight all about her. About *her* pleasure."

"You want to ease her into it?" I'm a little miffed he thought of it, and I didn't, but truth be, I'm not up to easing her into it. It might be the only chance I get. I don't do repeats. I might make an exception for Berklyn, but she already has me edgy and itchy. I'm not sure I can handle too much of a good thing—her. The more I have her, the harder it'll be to keep it physical only.

"Yeah. You okay with that?"

I'm not like him. I don't see this going beyond a night or two. I don't want to ruin it for him, but I'm not willing to miss out on those few nights either.

I saw her first, my possessiveness roars.

"If we get her naked and she's into it, I'm fuckin' her. I'm not taking a chance on losing this opportunity. I'm not romancing her, Walk. I'm not looking for happily ever after. I'm looking for a great fuck, as always. In her case, I'm not willing to risk my one guaranteed night for your shot at forever. If you're not into it, you can wait. She'll only put up with me for so long, then she'll be all yours anyway."

He frowns, his eyes flashing with doubt, maybe hurt too. "It doesn't have to be—"

"Yeah, for me it does. I'm not forever material. *You* know that. Soon she'll know it too." She already knows. I've no doubt, which spurs me on to fuck her before she slips through my fingers—with or without him.

My timers go off. "I've got to get back to work." I collect our dishes and stand. "I'll see you at home. What time are we picking her up?"

He's on his feet and holding the door closed before I can open it. "She wants me to pick her up."

I bite back a smile. "Great. What time?"

"No. Only *I'm* picking her up," he clarifies and steps away from the door.

Yep, I can't forget what this is—or, more importantly, what it's *not.* If she wants *anything* from me, it's my dick filling her hard and deep, which still remains to be seen.

"I'll see you both at Mel's then." I disappear inside, leaving him to follow or walk around the building to his car. I don't really care which at the moment.

She doesn't want me to pick her up seeps into every thought and taints my mood for the rest of the day. She may not want me at all.

Maybe she only said yes to get to Walk. The reality check is a gut punch I wasn't prepared for. There are reasons we don't do this—taking a woman out on a date before fucking her. It's counterintuitive to my "it's only sex" motto. I'd rather we pick a woman up at a bar—typically Mel's. Sometimes the grocery store, but that's an even harder sell.

Everything about tonight screams "Run!" as fast as I can in the opposite direction. I've let this thing with Berklyn get out of hand. We've pursued her for nearly half a year. We've—I've—never done that. Never allowed my desire to slay me like it has with her.

I'm so fucked. I fear, even if I do get her naked tonight, and we do fuck, I'm still going to be screwed and want more come morning.

That fucking itch is riding me hard for the rest of the day.

CHAPTER 8

BERKLYN

THE RAP ON MY FRONT DOOR CATCHES ME unprepared. I'm still in my bra and panties having gotten home late from the hospital. I've showered. My hair and makeup are done but—"Shit." I stub my pinky toe on the foot of my bed in a mad dash for my robe. *Crap, that smarts like a bugger bear!* I grit my teeth and hop the rest of the way to my robe, slipping black silk up my arms.

"Coming!" I limp to the front door, tying the sash, and take a breath, calming myself before peering through the peephole.

He's early. But his handsome face is forgiven when I catch him biting his lip, looking at the door like he can see me. I feel stupid for even considering an Uber. I wasn't against them picking me up. It's not like I don't have access to their personal information at the hospital. I feel safe with them, except maybe my feelings and my heart. Those are in danger of getting trampled as I open the door to the potential of what tonight could bring.

"Hi, Walker." I step back, opening the door further. "I'm sorry I'm not quite ready."

"Hey, Doc." His gaze starts at my feet and slowly slides up to my face before taking my invite and stepping past me. "I'm early, take your time."

I motion to the living room. "Make yourself comfortable." I manage to not limp as I follow. "There's beer in the fridge. Help yourself."

"Naw. I'm driving. Plus, we're not drinking tonight." He plops down on the sofa, arms spread out along the back, looking entirely too good in my home.

I start to head to my room and freeze, realizing what he said. *We're?* "Does that mean *I* can't drink?" Not that I'm a big drinker, but I could use a drink or two to calm my nerves and keep me from biting Jess' head off if he's in a mood or teases too hard.

He chuckles. "You can drink to your heart's content. We're in training, but I wouldn't drink anyway since I'm driving."

Good to know.

"Remote's on the coffee table," I offer before escaping his perusal of my silky robe as if it's see-through. I know he can't see what's beneath, but it sure feels like a caress all over my heated skin.

Once in my room with the door closed, I lean against it, closing my eyes. "Breathe," is my mantra for the night. I'm already overheated, feeling the Walker and Jess effect, even though he's not even here. I think they could make me come just from their heated stares. God, I want that. I want to be the center of their universe if only for a single night.

"Be present," I whisper. Take notes, etch this into your brain. It might be the only time you have two guys pursuing you at the same time. It's never been my dream, my fantasy. I've avoided even considering the concept because of my parents. What they have is great, but I want something just for myself—someone.

Two guys. Never. In. My. Wildest. Dreams.

Faster than I thought possible, I'm dressed and slipping on my sandals before checking out my flirty midi dress in the mirror. The pale teal floral print makes my eyes appear bluer than green. It's sleeveless with a white under-slip that shows above the rounded neckline and below the hem. I wear scrubs all day and don't go out often, so even this casual dress makes me feel feminine and pretty in the flowy shirt that ends just above the knee.

I leave my hair down but put a hair tie in my purse just in case I can't find the other ten or so I always think I'll need in case of a hair emergency. I've shaved everything that could possibly need shaving and blush at the thought of finding myself in an intimate situation where someone would care about the state of my hairy legs or other unmentionable places.

It's been so long…

On a deep inhale, I turn off the lights as I go and find Walker standing in front of my back window, staring out into the darkness. He seems distracted, deep in thought, but the soft clap of my shoes on the hardwood draws his focus.

I nearly lose my nerve when his gaze lands on me, full of heat and want. He does a once-over, slow and near indecent before stepping into me. "You…" He takes a breath and tries again. "You look incredible, Doc. Like a dream." Only his fingertips touch my arm, running down to my hand, where he links our fingers. "So beautiful."

My blush reignites as I try to absorb his generous words instead of dismissing them. "You look nice too."

He does. He's in stonewash jeans, brown work boots, and a white Henley with the sleeves pushed up that hugs every muscle of his chest, arms, and abdomen and highlights his natural tan and golden eyes. He's clean-shaven and the short, tousled dirty-blond hair only accentuates his jawline and delectably full lips.

As he leans in like he might kiss me—which lands on my cheek—I notice the small bandage over his right eye, nearly completely covered up by his loose curls.

"How's your cut?"

He brushes his temple, smiling. "It's good. Ready to get the sutures out."

"Only a few more days." I originally told him Monday or Tuesday next week, depending on how it's healing. But maybe I'll check it out later and see if it's ready. I'm leaning more toward no, just so he continues to take it easy and doesn't start sparring with a barely healed wound.

"Doctor's orders?" he asks, humor dancing in his eyes.

"Yes." *My* orders.

"Okay, Doc." He motions to the door. "You ready?"

As I'll ever be. "Yeppers," I casually reply and cringe at my lameness. He only smiles and guides me out the door, ensuring it's locked behind us, and to his truck.

When he opens the passenger door, I bite back the instinct to dismiss the effort. I'm so used to opening my own doors as so few men do it nowadays. His momma should be proud.

"Thank you." I take his proffered hand and hesitate as I contemplate the best way to step into his huge truck without flashing him. Maybe a dress wasn't the best idea.

"May I?" He pauses, waiting for my reluctant nod before bending and picking me up like I don't weigh more than the average woman my height and gently setting me on the seat. He catches sight of my heated cheeks and brushes one tenderly with the back of his hand. "Don't be embarrassed. I'm happy to pick you up and carry you everywhere, Doc."

I bark a laugh that turns into a cough. He simply waits till I catch my breath before handing me the seatbelt to fasten. "You good?"

"Yes, thanks."

"Don't mention it." He closes the door and casually walks around to his side and hops in like the nearly eighteen-inch step up is nothing. I suppose for his height of 6'6", it's not.

I'm a foot shorter. I'll have to figure out how to get in and out of his truck without showing my panties if we keep dating.

Are we dating? I know *this* is a date, but are we dating or simply working toward the *sharing me* part? I won't pretend I haven't already decided I want that. But how we get from *here* to *there*, I have no clue, and no idea how to encourage it without sounding silly or desperate.

Outside Mel's Bar and Grill, Walker opens my door and holds me by the waist as I attempt to slide out of his truck. I grip his shoulders and panic, my dress riding up when his hands slide to just under my breasts as my feet hit the pavement.

He quickly releases me, and my dress falls to its rightful place. "Damn, sorry 'bout that." Who's blushing now? "I should've picked you up like before."

"I should've worn jeans." I give him a half-hearted smile as I smooth out the back of the dress to ensure all goods are covered.

"Naw, your dress is perfect." His gaze tightens my chest as he dips to kiss my cheek and whisper, "You're perfect."

"Hardly," I reply on an awkward laugh, trying not to think about the extra he would have felt around my middle or the fact that he's held my weight twice in barely twenty minutes. *Perfect* is the furthest from what I'm feeling at the moment. Nervous and turned on, though, most certainly.

His smirk teases as he pulls me closer, his warm scent drawing me in until I catch myself. Behind my back, he closes the door and laces his hand in mine. His shining eyes seemingly see more than I'm ready to share. "You're perfect to me."

I don a smile and take the compliment, though I'm sure he's just being nice.

He's a gentleman. Despite his given career, his kindness is evident. His quiet soul tugs on the knot in my stomach, urging me to give him a chance.

A chance for what, I'm not entirely sure.

The first time I saw Walker, he came to pick up Jess from the ER after his car accident. His concern for his friend was evident as he asked me multitudes of questions, making notes on his phone. I tried to assure him the orders would be on Jess' discharge papers. He looked at me with open concern and determination and said, "If I take notes, Doc, I have a better chance of remembering. I'm sorry if I'm taking too much of your time. I just need to be sure Jess is okay and stays that way."

While Jess had been flirty despite his injury, Walker's focus was completely on his friend's wellbeing. He didn't give me a second look, at least not in the way he does now.

At Mel's door, the grinning bouncer gives Walker a fist bump and me a wink. "Have fun," he offers as we pass without paying the cover charge.

"That's Sloan," Walker offers as we step inside. "He's a teammate."

So, a fighter too. I glance back, catching Sloan's eyes trailing up my backside before locking on me. With another wink—of approval?—from him, I turn my attention back to Walker as we make our way through the crowd to a large corner booth that's busting at the seams with guys a big as Walker, and a few standing next to it, joining in on the conversation. It's wall-to-wall testosterone. Sprinkled in between the guys in the booth are three intimidatingly beautiful women who look up as we approach, their gazes all zeroing in on Walker holding my hand, their smiles growing.

But it's the mammoth of a guy who turns, stealing my breath as his nostrils flare and his jaw ticks, eyes scanning me and ending on our joined hands, that has me slowing my approach. Nervously, I release Walker's hand and stop beside Jess, whose gaze flits over me to Walker on my other side and then back to the table.

I don't even get a hello.

This. Is. Bad.

CHAPTER 9

JESS

WHATEVER I *THOUGHT* I'D FEEL WHEN WALKER arrived with Berklyn was wholly incomprehensible compared to the anger rising inside me at the sight of them holding hands like he's her lifejacket in a stormy sea, like she belongs to *him*.

It's what I want, right? For her to like him, to possibly be *his*—after. After we have *our* time together. Later. Not now.

I'm so deep in my head, I miss the introductions. I miss establishing her as my date too after she walked in with Walker. Not that *date* would be the word I'd use.

Mine feels more accurate. Instinctual. Like walking a circle around her, dick in hand, glaring while peeing, marking my territory, claiming what's mine.

It would be a horrible introduction to our friends. Actually, it would be right up their alley. As I take in our little group, the way Gabriel practically has Frankie on his lap to give us room to squeeze in the booth, the way Rowdy has Reese tucked under his arm, and the way Landry watches Taylor as she heads for the stage before he follows. I'm struck that these guys consider their woman *theirs*. *Mine* is not a foreign concept or a taboo word with their wives. Gabriel, Rowdy, and Landry are Frankie's, Reese's, and Taylor's too. No, territorialism at its finest is definitely at play here.

"Berklyn, what do you do? How'd you meet these two?" Frankie sips her OJ through a tiny stir straw, smiling at Berks like she just might be her new best friend.

I'm leery of her smile. I can't have these women—my family—becoming attached to Berk. Bringing her here for a group outing wasn't such a smart idea—especially before claiming her as mine—*ours*—and setting the ground rules.

On the other hand, seeing Frankie and Reese with their full baby bellies and their men being all possessive might just set Berklyn at ease, understanding we're just people. We might fight for a living, but it's what we *do*—not who we *are*.

"I'm an ER doctor. That's how I met Jess and Walker." Her eyes flash to me before looking at Walker and then back at Frankie. We simply nod our agreement.

She met me first. I was her patient. She didn't meet Walker until he came to take me home. The look on his face when I introduced them gave me the idea of asking her out for *us*. Every ER visit since was with the intent of bringing us to this moment where she agreed to a date with both of us.

And now, I'm fucking it up with my jealous pride. I didn't even greet her, never mind warmly. I ignored her as if her being here meant nothing.

It means *everything* despite my head telling my gut to shut the fuck up.

I clear my throat and ask if anyone needs a refill before heading to the bar to grab drinks. Landry said he'd take care of it, but he's busy singing with his wife on stage and the waitstaff is slammed. It's the least I can do, and it gives me a second to regroup and find my calm.

My phone vibrates in my pocket. When I see who the text is from, my heart starts hammering a beat faster than Landry's band.

Berklyn: *Are you going to be mad at me all night?*

Damn, I knew I was fucking this up, but I never expected her to call me on it. I'm impressed. And a little turned on. My Spitfire.

Me: *I'm not mad.*

Lies. All lies.

I look over my shoulder. Berk's attention is on her phone in her lap. She's trying to be covert. Cute.

Berklyn: *So, you ignore all your dates then?*

It's not a real date for me. Therefore, she's not *my* date. Though, a part of me really likes the idea.

Me: *Only the ones I like.*

Her head pops up, her wide eyes finding me instantly. The stillness of the moment steals my breath. I'm not sure, but I don't think she's breathing either. Her brow puckers before she breaks eye contact to reply.

Berklyn: *Reese says Mel's sangria is really good.*

Me: *Are you changing your order?*

Berklyn: *It is a woman's prerogative, isn't it?*

She's so cute, it makes my teeth hurt from all the clenching.

Me: *Question still stands.*

Berklyn: *Yes, please.*

Me: *I'm ordering food for the table. Any requests?*

Berklyn: *Fries. Lots and lots of fries. Doctor's orders.*

Damn, her cuteness level just switched to funny. Cute, funny, and sexy. It's a lethal combo. She's going to kill me. I've no doubt it will be as pleasurable as it is painful.

Me: *Done.*

Drinks in hand, I make it back to the table and reclaim my spot next to Berk with Walker on her other side. I slide her drink over. "If you don't like it, I'll get you something else."

"I'm sure I'll love it." She takes a sip and smiles with a thumbs-up. "Delicious," she says to me and Reese.

I hand Walker a Run Wild Non-Alcoholic IPA—our drink of choice when not consuming—keeping the other for myself.

After everyone has their drinks, Gabriel lifts his glass, making a toast, "To good friends, old and new."

In the mix of our resounding, "Hear, hear," "Cheers," "I second that," "Best of friends," I don't miss Berk's quiet, "To new friends."

The way she says it makes my heart hurt. Like she doesn't have any and would really like to be theirs. Avoiding her eyes, I press my leg against hers in silent comfort. I'm not really sure why, other than I think she needs it. I mumble, "Food's coming too."

"What'd you get?" Rowdy asks with hopeful eyes that match Reese's and Frankie's. Those two pregnant can eat any of us big guys under the table.

"Everything and a trough of fries."

"Yeah, fries!" Frankie seems nearly as excited as Berk.

"Thanks," my girl whispers.

"I also got you a burger and a chicken sandwich. I wasn't sure which you'd like."

Her smile is devastating. "I'm not picky. I'll take either or go halves if you want both."

"Halves it is." I couldn't decide which I wanted either, so this works.

I catch Walker smile, giving me a brow wag. He approves of my talking to her without sounding like I want to kill someone. Namely her, but not for any of the reasons anyone suspects. My anger is at myself for wanting something I have no business desiring.

I flip him off behind her back, my way of telling him to *calm the fuck down*.

"How was work?" Walker redirects our attention to our date. *No, not a date.*

"It was good. Crazy, but good." She proceeds to tell us about a nudist who came in with third degree burns from falling asleep while sunning on their roof deck.

"Is that the crazy part of your day?" Reese asked.

"Um, no." Berk twists her lips, color slowly rising, pinkening her cheeks.

Berk's blush is always arousing, but amongst my friends, I silently wrangle my body to behave.

"This couple came in with pink fur—fake—up their…" She points downwards with her hands. I don't know if she's unable to say those words or prefers not to with the mixed company staring at her like she's about to give away the secret to life. But she's a doctor. Those words should come easy to her, right?

"Vagina?" Frankie cringes, a sneer on her lips as a laugh bubbles free.

"Asshole?" Gabriel offers with a barely contained laugh.

"Yes," Berk points at them, eyes teaming with humor, "and yes."

"Pink fur from what, exactly?" Reese inquires.

Rowdy leans in. "Kitten, I'm not sure *I* want to know. I'm pretty sure *you* don't want to know." He kisses Reese's temple, tightening his hold around her shoulders.

My gut inexplicably constricts. *That's not for me.*

"*I* definitely want to know," Frankie chimes in, smirking at Gabriel's scowl.

Berklyn's gaze circles the table to confirm everyone wants to hear before continuing, "It's called Plushophilia. People who get sexually aroused by plushies—stuffed animals. Apparently, they covered a vibrator in fur and proceeded to…"

Jesus. I swipe my face, not wanting to hear more. Not because of the act but because of the visual of her involvement in the retrieval of said pink fur. But… Also the act… Fur. I mean, seriously.

"Pleasure each other?" Walker happily concludes, eyes gleaming. I want to bop him upside the head. He better not get any ideas.

"Yep," Berk pops the P. "It kinda fell apart from overuse, I guess." She shivers at the reminder.

Everyone bursts out laughing. Everyone except me. My insides roll and my jaw clenches at the thought of all the bizarre and potentially unsafe situations she must find herself in, working in one of Vegas' busiest emergency rooms. This is Sin City. Is she ever in danger? Has she been hurt while on the job?

Berk's laugh dies when she catches my glare. "What?"

My brow pinches, and I shake my head. "Nothin'." I'm being unreasonable. It's not my concern. *She's* not my concern.

Berklyn leans in, forcing her glorious scent up my nose. "Was my story too much? Did I embarrass you?" She sits back, wringing her hands. "It was, wasn't it?"

I cover her hands with mine, "No," and barely brush my lips across her temple. "It was funny."

She turns, bringing her lips dangerously close to mine. "Then why aren't you laughing?" Her incredulous gaze searches mine.

Squeezing her hands before pulling away, I break eye contact, grumbling, "Because I'm an ass." Plain but not so simple.

Worry for her seeps into my blood, coursing through my system like a lit fuse.

The silence pings between us as the conversation continues around the table. Walker pulls her into his discussion with Rowdy and Reese. All I hear are mumbled words and the harsh reality of how bad this *date* is going.

She'll never want me.

She's better off with Walker—*only* Walker.

Yet, as her attention is on anyone else but me, her hand silently settles on my thigh, squeezing once before simply remaining, palm down and open. Her heat radiates through my jeans, warming my skin, burning the impression of her hand on my skin.

Silent. Deadly. And desperately wanted. Her touch—is everything.

I'm back in this fight, unable to give up—not even for Walker.

I steal a steady breath and then another. Take a sip of my non-beer and witness her infiltrate my family by choice. Not so silently, still deadly, and oh so beautiful.

CHAPTER 10

WALKER

I CAN'T STOP SMILING. SHE'S GONNA THINK I'M HIGH if I don't stop. It's not even what she's saying—though her smarts are showing. It's her shy smile and her passing glances as if she needs assurance that she's doing okay getting along with our friends. Mostly it's her silent communication with Jess. I spotted her hand on his thigh, his on and off touches, and their shared glances. It's everything I've wanted—she's everything I want. For me. For us.

Jess and I have shared women for years. But they were one-nighters, few repeats, and never got my head going to where it's going now. Doc could be more. I want her to be more, not just for me but for Jess too. He needs someone to love, someone who will love him hard and deep and never, never betray that love.

Doc is the one. I'm sure of it. She can break his self-imposed curse he's chained to his heart, his love life, his future that is nothing more than work and baking—which is work too. Besides his gran and his friends—family by choice—he's looking at a future of empty sex and lonely nights. I can't hold out for him forever. He needs to get onboard, and Doc is the ticket.

She's a good person. Smart. Beautiful. None of us are kids—we all know what's going on. She's a full-fledged adult with emotional intelligence. She'd be good for us, and I think we'd be good for her. She's a busy woman. I doubt she has time for fun. I could give her fun and lighthearted. Jess—well, he can give her intensity and focus. I don't know if she needs those things, but I'm hoping we have something she wants.

When food arrives, I dig into my fully loaded bacon cheeseburger—thanks to my roommate for knowing me so well. I'm halfway through before I realize Doc and Jess are sharing a burger *and* a chicken sandwich. By the moaning going on, I think she's enjoying the burger more and maybe the French fries too.

"Just try it." She nudges me, motioning to the bottle next to me. "Can you pass the ketchup?"

"Yeah, sure." I hand her the bottle and watch as she squeezes a pool of the ruby goodness next to her pile of fries, not on them like me, then hands it to Jess, who I know doesn't use the stuff.

Only to my surprise, he does. I've never seen the man use ketchup, not on fries or even hotdogs. Not that the health nut eats hotdogs. Shocked, I sit back and watch as he pokes a fry in the ketchup and takes a bite before putting the whole thing in his mouth.

Berklyn smiles while she does the same, mumbling, "I can't believe you don't use ketchup. It's unAmerican or something."

"It's unnecessary sugar," he retorts around his second fry with *unnecessary sugar* on it.

I don't even try to hide my smirk. She's good for him.

"You have to admit, it's good," she insists, teasing him with a hair flip and nibbling her bottom lip. She cares what he thinks. It's sweet.

Jess shrugs, completely missing her flirting. "The question is, would you rather have vanilla ice cream or ketchup?"

She gawks, a fry halfway to her mouth. "Seriously?"

He chuckles and urges her arm to finish its path to her mouth. "You're a doctor. You have to know this."

She aggressively bites her fry in half. "I'm a doctor, not a nutritionist. But there might be some vague recollection of this knowledge somewhere in my brain." She dips the other half of her fry, swirling it around. "I'd prefer to have both, honestly."

Their eyes lock, and if I wasn't so invested in their connection, I'd look away. The heat penetrating his gaze before lowering his eyes to her breasts and back up has all kinds of dirty thoughts swirling in my head. Thoughts I'm not bold enough to say, especially not with an audience. Suffice it to say, it involves Doc and licking ice cream off her breasts and her—

"Honestly," he leans in close so only she and I can hear, "I like the look of both on you."

Damn. That's my boy. The Closer.

Her blush is authentic and endearing. He only complimented her body. What would she do if she knew what I was thinking of doing to it?

Jess looks at me with a slight nod before focusing back on his food.

"Speaking of ice cream," I nudge her with my shoulder to get her attention, "what's your favorite?"

She smiles as she sits back, considering. "There are so many. It depends on the brand, but pretty much anything vanilla with chocolate. Chocolate fudge is a bonus. I'm not so crazy about nuts in my ice cream, but it's not a *no*."

"So, nuts aren't a deal breaker." Of course, all I can think of is her licking ice cream off my balls. "Noted."

Out of the corner of my eye, I catch Jess shaking his head. He caught my inuendo or at least the dirty path my brain is heading down.

"I like caramel too," she adds.

"If you had to choose, fries or ice cream?" Jess asks.

Her brow puckers as she takes a sip of her water, narrowing her gaze on him. "Why do you hate me?"

He laughs. "That hard to choose, huh?"

I like the way she looks to me before turning back to him, like she wants to be sure I'm included in the conversation. "If you're going to make me choose, fries, hands down."

"Doctor's orders." The glint in Jess's eyes gives me hope.

"Now you understand." She motions between us. "What about you, salty or sweet?"

"Salty," Jess chimes in before I can.

"Both. Though I'd prefer steak over fries." Mmm, we should grill steaks next time we get together.

Her face lights up. "I didn't know steak was on the table."

"Beef is *always* on the table, Doc." I waggle my eyebrows in emphasis.

She bites her lip, giving me a once-over. "Good to know."

BERKLYN

I'm being a shameless flirt. I'm feeling it tonight with these two. It was a rocky start with Jess, and I'm hoping I don't say or do something that turns off his attention. Because being the focus of his attentiveness is hot on so many levels. Probably, mostly, because I know he can turn it off with a flip of a switch. I've been in that dank coldness before. I didn't like it. I don't want to go there again.

Let me be worthy of his attention. It's sad how much I crave it, how much I want it, how much I want him.

But then there's sweet Walker with his kind eyes and jovial nature. He has a wicked naughty streak that steals my breath and has me wanting to crawl under his skin to find out what he's thinking behind those mischievous golden eyes and kissable lips.

"Dance with me." Jess' warm breath teases my ear as his eyes lock on mine, waiting, nearly pleading.

"Okay." He wasn't really asking, but his eyes say he was. I kiss Walker's cheek before sliding out of the booth behind Jess, taking his offered hand.

As we make it to the dance floor, the song changes to something slow. Jess pulls me into his chest, scooping my arms to rest on his shoulders before his hands slide down my sides to land on my hip and lower back. I suck in a breath when he tightens his grip, his eyes holding me happily hostage as he starts a slow and seductive dance while his friend Landry sings "Hurt Somebody."

I'm not sure I take more than a handful of breaths the entire time. It isn't until the song switches again that he breaks eye contact and moves into a two-step around the floor that I finally give in to my need for air.

I've never been much of a dancer, but under his capable hands, I feel light on my feet and graceful. It's an illusion I'm afraid will crumble the moment I open my mouth. So, I stay silent and let him lead through song after song until we're sweaty and in need of cool drinks.

But instead of heading back to the table, he secures me a seat at the bar with two ice waters set in front of us by the bartender. Jess' front presses into my side as he stands between me and the guy behind him, his arm around my back as we down our drinks. It's close proximity, but after dancing sequestered in his arms, it feels right.

After refills and I dab the sweat from my face and neck, Jess leans in. His intensity is back, his focus all on me. "Why didn't you want me to pick you up tonight?"

I'm thrown back to our arrival—Walker and I—and Jess' cold

welcome. "Is that what you thought—that I was rejecting you?" I frown at his assumption. "Is that why you were angry?"

He glances over my head, scratching his jaw in consideration. "Maybe."

I don't want to cause issues between him and Walker, so I only say, "I guess I assumed you didn't want to since you didn't show up with Walker." I play with the condensation on my glass. People are loud and animated all around us, but this space between us feels intimate and throbbing with tethers that, if pulled, could go down multiple paths—good and bad.

He tips my chin, his green eyes locking on mine. "I wanted to."

I shudder under his gaze, taking in the weight of that confession. "Noted."

I save that tidbit for consideration when I dwell on the details of tonight, when I'm home alone in my bed, wondering if he wished he'd picked me up on his own or with Walker? Does he really want to share me? Does Walker? Or is sharing their kink?

If he leans in any farther, his lips will touch mine, or if I lean in, just a little, we'd be kissing. But I don't. I don't want to make the first move. Welcomed or not, even under his spell, I'm uncertain of the next steps. How to move from A to B with a man who acts like he could eat me alive with passion one minute and spit me out the next.

My head spins with the notion, and I'm not even tipsy, my sangria long forgotten and watered down at our table.

A warm hand snags up the back of my neck and sinks into my hair seconds before Walker's face comes into focus at my side, facing Jess. I'm in the middle of a Walker and Jess sandwich. God is good.

"You ready to get out of here?" Walker's hopeful gaze doesn't leave me as Jess' hand slips lower, drawing lazy circles right above my butt where my underwear would be if I were wearing any.

"Yeah," I let out on a sigh.

I guess Walker has a plan on how to get us from A to B.

"Let's say our goodbyes." Jess presses his lips to my temple, and my whole body heats.

I flash to Walker, concerned about the show of affection. But he only winks and offers me his hand. "We'll be quick."

My surprise must show as he leans in, kisses my cheek and whispers, "Promise we won't be quick about *that*, Doc."

CHAPTER 11

JESS

WHEN WALKER LIFTS BERKLYN INTO HIS TRUCK— and she lets him—I bite back a roar of possessiveness and slide in after, lifting her onto my lap. I still her complaint with a grip on her thigh. "We're not far."

I secure the seatbelt around us and ease her into lying back with her head on my shoulder so we're cheek to cheek and every bit of her backside is pressed against my front.

"This is illegal and dangerous. I can sit in the back." She squirms and gasps when she rubs her ass along the hard ridge of my cock.

Yeah, baby, that's for you. "Be still," I groan in her ear and press into her, resisting the urge to rut into her like a horny teen.

We leave my Charger at the bar. I'm not missing this opportunity to ease her into what happens next.

I slide my hand up her thighs, easing her legs apart. She resists for a moment and then relaxes. "Anything you don't like, all you have to do is say so, and it stops." I squeeze her breast as my other hand continues up the inside of her thigh, testing the waters. She gasps. I don't stop. "I won't ask for permission, but that doesn't mean you can't say no." I suck and nibble her earlobe, drawing out a slow moan. "Understand?"

"Yes," she practically pants, letting her legs fall open on either side of mine as my hand nears the promised land.

"Walker, anything you want to mention?" He's part of this too. I might be playing while he drives, but that won't always be the case.

He groans from the driver's seat, "Y'all look so hot."

I catch his gaze falling to her lap and tap his arm. "Eyes on the road, or I stop."

"Don't stop." He places both hands on the steering wheel, probably trying to keep from touching her or himself. "Are you wet for us, Doc?"

His attention is back on the road where it needs to be, but his mind is racing, just like mine. I stop millimeters from her pussy, her heat radiating, calling to me. "Answer him, Berklyn, or I stop."

"Yes!" she cries seconds before I make contact.

Fuck. Fuck. Fuck. She's not even… "Berk, where the fuck are your panties?" Anger rises as I slide my fingers through her uninhibited slickness and growl my displeasure at finding her bare. It's a mixed bag. I'm hard as fuck and turned on by the easy access. But I'm pissed she went out in public in a semi-short dress that could have given a free show had I twirled her on the dance floor a little faster.

She grinds against my hand. "Laundry day?"

I want to spank her sassy ass. Instead, I sink a finger inside her and suck on her neck to squelch my groan. She so fucking wet and hot. I can't wait to dip my cock inside. "You don't go without panties unless we say so. Got it?"

"Yes," she moans as I fingerfuck her nice and slow, gripping her breast and teasing her nipple.

I don't know if she's too turned on to answer honestly, but for now, I'll accept her acquiescence and reward her with another finger. Sliding in and out, my palm pressed against her clit. "So fucking wet, baby."

"I can hear it," Walker groans.

"Can you smell how turned on she is?" I lathe her neck and shoulder with open-mouth kisses, grinding into her, pressing her against my hand, fucking her in my mind, deep and hard. "When you come, whose name are you gonna call?"

"Um, yours?" She writhes on my lap, trying to control the pace.

"This time. It'll be Walker's when he's the one bringing you pleasure."

Her head falls to the side. I imagine her watching his jaw tick as he focuses on the road. "Do you want to touch me?" she breathlessly asks him.

Damn, she knows how to play.

His eyes flash to her. "Yeah, Doc. As soon as we're home, there will be so much touching."

And fucking.

"We're almost home, baby. You gonna come for us?" I increase the pressure, rubbing that special place inside that has her keening and clawing at my arm and the center console between us and Walk.

Fuck. The sound of her wet pussy sucking my fingers so tight is nearly too much. I close my eyes, lost in the feel of her grinding in my arms against my hard cock. Her labored breaths are music to my ears. Seconds stretch into eternities and then snap back into place when she stiffens and says my name on a long exhale as she peaks and falls over the edge for me. For us.

"Holy fuck," Walker exclaims as he stops the car and throws it into park. He opens and slams his door, and before I can get the seatbelt loose, he opens my door and pulls her off my lap and into his arms. Berk wraps her legs around his waist, grinding against him, working through the last of her orgasm as his mouth slams over hers.

I slip out behind them, pressed to her back, and guide them through the garage door to our apartment, never breaking their heated kiss. His hand slips to her ass beneath her dress, and I growl my approval as he groans when he touches her wet pussy. She's drenched, I know it, and I can't wait to taste her.

WALKER

"Walker," she moans as my fingers slip through her wet folds before sinking inside.

"So fucking wet, Doc. So fucking sexy." I barely break our kiss, thankful for Jess guiding us to his bedroom.

He has the custom, made-for-a-giant bed that's perfect for fucking. But just inside his door, he stops me. We don't even make it to the bed before he's ripping her dress up over her head and relieving her of her bra.

I slowly lower her to her feet, trailing kisses along her jaw and neck before Jess turns her around and drops to his knees.

"Jess!" She sucks in air and grips his hair. "Jesus, give a girl warning." Her head falls to my shoulder, and she gasps, "Oh my God."

He doesn't let up. He lifts her leg, resting her foot on his shoulder, spreading her wide. I capture her mouth, losing myself in her taste, her gasping moans and shuddered cries. I caress her everywhere I can touch, grip, or hold on to while pressing my front to her back, keeping her standing on one leg as he devours her from below. I've never seen Jess so ravenous, so out of control. And it only turns me on more.

What happened in the truck was fucking epic. I nearly came in my jeans when she did. If she'd held out a few seconds longer, I would have made it into the garage in time to slip my fingers inside her too and feel her come.

I could do that now, or I could—

"Oh!" Doc breaks our kiss, and her eyes fly open. "Is that you?"

I rim her asshole again. "Yeah, is that okay?"

"Are you asking for permission?" She seems surprised.

"I am." I'm not as bossy as Jess. I know he won't force her to do anything she doesn't want, but he also won't ask as much beforehand. I don't want to make her uncomfortable. One of us has to think ahead and ask permission when it's warranted, and with ass play, it is warranted. "Have you ever been fucked in the ass, Doc?" I'm also direct.

"Once—" Her head falls back, and her grip on Jess' hair tightens. "Oh God!"

Jess growls his approval, working her harder.

I'll go easy on the ass play until we can discuss it when she's able to think clearly. Jess presses my hand to her hole, encouraging me to warm her up to the idea. I think she's already *warm* to the idea of whatever we want. She's on the verge of her second orgasm, and he and I are still fully clothed.

I use the moisture from her soaked pussy to lubricate my finger and gently press through her tight ring as Jess works her pussy from the inside out.

"Yes," she grips the back of my neck and kisses me, sucking my tongue, and moans, "Walker," into our kiss.

I delve deeper, only a finger, as far as I can while twisting and pulling at her nipples and devour her mouth. I can't get enough as Jess eats her pussy. Desperate, I grind my hard cock against her to find some relief.

On a sated cry, she comes, moaning our names. My eyes burn with the urge to cry at the sound of my name on her tongue as she falls apart in ecstasy. I've wanted this for so long. Maybe not as long as Jess. But right now, I don't think I could want this more, be harder or more desperate to fuck her until I fill her up again and again.

Jess lowers her leg and holds her hips as he stands, pulling his shirt off and wiping his glistening face. "Don't stop fucking her ass," he grouses as he leans close, lingering like he might kiss her.

Do it. I hold my breath, wanting him to take the chance, to commit to this, make her ours. He wavers, then brushes his lips across her cheek. "You okay? Can you take more?"

I'm disappointed he didn't kiss her, but I'm impressed he's asking for a status check.

She cups his cheek and smiles. "I can't believe there's more."

I chuckle and nod to Jess. "You're about to get a whole lot more, Doc." I slowly move my finger in her ass, smiling at her gasp and trail my other hand down her stomach through her pussy lips before delving inside. "Look at him." I nudge her head that's lolled to rest on my shoulder.

She perks up and swivels her hips as Jess unbuttons his jeans with one hand. Then he toes off his shoes before pulling off the rest of his clothes. I've seen Jess in all states of undress. I'm a straight guy, but I have to admit, seeing him hard with lust in his eyes is a turn-on, namely because I know what he can do with that cock and how he's gonna make her scream her consent over and over again. And I get a front row seat.

CHAPTER 12

BERKLYN

I CAN'T STOP MY KNEES FROM WOBBLING AS JESS strokes his beautifully hard cock and steps up to me. I've never seen a more magnificent creature in all my life. I've no doubt Walker is just as impressive. I don't need to see him naked to believe it's true. I can't imagine both of them naked before me, wanting *me*.

I can't stop staring in awe as Jess tweaks my nipple before bending to draw the tight bud into his mouth.

I grip his shoulders and moan, "Oh God," for the hundredth time. They must be sick of hearing it.

"No, never." Walker trails kisses along my neck, making me shake with need. "You keep moaning your pleasure, and we'll keep making you come."

God, that's the best promise I've ever heard.

He chuckles. "You're saying your inner thoughts, Doc. Just want to be sure you know that."

I can't help it. I can't be held responsible for my actions or what I say.

The intensity of their touches has me on the verge of coming for a third time. "Please," I beg to whoever is listening.

Walker slowly removes his fingers from inside me, keeping the one in my ass. The sensation is so much stronger now that it's the only one, until he circles my clit with his wet fingers. "I want you to come again before Jess fucks you."

Yes. Yes, do that. "I'm not sure I can," I mumble, though I'm pretty sure I'm about to find out.

"You can." Jess runs his hand below Walker's and slips inside me, growling his approval when I clench around his digits. He bites my nipple before licking the sting away, then kisses across my chest to my other breast. I cry out as he sucks it deep, flicking his tongue and twisting the other nipple between his fingers.

I pull Walker into a kiss even though I want to know what it's like to kiss Jess, but his mouth is busy, and I'm not about to stop his ministrations. A moment later, a warm mouth lands on my neck, kissing and teasing my sensitive flesh as I'm kissing Walker.

Jess fingers me faster. "Need you to come, baby." Jess's voice is deeper, commanding and needy.

"Just fuck me. You don't need to wait." No need to be greedy.

The next second, I'm lifted in the air, all fingers exit my body, and I'm crushed between Walker—who's backed up to the closed door—and Jess, whose cock slams into me before I can get my legs around his waist.

"Fuck," Jess groans into my neck and swivels his hips. "I can't wait any longer."

My response dies on my lips as he pulls out and thrusts forward, pushing me into Walker, who grips my hips and whispers in my ear, "You've made him crazy with lust, Doc. Feel how hard he is for you."

"Walker," I moan as his words trail over my skin and Jess fucks me like he can't get deep enough. He's frantic, and it's such a turn-on. I've made him lose his mind. Me.

"Want you to come on his cock, Doc. Can you do that for me?" Walker snakes his hand between Jess and me and rubs my clit, murmuring, "Fuck, I can't wait to feel you wrapped around me."

That's all it takes to have me screaming my release, bucking in their arms as my body tightens in all the right places and strangles Jess' cock. But he doesn't come. He slows, biting my neck, sending another wave of flutters through my body.

"Fuck, Berk," he growls and licks the sting, stilling deep inside me as I quiver in his embrace. "Not done with you."

JESS

On shakier legs than I'd like, I pull Berk out of Walker's hold and lay her on the bed. She collapses, arms wide, hair splayed across my pillow, nipples tight, begging for attention. Kneeling between her spread legs, I slowly push back in, filling her to the brim. I start to fuck her slowly, letting her catch her breath and letting my body calm so I can go longer without coming in sixty seconds flat. I grip her hips, pulling her to me with each drive, kneading her flesh as I surge forward. Enjoying the view of my cock wet with her juices, I slide in and out of her bare pussy, her tits bouncing with each thrust.

Her hands land on mine and slowly make their way to my thighs as she arches into me. Her gaze slips to the side where Walker is watching. Her brow furrows before coming back to me.

"He likes to watch, Berk. Don't worry. He'll get his turn." The thought has me thrusting harder.

"I thought you wanted to share me." Her attention slips back to him.

"Walk, our girl needs your reassurance." I don't stop fucking her as he kneels on the bed, getting in her face.

"I'm right here, Doc. Enjoying the view." He runs his hand along the side of her face and into her hair, his forehead pressed to hers.

It's intimate and tender. *I can't give her that.* The reminder only makes me fuck her harder, gripping her hips tight enough to leave marks to remember me by. That I can do. "Tease her clit," I bark through clenched teeth.

Walker complies. His eyes never leave hers as she presses her head into the pillow. She moans her approval as his fingers circle her needy nub and she clenches around me.

"Fuck, that's it." If I could freeze this moment, I would. On the verge of flying, tipping the edge. The feel of her is… Everything.

He lies beside her, stealing a kiss that should be for me. She grips his hair, keeping him close as he fucks her with his tongue in time with my cock.

"Fuck, Berk." I throw my head back and fuck her faster, harder, closing out the sight of her giving him what I can't take.

"Jess," she moans into their kiss, and I feel triumphant, exonerated for all the times I was an ass to her, for all the times I didn't think she'd want me like this.

Faster. Faster. Faster.

I slam into her over and over again, watching them kiss and his finger moving on her clit. So tender, so loving, only for her gratification.

Heady pleasure and tunnel vision wrap around me when she comes, stealing my soul and sucking the cum from my cock, making me grunt my worship in the form of her name, "Berks, fuck, baby." I thrust through each spasm of my release and hers until her body stills and I pull out, watching my cum slip out of her well-used pussy. I run my thumb along her opening, pushing it back inside. *This.* I can give her this.

She trembles and jerks, breaking their kiss, and her eyes land on me. My cock bobs, still semi-hard, and her gaze falls to it. Her brow arches, and I smile. "Not done, baby. We're just getting started."

CHAPTER 13

WALKER

D OC NAKED AND SATIATED LYING BEFORE ME IS A
dream come true. Sharing her with Jess, a fantasy. She runs her
hand up my chest, gripping my shirt, pulling me to her. "Will you
get naked now?"

Wild horses couldn't stop me. "Yeah, Doc." I kiss her gently, taking
the time to enjoy her sex haze before I get so deep into it, I forget to take
a mental picture of this gorgeous sight. "You need anything?"

"You inside me."

I smile against her mouth. "That's absolutely gonna happen, but I
mean do you need a drink or the bathroom?"

"I'm not sure I can walk, to be honest."

I should laugh, but she's so sincere. "I can carry you." I've never
helped a woman pee, but it's not something I'd shy away from.

"I'm good," she insists.

Jess rolls to his side on a grunt, mumbling, "I'll get us some water."

While he's gone, I slip the covers off from below her and push them to the foot of the bed, something we should have done before Jess fucked her. There has to be a massive wet spot on his comforter. A fact I'm sure he couldn't give a shit about.

I tug my shirt off, my shoes and socks long gone, and undo my jeans, giving my cock room to breathe all while her eyes never leave me, trailing a heated path along my every groove and hard edge. I lean down and take her mouth for a slow, savoring ride.

Her hands scorch my skin as she feels her way around my chest to my back and lower, gripping my ass below my jeans. "I want to taste you," she breathes across my lips.

Well, fuck. She doesn't have to ask twice. Rising to my knees, I push my jeans and boxer briefs far enough to free my cock. Before I can settle, she lunges, her hand gripping my shaft as her tongue licks my crown like an ice cream cone, once, twice, then sucking me deep.

"Fuck, Doc." I grip her hair to slow her roll. Her aggressiveness is going to end me before I get inside that pussy of hers. "Make it last, Sugar."

She slows, running her tongue along the underside, pulling me deep as she sucks like I'm a fudge pop. *Fuck. Fuck. Fuck. That's not any easier on my restraint.* "Too much," I hiss and pull out of her mouth.

"What—"

I stop her protest by slamming my mouth to hers, shoving my jeans and underwear down. When they get to my calves, they're tugged free. "Thanks," I mumble to Jess, knowing he's the one who finished the job.

"There's water on the end table when you need it." His words are helpful but distracting.

I settle between Doc's thighs and groan when she wraps her legs around me, grinding her wet heat against my desperately hard cock.

Without protest or asking, I breach her entrance, pushing through her swollen flesh, eating up her cries with our kiss.

Deep, so fucking deep, I fuck into her, grinding my hips, getting maximum clit contact while stroking her insides with each thrust. I bend my knee, opening her more, sinking deeper, barely holding my weight off her with my arms. Her silky hair caresses my hands as I hold her head, deepening our kiss as we fuck each other's mouths.

Her moans, gasps, and needy hands spur me on, but it's Jess settling in beside us that has me breaking our kiss, catching my breath, and watching as he snakes his hand between us, squeezing her breast, twisting her nipple.

Doc throws her head back, loving the contact, which has me switching gears.

I turn her to face Jess, lift her top leg and sink back in. "Walker," she sighs, reaching for me, caressing me with her heated gaze and wanton moans.

I lean forward, spreading her wider, and kiss her mouth until Jess nudges his way to her breasts. She grips the back of his head and wraps the other around my neck, keeping me close, but I don't kiss her. I watch as he flicks her nipples with his tongue before sucking each one, gripping her breast, forcing a silent cry from her lips as she arches into him.

My hips slam forward, harder, but not faster. I'm not ready for this to end. I'm not ready to come, though it's a losing battle. There's no way I won't come when she does, and by the way she's gripping my cock, neither of us will last much longer.

I don't miss the sensation of Jess grinding against my thigh. He's ready to go again, and that only heightens my desire to watch her come around his cock again.

The tingle up my spine alerts me there's no way I'm not coming unless I stop fucking, and there's no way that's happening. But she needs to come first. I direct Jess' hand to her clit before I put all of my weight on her leg and my arms, leaning in to devour her mouth.

When she falls apart, I groan through the vise around my cock, thrusting harder, giving her my focus until she crests. Then I sit back on my knees and grip her leg, fucking into her with a frenzied need until she's screaming my name and taking my cum deep as I bathe her insides with my release.

JESS

As soon as Walker falls to his back, I urge Berk to straddle his lap, his used dick squished between them. It'll get him hard again, and this time, he's not only going to watch me fuck her, he's going to feel it.

I press on her back, keeping her against him, giving her a chance to recover. We've been enthusiastic with her. I doubt her body has ever been used this much or felt this much pleasure. But damn if she doesn't press her ass into my hard cock as she looks over her shoulder, biting her lip.

Running the head of my cock along her drenched folds, I can't help but think of mine and Walk's cum dripping out of her. We briefly discussed condoms and were elated when she agreed to go bareback, which we never do. But with Berk… It's different.

This connection with Berk is making me do all kinds of things I've never considered before, only I write it off to endorphins teeming through my body. Maybe when I'm not hard for her, I'll think differently.

"You good?" Walker asks seconds before I push inside her heat. I don't answer. I start fucking. That's answer enough.

"Fuck," he groans. His hands come up to grip her hips, urging her forward and back. "You're so fucking wet, Doc. Our cum is coating my dick, making me hard."

Berk presses up and looks down, watching as we move her back and forth on our cocks, only I'm inside her, relishing the feel of her, so fucking hot and wet, sucking me in like she can't get enough.

Walker takes the opportunity to play with her tits, pulling a sigh from her lips.

"Please don't stop." Her head lolls to the side. "It feels so good."

I grip her thighs and lean back just enough to thrust harder, longer. "Nobody's stopping, Berk." I run my hand up her back, squeezing the back of her neck, causing her to tremble. I bend down and kiss her shoulder and up her neck. "I think you need us both inside you."

She turns her head so fast, our lips clash, but instead of pulling away, I pull her back so she's flush with my chest and eye Walker as he looks down to where we're joined. He trails his gaze up her body, catching on her breasts he continues to tease, and asks, "Think you can take us?"

Before I hear her answer, I pull out and hop off the bed to retrieve lube from the nightstand. She's wet as fuck, but you can never have too much lubrication, especially when two dicks are rubbing against each other. I look up to find her eyes on me. My brow punches. "We need a yes or a no, Berk. There're no passive agreements in our beds." That's another rule she'll need to remember. I may not always ask for permission, but when I do, I expect an answer.

Her concerned gaze flicks between us. "Both of you inside me... Where?"

I kneel beside her and squirt lube on my fingers before slipping between her folds and pressing them into her. "Here, baby. Your ass will require more than lube to prepare. We're only talking about your pussy." I kiss her shoulder. "We'll discuss your ass at another time."

"Okay." She nods and grabs the lube, squeezing some in her hand, and grips my cock. I thrust into her hand as she coats my shaft, and I continue to finger-fuck her.

When I'm thoroughly lubricated and ready to fuck her into next week, I motion to Walker and return to my position behind her, chuckling at her grumble as I remove my fingers from her pussy. Greedy girl.

CHAPTER 14

Berklyn

R IDING WALKER IS A WHOLE NEW EXPERIENCE, especially all slicked up. I didn't think it would feel different, and maybe it's just mental, knowing what's about to happen as Walker stills my movements and Jess pushes me into Walker's chest.

"Take a breath for me, Doc." Walker snakes his hand into my hair, capturing my attention. "Relax. It'll be tight at first. Then you'll stretch to accommodate us. Remember, babies come down this path."

He groans when I clench around him at the thought of getting pregnant by these two. We're not using condoms. Birth control is not one hundred percent effective. But the idea of not feeling them when they come inside me after having experienced them in all their glory isn't something I'm interested in. This feels like a once-in-a-lifetime opportunity, and I want the full package.

"Rub her clit," Jess barks from behind me, his cock primed and ready.

I slam my hand on Walker's chest, biting back a moan as his thumb coasts across my clit.

"Don't fight it, Sugar. Let us hear you." Walker tweaks my nipple, his eyes pleading with me, begging me to take it—to take him. *Him* being Jess.

"That's it, push back," Jess groans in my ear.

I didn't even realize I was, but I do it with purpose and scream, "Jesus F!" when Jess slips in with Walker's cock already inside me. "Oh my..." My vision darkens for a moment, and I close my eyes. It's too much.

"Breathe, baby." Jess kisses along my shoulder as he kneads my hips. "Just breathe."

The intensity of Walker's mouth on my breast brings me back to them. I open my eyes and swipe at wet cheeks.

"You okay?" Jess comes into view as he cups my cheek, swiping at the tears.

"I don't know why I'm crying." My chin wobbles, and my voice cracks as I fight back a sob. Gah, this is embarrassing. I mean it hurt, but that's not—

"You're safe with us, Doc." Walker cups my other cheek.

"It's not unheard of, crying during something so intimate, so intense. You're vulnerable, opening yourself up to us," Jess adds. He kisses my temple, taking a deep breath. "You say the word, and we stop."

Their tenderness is unexpected, and instead of making me cry harder, my tears dry up. I want this. I want this with them. "I'm okay."

Jess studies my face for another second before kissing my cheek and pulling back to grip my hips. "We'll go slow. Let me lead," he urges.

I nod my consent and focus on Walker, watching his face morph into one of pure bliss as Jess begins to move. Slowly, he pulls out and pushes back in, little by little, short strokes that have me moaning and arching into him, asking for more.

He doesn't disappoint. His mouth lands on the back of my neck, his whispered praise raising goosebumps along my skin and puckering my nipples under Walker's care.

Soon they alternate their thrusts, and I fall into a state of euphoria that knows no bounds, no limits, as I take them into my body and release the pleasure in panted breaths and cries for more.

The smells and sounds of sex fill the air, and I'm lost to their groans and growls of carnality. Their focus is intense and all consuming.

Harder.

Faster.

Wetter.

Slaps of flesh meeting flesh.

Cries of ecstasy fill my ears with grunts of need driving them forward, deeper, deeper, deeper.

Walker sucks and nips at my breasts as Jess fingers my clit, griping my hip, taking me.

Faster.

Faster.

Faster.

The feel, the feel, the feel of their possessive touch, complete and utter ownership of my body and my enjoyment of theirs. On a cry that rips up my throat, I come so hard, the air around us ignites and sparks in my vision, racking my body in violent tremors with no control over my limbs.

Jess presses me into Walker as they come, barking their praise, their adoration, their endearments that have my heart fluttering and my tears falling free and unfettered.

I wake in a heap of muscles, limbs, and hot bodies. My own aches like I've never had sex before. Though, I suppose I've never had sex like *that*

before. I groan and hide my embarrassment in the chest I'm using as a pillow. I open my eyes long enough to see who it belongs to.

A big, warm hand runs up my back and into my hair, massaging my scalp. I softly groan, and Jess' chest rumbles below me in approval. His other hand starts on my back moments before a third hand rubs my thigh up to my ass, over and down the other leg.

I arch into their caresses, drawing groans from them as they roll into me from below and behind. The hard press of their cocks, making me want what my body has no business wanting again so soon.

"She's sore," Walker's morning timbre wafts across my back, his mouth taking up residence where a hand isn't touching.

"She can still come," Jess' grumble sends a tremor down my spine.

"Why are y'all talking about me like I'm not here?" I roll to my back, forcing Walker to make room so I'm not sprawled on top of him, then catch each of their sleepy gazes.

"Believe me, we know you're here, Berklyn." My name on Jess' tongue has my core weeping for attention. He doesn't disappoint. Lifting onto his elbow, he zeroes in on my left breast, licking the tender peak before flattening his tongue, running circles around and over it then sucking it deep.

"Oh, God." I arch into his touch, reaching between us and wrapping my hand around his hardness.

His growl of approval is all it takes for me to turn to Walker and do the same as he latches onto my other breast. With my head thrown back on a moan, they lift my legs to lay over theirs.

Walker tosses the covers off, revealing our nakedness to the breeze of the ceiling fan. I shudder as their hands roam my body, avoiding the apex of my wanton need. I undulate my hips, trying to draw them closer. Thumbing the heads of their cocks, I spread their moisture, making me clench around nothing and silently beg them to touch me.

A quick swipe across my opening, then over my clit, passing to one side then the other, down my thighs, gripping and kneading, flexing their cocks into my hands as my hips reach and reach for nothing but air. "Please," I beg out loud.

One of their hands cups my pussy, running their fingers through my wetness to tease my clit and back. Another hand does the same and stills on my opening, rubbing just above it, over it, and below. Finally, finally, fingers concentrate on my clit, circling slowly as another enters me, just barely, but enough to have me arching off the bed, begging, "More." I squeeze their cocks. "Please."

"Fuck." Jess's eyes pop open, locking on me, still sucking my breast and the finger goes deeper. I guess that's his hand as the one on my clit stays steady.

"Yes." I rub the head of his cock, and he adds another finger. "I need you inside me," I plead, undeterred by the pleasurable ache of my overused pussy. "Please."

Jess rises over me, releasing my breast, spreading me wide as he kneels between my thighs with my ass lifted in his hands, squeezing before guiding his cock to my entrance. "I don't want to hurt you." His pained expression eases as he slowly enters me on a groan that matches my own. He thrusts slowly, leaning over me, pulling my hand off Walker's cock. "Suck," he commands.

Walker comes to his knees beside me, his hard dick in his hand, near my face. "You okay with this?"

"Yes, but—" I lose my words on a moan when Jess starts rubbing my clit in time with his thrusts. It takes me a second to realize I'm being selfish, taking and not giving. I lean over and take Walker in my mouth, sucking him harder than he's probably prepared for as I bob up and down, taking him down my throat as Jess' cock fills me to the brim.

It's too much.

So full.

Walker's adoring gaze as he thrusts into my mouth, squeezing and pinching my nipples, groaning, "So fucking hot, Doc. You take us so good," has moisture flooding my core on a muffled cry.

"Fuck, baby, yes. So goddamned wet," Jess growls, squeezing my hip and fucking me deeper.

Walker's head falls back, his other hand locked in my hair, holding my head up off the pillow. "Not gonna last."

"Need you to come, Berk." Jess thrusts harder and rubs me faster, bringing a tingle to my spine that surges and spreads.

"Jess!" I cry seconds before I come.

Walker pulls out of my mouth and latches onto my breasts, biting and sucking, throwing me over the edge. I scream my elation, the sound echoing in my ears, reverberating in my bones as I shake through Jess roaring his release. He grips my hips, pounding each rush of ejaculate into me, sending chills along my body.

Still deep inside me, Jess leans down, kissing up my stomach to lathe the breast not occupied by Walker with his tongue before trailing up my chest to my neck and along my jaw to my ear. "You're fucking perfect, Berks."

I shudder under his praise and long for his kiss that never comes.

Jess pulls out of me, his lips still on my neck, mumbling, "Walker," before he falls to my side, his hand replacing his mouth on my breast.

Walker leans over me, turning my face to him, running his fingers over my mouth. "Your mouth is perfect, Doc, but I'd really like to come buried deep in your pussy."

God, these men and their words of praise. I cup his cheek, running my hand into his hair. "How could I say no to that?"

His smile is devastating. His kiss is tender as he plays with my breast before lifting my leg and entering me slowly, twisting my hips to take me from behind. His hand slides down my stomach to splay over my pussy, touching my clit and probably himself as he glides in and out on a groan that has my nipples hardening.

I grip his ass and arch into his thrusts, moaning my pleasure.

Jess moves closer and sucks my breast while kneading the other, his cock between us, grazing my thigh as he thrusts in time with Walker.

Tilting toward Jess, I lift my leg, reach between us and guide him to my entrance to join Walker. But instead of entering me, he holds his cock to my clit and thrusts against me, saying, "You'll be too sore, baby." His lips find my neck, and he sucks and licks, whispering dirty words of praise along my skin.

Walker reaches over me, gripping Jess' back, and Jess does the same, sandwiching me between then, completely on my side, not a breath of space between any of us. Walker fucks inside me from behind, and Jess fucks against me face-to-face, rubbing my clit and I imagine parts of Walker with his cock and balls. The thought only turns me on more, the fact that they worship my body so thoroughly and don't mind their swords crossing is an unexpected turn-on, more so because their pleasure is lost in pleasing me and not each other.

Our bodies undulate to a rhythm they create, accompanied by our gasps, moans, and verbalized "Fucks" and "Oh Gods," increasing in tempo. They drive me into a frenzy, and my hold on Jess tightens, my foot locked against his ass as I near the edge of ecstasy. In turn, his firm grip on Walker ensures the friction we both need never wavers and only increases with each thrust from Walker and Jess meeting my clit over and over again.

I come on a strangled cry, relishing the feel of Jess coming on my stomach as he sucks on my neck and the bite of Walker's grip on my hip as he groans his release with a slap on my ass and a final thrust that has my insides bathed in his cum.

"Fuck me," Jess exhales into my neck, moving his head to rest between my breasts.

My hips still move, enjoying the contact, the small tremors that feel so good.

Walker kisses my neck. "You could come again, couldn't you?" He doesn't wait for my reply before snaking his hand between us, rubbing my clit with purpose.

I moan and strain, reaching, reaching, already close, so turned on knowing he's not avoiding touching Jess' cock still stuck between us to pleasure me. The lubrication is a mix of Jess' cum, mine, and Walker's.

Jess thrusts, growling, "Fuck," and bites my nipple before sucking it hard.

Walker starts to move, filling me slowly as he hardens inside me, but increasing his tempo as my moans grow in intensity. I start to climb again because these two men find me sexy enough to get hard all over again.

It's a heady experience. One I'm not sure I'll ever forget or fully recover from.

When I come, it's so intense, I lose sight and hearing except the rush of the blood in my ears and the feel of their cum pulsing inside me and on my skin as they join me in a chorus of euphoria and reverence.

CHAPTER 15

BERKLYN

AFTER A QUICK SHOWER, ALONE, I DRESS IN THE t-shirt and boxer briefs Jess left on the bathroom counter. I'd hoped he or Walker would shower with me, but after feeling the heat of the water hitting all my sore and overused muscles, I'm thankful for the reprieve.

It wasn't a joke last night when I said I wasn't sure I could walk. I barely made it to the bathroom after Jess showered and left the room, giving me privacy to crawl out of bed without being witness to my weakened limbs, lumbering like a newborn fawn. Walker had already headed to his room to shower. Before they left, I hadn't considered having to get up naked in front of them to find clothes or escape into the bathroom.

If there's a next time, I'll have to figure out how to do that if I'm not afforded the same privacy as today.

Next time?

I'm not sure I could handle more of them, but I can't imagine never feeling their touch again.

I don't see how any man could beat the intensity of their lovemaking. No. Not *lovemaking*. Sex. It was just sex.

Just. Sex, I repeat as I brush my teeth with the new toothbrush Jess placed on top of the t-shirt. When I'm done, I loosen my hair from the messy bun to let it cascade down my back in soft waves. I run my fingers through it and shrug at my makeup-free face. They've licked, sucked, fucked, or caressed every inch of me and every hole. If they can't deal with my all-natural state, then that's their problem.

I'm not going to stress over it and pretend I wake up with a full face of makeup, even if I had it all with me to do it fresh. I just can't be bothered. This is me.

Now, if I could only feel that comfortable with the body when—if—I have to get out of bed with them watching my naked ass and thighs jiggle.

That's a problem for Tomorrow Berklyn. Today Berklyn is going to savor my sex-sore state, relish the tingle along my skin, the pinkness of my cheeks, and the brightness of my green eyes. I've been truly sexed up for the first time in my life, and I'm not going to ruin it with doubt and insecurities.

Yay me!

Barefoot and braless, I find Jess and Walker in the kitchen talking softly as Jess hovers over the stove. The smell of bacon hits me first, followed by coffee. "Morning." I smile as their heads jerk my direction.

"Morning, Sugar." Walker presses a kiss to my lips while squeezing my ass. "You good?" He releases me, leaning against the counter.

"Yeah. You?" I look at Jess, trying to anticipate his response to me still being here. I hadn't intended on sleeping over, but after our escapades last night, I collapsed like the dead and didn't wake up until this morning and then… Well, morning smexy happened.

"I'm perfect." Walker brushes the back of his hand down my cheek.

Jess leans in, kissing my forehead, mumbling, "Morning, baby," across my skin, making me tingle. He smiles, squeezing my waist. "You hungry?"

"Ravenous." I relax at Jess' open demeanor. I expected Walker to be nice. I wasn't sure about Jess, though nothing about last night gave me the impression he didn't want me here. Maybe grumpy Jess is gone.

Maybe sexed-up Jess is full of endorphins and grumpy Jess is hiding and waiting. That's probably more likely.

A tiger doesn't change its stripes. I have to remember that.

"Coffee?" Walker hands me a cup.

"Yes, thanks." I take it and enjoy the rich smell.

"Sugar and creamer are behind you." Jess motions over my head. "Food will be ready in a minute. I hope you eat meat and eggs."

I want to reply with a dirty joke about eating their meat but decide against it. "I'm a complete carnivore. I love fruit and veggies, but this body doesn't survive on salad alone."

Jess' gaze drops to my chest and down to my thighs, heating my cheeks. I didn't mean to draw attention like that. I turn away, adding sugar and creamer to my coffee, stirring in the silence that follows my awkward statement.

A hard press of a body to mine with a grip on my hip has me stilling. A warm mouth traverses my neck as my hair is pulled to the side. "Whatever you're thinking stop," Jess growls in my ear. His hand runs down my ass to my thigh and squeezes. "You won't hear any complaints from us about what you put in your body, except our cocks. You should definitely take more cock—our cocks, to be specific."

I gasp a laugh and catch the gleam in his eye. "Duly noted."

Walker takes my hand, leading me to the table. "Sit, Doc. Let us feed you."

Halfway through the best cinnamon rolls, bacon, and eggs I've ever eaten, I catch Walker staring at me with a shy smile. "What?"

"You doing okay? Were we too hard on you? How sore are you?" His brow crinkles with concern.

I wipe my mouth and sit back, considering his words and Jess' attentive gaze. Is he worried too?

"I had a great time. Better than great. Yes, I'm sore." I look away, embarrassed by the heat radiating off my face. "But it was…"

"Amazing?" Walker prompts.

"Addicting?" Jess suggests, his open gaze turning reserved as if he didn't mean to say that out loud.

I blink at him, surprised by his candor as much as he is. They are addicting. I could get hooked. But I can't. It's just sex.

Just. Sex.

"Life-affirming, mind-blowing." I shrug and break eye contact. "Maybe even life-altering." I take bite of cinnamon roll and hope they change the subject.

"Mind-blowing. I like that." Walker smiles.

"Life-altering." Jess' gruff tone reveals that perhaps he doesn't like that statement, not because it's not true, but because it could be true.

I don't disagree. I wasn't looking for life-altering. I don't have room for that, and apparently neither does he.

"Though, I have to say, the highlight was when Walker reminded me where babies come from." I smirk at Walker, loving his wide eyes and gasping laugh.

"Damn, I was trying to be helpful. You looked like you were about to panic."

I laugh with him, relaxing when Jess joins in. "It was kinda funny."

"It was." Though I didn't laugh at the time. It actually did help me calm down and remember larger things than their combined cocks are meant for the vaginal canal. I'm a doctor; of course I know that. But in the moment, I was just a woman trying DVP for the first time. I was scared and thankful for his rather rudimentary statement that brought me back down to reality.

I wink at Walker, and his returning smile tells me my teasing didn't hurt his feelings one bit.

"So, Doc. What are you doing next Friday?"

CHAPTER 16

JESS

I FIGHT THE SMILE MY FACE THREATENS TO DON for the rest of the weekend. Our time with Berklyn was remarkable. Remarkably sexy.

Remarkably scary.

Remarkably life-altering.

She wasn't lying when she said those words—*life-altering*. The seismic tremor she set off rocked me to the depth of my soul, threatening to crumble the wall around my mangled heart.

Brick by brick I've sheltered my heart. Never letting any woman in after the first who proved women can't be trusted, like my dad touted. Though, he was a sonofabitch and wasn't to be trusted either.

Berklyn got close. So damn close, I nearly fucking kissed her multiple times. I ravaged her body in nearly every conceivable way, except her ass.

That's next.

If I can manage to keep myself in check. Keep Walker's expectation to a low roar and don't, under any circumstances, fall for her—or let her fall for me.

I was myself around her. The self that was trusting and open to possibilities, to the experience of what we were creating together. That softened person doesn't have any place in a transactional, sex-only encounter. Whether it's a one-time thing or multiple times. The quantity doesn't get to change my deep-rooted rule of *it's only sex*. The heart, the soul, any amount of vulnerability or hope does not have a place in that type of arrangement.

The *only* type of arrangement I can have with Berklyn: transactional.

It pains me to think of her in that way. But I can't trust myself to not hurt her, letting her think I'm capable of more. Or worse, that I am capable, and she goes and proves me wrong for trusting her.

I just can't go there. I'm not built to be the man she needs, even if it's half a man and Walker is the other half. She deserves a whole man or two to love and cherish her, not Walker-and-a-half.

I'll cherish her from afar, a reserved and safe distance.

By Sunday night, Walker's moping because I'm not suddenly a changed man. The incredible sex with Berklyn has me on edge and needing to hit something or someone. He doesn't get it. He wants to keep her—forever. But he knows I'm not a forever kind of guy.

Yet I'm not ready to give her up so he can pursue that fantasy. I've only just gotten a taste, and if I let his bleeding heart loose on her now, I'll lose her before I'm willing to—before I've made peace with the idea of giving her up for him.

That's what I'll have to do. It's where this is heading: his happily ever after with her.

I'll get there. I'll make myself get there. Just. Not. Yet.

I'm back to the place where I need to let off steam, and it can't be with Walker. I'll hurt him. I've got a tight grip on my resentment of how easily he falls, how easily he trusts, how easily he sees forever in her eyes. I can't let that loose on him. He deserves better.

So, I'm heading to the Black Ops Gym hoping someone is there to spar. Someone who can take my crap and give it back tenfold. Someone like Gabriel. I sigh in relief when I see him working out on the heavy bag. It's late, not his usual time for working out. Maybe he has a little frustration he needs to exorcise too.

"Hey, man," I greet, speaking louder than his heavy metal music he has blaring through the sound system.

I get a chin nod until he finishes his combination. "Hey." He steps back, bouncing, shadow-boxing an invisible opponent.

"You're here late," I state the obvious, wanting to feel him out.

That earns me an eyebrow raise and a death glare that would have lesser men quaking. "Yep."

Okay. Maybe he's not up for company. I move to the bench across the way and set my keys, water, and towel down before grabbing a jump rope. It's a quick way to burn off steam, warm up the muscles, and get the heart racing. I do a few stretches first to work out the kinks from Friday and Saturday's activities with Berklyn and Walker. The vision of her taking my cock already has my body aching for more.

Twenty minutes into my jump rope warm-up, I'm dripping sweat and cussing myself for skipping yesterday's workout. Sex is great, but it's not enough cardio to keep up the level of fitness required for my next fight.

It's not a championship bout, but it's one of the bigger matches I've garnered. With Gabriel still fighting and keeping Wicked Tuff's Heavyweight Champion title, there's not too much further I can go unless I want to fight him. And that would never happen. One: Cap wouldn't pair up two of his own fighters for the championship. Two: I don't want to fight Gabriel. I'm not sure I could win, and that doubt is enough to know I don't want to try. Give him a few more years, maybe another kid, and he'll be ready to hang it up.

Until then, I work hard and take every fight Cap secures, building up my experience and ranking, biding my time. Plus, I'm not the only one waiting. Rowdy is biting at the chance to take Gabriel's place. It would be cool if a Black Ops MMA fighter won every title for the foreseeable future. That's a feather Cap deserves to wear in his proverbial hat. One we'd all love to give him.

As I move on to free weights, deciding it's better to not do any lifting that requires a spotter since Gabriel obviously doesn't want to be disturbed, the door swings open, and Rowdy comes stomping in, heading straight for his brother-in-law.

"What the fuck?" Rowdy glares at Gabriel. "You came without me?"

"I needed to fuck or hit something." Gabriel picks up his water bottle. "And given that my Angel is pissed at me, I'm here."

Rowdy scrubs his face, kicking off his shoes, cracking his neck. "You wanna spar?"

Gabriel glances at me. "I think Mustang needs it more than I do."

Is that his form of an apology for being an asshole? Not that I'm one to judge.

Rowdy's hopeful gaze lands on me. "You up for it?"

"God, yes." I rack my free weights, adrenaline rising in anticipation of landing and taking some hits.

Rowdy and I get busy wrapping our hands. When I'm done, I wipe the sweat from my face, chest, and arms, feeling like I have an advantage in already being warmed up. But he's coming in fresh, so it's a tossup on how this will go.

When the music switches to "Follow You Home" by Nickelback, I hop in the ring, waiting on Rowdy. I take it as a good sign Gabriel chose my fight music and not Rowdy's.

Honestly, his would have been fine too. When I'm fighting, I don't hear the music. I only hear the voice in my head telling me I'll never amount to anything except a no-good drunk like my dad. The lying, cheating, motherfucker he is—or was. He could be dead for all I know.

"Ready?" Gabriel levels me with his stare. "Winner fights me."

I crack a smile. My night just got substantially better. "Bring it," I egg Rowdy on.

"You shouldn't tease the beast, Mustang. I've got a lot of frustration to work out." Rowdy's smug face eases the tightness in my chest.

He's a means to an end. Both of them are. Whether I win or lose, I know I'll be a better competitor for having fought either of them. Gabriel is the best of the best. He doesn't spar with just anybody, and I know if Rowdy didn't show up, eventually Gabriel would have offered. Otherwise, he wouldn't have offered himself up as the prize for winning against Rowdy.

"Bring it, Texas," I taunt.

"You're going down, Horseboy."

I chuckle at the sad state of our smack talk. It's obviously not up to par for an actual match.

He comes at me. I duck and sweep his leg out from under him, coming back, smiling. Bouncing on the balls of my feet, I wait, relishing the anticipation of what he'll try, what move he'll send my direction, trying to take me out, take me down. I'm nearly elated, relieved I held it together with Walker. He doesn't deserve my shit. He loves fighting as much as I do, but he doesn't need it like I do. His sanity doesn't hinge on this type of release. He gets endorphins from it. I get a release. A release of anger, of uncertainty, of feeling like I'll never be enough, not good enough, not whole because I can't—

Thwap.

"Fuck." Pain flares across my cheek, an evil grin parting my lips, displaying my mouthguard that's probably bloody, "Again." I urge, taking a few more hits before I go on the offensive.

I need the pain to remember who I am and who I'm not.

I'm my father's son. A piece of shit fighter from the wrong side of the tracks. Solid on the outside and hollow in the center. I don't need more than this.

I have great friends.

A family by choice.

I'm a baker.

I'm a fighter.

I'm no lover.

CHAPTER 17

JESS

LAST NIGHT'S SPARRING WITH ROWDY AND THEN
Gabriel left me feeling more confident than I have in a while. Though
I didn't win against Gabriel, I didn't expect to. Plus, I was pretty
worn out from Rowdy. It would have been nice to beat them both, but I
also know Gabriel could have been way harder on me. In the end, it was
a draw. I'll take it as a win.

I pull up outside of Berklyn's house. We brought her home on
Saturday after our late breakfast. Walker lingered, wanting to stay, but I
knew it was time to part ways before I got any more attached. Last night
got my head on straight.

I hope Berklyn doesn't read too much into why I'm here today. Walker
could have easily completed this task. The idea of leaving it to him rubbed
me the wrong way. So here I am outside her house at six in the morning
when I should already be at the bakery. Thankfully, I had energy to burn
last night after sparring and went to Sugarplums to make the batches of

dough needed for today. Maybe I'm actually ahead of schedule. But I still don't have time to linger.

Knocking on her door, waiting for her to answer has unwanted nerves tightening my gut. I hate how easily thoughts of her sway my body and mind. It's a constant battle of wills between what I *want* and what I can *have*.

What about what she deserves?

Shit. I shove my hands in my pockets, looking up at the rising sun. And sigh at the realization. The answer is the same. She deserves a whole hell of a lot better than a man like me.

When the door swings open, I'm met with Berk's makeup-free face and eyes full of surprise and hope.

Don't look at me like that, baby. I'm not that man.

"Jess? What are you doing here?" She pulls on the hem of her scrubs top, smoothing it like she just pulled it on to open the door.

"Can I come in?"

"Sure," she steps back, "I don't have long."

"Me neither." I can't resist pressing a kiss to her forehead and breathing in her clean floral scent as I pass.

"What's up?" She closes the door and turns, crossing her arms, shutting down the openness that was on her face a moment ago. If she was happy to see me when she opened the door, she's anything but that now.

I hold up the bag in my hand. "We discussed having anal when we get together on Friday. I'm here to prepare you."

"What?" She backs up, arms falling to her sides.

I capture the back of her neck and gently lift her chin with my thumb. "The panic you're feeling is natural. It's also why we need to prepare. We can't just jump into it and hope for the best."

"But I have work."

"As do I."

"I—"

"We don't have to do this today. We can discuss it and figure out a better time to prepare your body if you're interested in proceeding." I rub her bottom lip, relishing the soft, plump flesh. My cock twitches at the idea of her mouth on me. Walker got to fuck these lips. I haven't had the pleasure. "Fuck, I want this mouth," I growl, nipping at it, and quickly pull away, catching myself before I do something I can't take back—I can't erase.

"I'm not saying no…" She frowns, her gaze studying all of me before landing on my mouth. "You want to kiss me?"

Kissing is too intimate. "I don't do that." I release her and step back, ignoring the hurt in her eyes.

"What? Kiss? Why?" She waves her hand, stopping my response I had no intention of giving. "Never mind." She skirts around me and heads to the kitchen. "I literally don't have time for this. I have to get to the hospital." She grabs her keys, purse, and tumbler and turns, watching me expectantly.

I'm screwing this up. I should have let Walker do this. He would have handled it with more care.

He would have *kissed* her.

He probably would have fucked her too.

Would she brush him off like she is me?

"Can I come back tonight?" The words leave my mouth in a rush, bypassing my better judgment to just let it go—let *her* go.

"Um," she swallows, staring at the floor for a moment before locking eyes, "not if you're going to be an a-hole."

I nod, knowing I can't make that promise. I can't make her *any* promises. "Okay." It's not really a lie. I want to be nice to her but probably not in the way she hopes.

I follow her to the door and catch her around the waist before she opens it, smiling into her neck, remembering the last time I saw her in scrubs. They were tighter than what she's wearing now, not that I minded. Though I made her feel they were indecent.

"What time?" I kiss the tender spot below her ear, running my hand down her stomach to cup her pussy and grind against her, letting her feel how hard she makes me.

"S-six," she gasps, flexing into my hand.

"I'll bring dinner." I brush her ponytail to the other side and suck her earlobe, drawing my hand up her stomach, toying with the waistband of her scrubs before slipping beneath her panties to her bare pussy.

"Jess," she moans, leaning into me, gripping the back of my head, widening her stance.

That's my girl, I silently praise, unable to gift her such niceties. "Fuck, baby. You're so wet." I pinch a nipple through the fabric of her top and bra. "I could fuck you right here, leaving you dripping with our cum."

"Ohmygod," she gasps as I sink my fingers into her needy heat. Her purse and keys hit the floor. I nab her coffee a second before it joins them, setting it on the entry table.

"Arms up," I command, testing her limits.

Instantly she raises her arms.

I pull her top off over her head, unhook her bra, and let both fall to the floor around us. In quick succession, I pull her scrubs and panties to her ankles and unleash my cock.

Still fully clothed, I growl across her skin, "Brace yourself against the door," and run open-mouthed kisses from one side of her neck to the other as I palm her tits and twist her nipples, earning a slow mewl that has my cock dancing against her backside.

When she's on her tiptoes, leaning forward, I run the tip of my cock along her dripping folds, then slap it against her pussy a few times before pushing inside frustratingly slow.

"More," she pleads, pressing her forehead against the curtained window of her front door. She parts it, giving me a clear view of the neighbors' house across the street, their lights on, shadows moving beyond the shaded windows.

Could they see us if they looked out?

I slam forward, excited but not happy about anyone besides Walker witnessing her pleasure, what I do to her, as I start to fuck her hard.

"Jess!" she moans against her hand, trying to muffle her cries.

My grip on her hip and breast tightens as I increase my pace, practically lifting her each time I slam forward.

She gives up trying to muffle the endless stream of gasping moans that joins my grunts the harder I thrust, filling her so deep, I'm sure I'll come inside her uterus. The idea only has me growing harder and my balls rising, preparing to come.

I lock on to her shoulder, sucking her flesh as I release her breast to rub her clit, ensuring she comes before I do, knowing she would for sure if Walker were here to suck her nipples to completion.

"Fuck. Fuck. Fuck," I chant, getting closer. "Need you to come, Berklyn, before I fill you up."

"Oh. My. God!" She arches into my thrusts, locking her arms. "Yes!" she screams. "I want to feel you coming inside me."

As she trembles from head to toe, her orgasm rips through her, squeezing me so good. Seconds later, I growl my release, pumping streams of cum into her with frenzied strokes. Her pussy strangles every inch of my cock, and I rub her clit until she's begging me to stop.

Pulling out, I carry her to the bathroom and make quick work of cleaning us up before helping her dress and ignoring unhelpful thoughts of doing this again tomorrow and maybe the next day... And maybe...

CHAPTER 18

BERKLYN

ELBOWS DEEP IN TRAUMA, IT'S OFTEN HARD TO see the big picture when covered in blood, heart pounding, and just trying to keep the patient alive, reacting to each issue as it arises. It isn't until it's over, the analysis of what happened hits. Often the trauma of it, the sights and smells, the emotions, the fear of *what-if* come crashing down in the lull—the aftermath.

That's how I felt after driving away from my house, driving away from Jess. In the heat of his touch and rousing words, I'm lost, trying to survive the onslaught, trying to catch my breath, trying to keep my head, my emotions in check. Now, hours later, the postmortem of our joining is sobering.

He doesn't kiss?

Or he doesn't want to kiss *me*?

Yet he easily burns kisses into my skin with heated lips that touch me—everywhere—except my mouth.

He said he wanted my mouth. Did he not mean he wanted to kiss me?

I pop off my gloves, tossing them in the trash, and pump sanitizer into my palm, working it into my hands, and face my patient. "Olivia, can you remember not to touch your owie?"

"Yes, Dr. Berk." She nods, her eyes wide with awe. Dr. Fortier was too hard for her to say. She's only five with the sweetest lisp she'll more than likely outgrow.

My little brother used to pronounce the TV remote as *marote* and yellow as *lellow*. It was too cute, and I hated it when he started saying them correctly. It would be hard as an adult to continue to mispronounce those things, but, damn, it would have been so cute. Just like he used to call me Sister, then one day he sadly started calling me Berklyn. Growing up sucks sometimes.

Turning my attention to her parents, I advise, "She'll need to see her primary care doctor in ten days to have the stiches removed. No baths until then. A shower is okay in twenty-four hours as long as you use a waterproof bandage to cover the laceration. Watch for signs of infection." I continue my spiel about keeping the wound clean and changing the bandage—all of which will be in the discharge paperwork, but I figure if they hear it at least once, they have a chance of remembering it.

I liken discharge paperwork to manuals. People rarely read them.

Five more patents, a slew of charting, and another coffee. I'm about to head to the cafeteria for lunch when my phone vibrates with an incoming call. My heart jumps when I see the name.

"Hello?"

"Hey, Doc. Are you free for lunch?" Walker's rough voice does silly things to my girlie parts, wanting him to whisper all sorts of dirty things in my ear and across my skin as he takes me like he did on our *sleepover.*

"I was just heading to the cafeteria."

"I can do better than that. Can you come outside? I'm at the ER drop-off."

"Let me grab my purse—"

"You don't need anything but yourself. We're not going far. I know you don't have long."

"I'll be there in a minute."

"I'll be waiting."

We've recently implemented overlapping shifts to allow nurses and doctors to take breaks during the lulls. There are days there are no breaks, but luckily today is not one of them.

When I step outside, the warmth hits me immediately despite the covered entry. Walker's black Ram truck pulls up with the front passenger window down.

"Hop in," he calls from the driver's side.

Thankfully, in my scrubs, I can make the climb with ease, not having to worry about flashing anyone in a dress or skirt. "Hey." I plop down and secure my seatbelt.

"I hope you don't mind burgers and fries. I knew you liked 'em and didn't want to chance getting something you don't like."

Fries. My dear friend. "You can never go wrong with burgers and fries."

"No, you can't." His smile is endless and calms any nerves I had in seeing him again.

He pulls out and circles the hospital grounds, coming to the main parking garage for the hospital, and enters. Skillfully, he drives up to the top floor, finding a secluded corner that faces the mountains, and parks.

"I hope you don't mind lunch in the car. I figured you wouldn't have much time for something more adventurous."

"I don't mind at all."

He motions to the backseat. "Your food awaits."

WALKER

I can't help but smile as she devours her burger like she hasn't eaten in weeks. It's only been a day since we've seen each other, but I missed her.

I missed her smiling eyes when she laughs.

I missed the sultry curve of her lips.

I missed her gasps and moans as she comes on my cock.

Clearing my throat and mind of such thoughts, I broach the possible elephant in the room—err, truck. "I heard you had an early morning visitor." I decide to lay it out there. I don't want her to worry about whether I know or not. Jess and I don't keep secrets, especially about sharing women. That kind of intimacy requires trust and honesty between us and them.

"I did. Is that okay?" She nibbles her bottom lip. "Is it against the rules?"

"Rules?" I shake my head. "No, we're both seeing you, as long as you're open to it. There will be times it will be like this, just the two of us, or you and him, and there will be times like Friday where we're all together. We don't want you feeling guilty about being with one of us and not the other. What happens is completely up to you."

Her eyes widen in shock. "Really? It doesn't bother you?"

"That you fucked Jess this morning?"

She coughs around a fry. Once composed, she frowns. "I think he'd say he did the F-ing."

True. He would. And he did.

"I don't mind. I want you to have time to get to know him without me. My only regret is not being there to watch."

"You really enjoy watching?"

My body hardens at the mental image. I brush my thumb along her cheek and consider pulling her ponytail for half a second. "Yeah, Doc. I do."

"Do you want to come for dinner tonight?"

I'm thrilled she's asking. "I can't. I'm working the door at Mel's tonight." Even if I wasn't, I wouldn't. She needs this time with Jess, for her to let him in and for him to do the same. Though his walls will be far harder to crack.

"Do all of you have multiple jobs?"

I shrug. "Some do. Actually, most do. Unless you're independently wealthy like Rowdy or have big sponsors like Gabriel, who's the current heavyweight champ, you need other income."

"Thought you did computer stuff."

Computer *stuff*. Cute. "I do. I have my own consulting business, but I also help Landry out at Mel's. Most of the Black Ops guys do. So, it's fun to hang out with them, listen to music, and make a little cash on the side, keeping the peace."

Not to mention the chicks.

We primarily find our women there. No reason to bring that up. Especially since we're not looking for another woman while we're focused on Doc.

Food devoured and garbage collected, I slide her closer by her hip. "How long do you have?"

"Not long." She tips her chin, her green eyes tracing my lips.

"Can I kiss you?" My heart thunders in my chest, not because I fear she'll say no, but because I sense she wants to say yes.

"God, yes."

"Good answer," I breathe across her lips before wrapping her in my arms and breaching the distance, claiming her mouth, taking a taste, a moment, a memory all for myself.

If kisses were lifelines, she'd be mine, unyielding, vibrating with need and echoing of possibilities.

"Walker," she sighs. "I wish I had more time. I want you."

The thrill of hearing her say that sends me into overdrive. Deepening the kiss, I pull her into my lap sideways, not sure I could handle her straddling me, knowing I can't have her.

"I want to make you come." I suck her bottom lip. "Do you want that?"

She has time for an orgasm, surely.

Her harsh breath slips along my skin as she kisses my neck, making me groan. "I want you inside me, Walk."

Fuck. Her using my nickname that only Jess uses kills me, makes me harder, feels intimate in a rather unintimate place. It's dark in the corner, the light is out, but anyone driving by could see us. My windows are dark, but not that dark.

"Doc," I groan as she grinds her ass on my lap.

"We could be quick." She pulls back, cupping my face. "I know what your hips and cock can do. You can drill me into an orgasm in minutes." She slides off my lap, catching my gaze. "Actually, I don't even care if I come. I just want to feel you inside me, even if only for a minute."

"Fuck, Sugar, I'm never going to say no to you. I just don't want you to regret it when you're late." Plus, there's no way I'm letting her on my cock without her coming at least once. It's a Walker Rule she'll need to learn.

She slumps down in the seat, toeing her shoes off and tugging at her scrub bottoms. "Take your cock out. I need to feel you. Please."

Fuck. Fuck. Fuck. We're bottomless in ten seconds flat. The whole time I'm undressing, I consider the best position so she can't be seen by a drive-by. I won't risk her job no matter how badly I want inside her.

Face to face, we lie on the bench seat. It's tight fit for me, but I manage.

I lift her top leg and run my cock through her wetness. "Ready?" She feels ready, but I need her words.

"Please." She arches toward me, taking my tip inside her wet heat.

"Fuck," I groan and surge forward, gripping her ass, thrusting deep, pressing her into the back of the seat.

"Walk," she cries, digging her nails into my ass. "That, ohmygod, feels so good. Please don't stop."

I kiss her swollen lips. "Not stopping."

With a heady rhythm, I fuck into her in a circular motion, rubbing her clit with my pelvis with each swivel of my hips. Time is endless. I'm in no rush, other than the race to make her come and get back to work on time.

I steal her cries of pleasure in our kiss, sucking her tongue and lips, pulling her closer, drilling deeper. The scent of sex and the sounds of our fucking fill the cab, enclosing us in a bubble of our making.

It's only her.

Her eyes begging for more.

Her pussy taking my cock so fucking good, writhing against me, feeding the empty recesses inside me only she's been able to reach.

"Ohmygod!" She tightens, squeezes. She's close.

"Berklyn, fuck, baby. You feel so good. You're gonna make me come." I clench my jaw, holding out for her.

"Yes!" she cries, gripping the back of my neck, not letting my lips get far from hers.

"You want that, don't you?" My eyes lock on hers. "You need to know you drive me so crazy that I'm ready to come after only being inside you for a few minutes?"

"Oh, God. Yes, please. I'm—" Her eyes close, and her head falls back on a long moan.

"Fuck, yes." I capture her mouth and fuck through her orgasm, feeding on her gasps and cries.

She nips and kisses me back. Gripping my ass, surging for me, taking me, taking me, taking me.

"Doc," I growl, jolting, drilling inside her, filling her with my release with every spasm of her pussy sucking me in, and in, and in.

One minute. It's all I allow us to bask in the afterglow. When I pull out, she groans her discontent.

"Sorry." If I could take my time, I would. "You okay?"

She runs her fingers through my hair. "I'm great. I just want to lie here in your arms. Maybe do that again in a few minutes."

My heart leaps at the idea. I kiss her forehead. "I want that, Doc, I truly do. But I need to get you back so you can save lives. Hold on." I sit up, snagging an extra t-shirt from my workout bag and place it between her legs, urging her to sit up so the rest of our cum comes down instead of dripping down her leg or in her panties when she stands.

She sheepishly gives a, "Thanks."

"Don't mention it."

I clean her up as best I can, wishing I had some of those baby wipes the guys have for their kids. They'd come in handy right about now. I help her get dressed before getting decent myself. Once she's presentable and in the front seat, I start the engine, exit the garage, and circle around to the ER drop-off area.

Before she steps out, she grabs my hand. "That was pretty amazing, Walk. The best lunch I've ever had."

I bark a laugh and squeeze her hand. "Anytime, Doc. Anytime."

A quick kiss and she's gone, taking my heart with her.

CHAPTER 19

BERKLYN

MY DAY FINISHED PRETTY MUCH HOW IT
started: with too much work to go around, a yawn, and an empty
stomach ready to devour. And the need for a shower. I've had
sex twice today. I never thought I'd be that girl to have sex over lunch,
or in her front entry, for that matter. Who am I? What have these men
done to me? They've lit up my body in ways I had no idea were possible.
They've made me feel cherished and special… And needy for more.

It's just sex, that inner voice reminds me. They never promised anything else.

Often, I just grab a utilitarian rinse at the hospital, but with Jess
coming over, I opt to wait until I get home so I can take care of other
business while washing away the day.

Someday, in my dream home, I'd love to have a mudroom with a
luxurious shower so I could step in from the outside, strip, shower, and
throw on some cozy clothes before traipsing into the rest of the house.

Working in healthcare, I'm cognizant of bringing germs home on my clothing. Despite wearing gloves, masks, head covering, washing hands, and taking every precaution given I don't work for the CDC, I could be carrying all kinds of germs from the top of my head to the soles of my shoes. Leaving all of that in a mudroom with its own washer and dryer, shower, and stash of clean clothes is a dream.

Someday. I sigh as I strip in my laundry room before walking naked to my bathroom. With only thirty minutes before Jess is supposed to be here, I shave, wash and condition my hair, and clean every nook and cranny. I can't believe I'm considering he might want me again. I mean, he might not, but I'm cleaning up like he might. Like I know I want it if he's game.

With my hair barely dry, I twist it into a top knot, so it'll produce soft waves when dry by morning. Not that I'll be showing off the waves once it's secured beneath my scrub cap. I pull on cutoff shorts and a tank top, not feeling the desire to dress up. I'm a come-as-you-are kinda girl. I like to get dolled up, but not after a long shift, and especially not to relax at home. I do take a moment to put on a coat of mascara, so it looks like I put in a little effort.

Right at six, there's a solid knock on my door. Did he arrive early, waiting until it was exactly six before approaching the house and knocking? Jess seems like a right-on-time kinda guy.

"Hey." I smile at the hulk of a man on my doorstep, ignore the zing of want fueled by flashes of this morning, and motion him inside.

"Hey, Berklyn." As he enters, he leans in like he might kiss me but pats my arm at the last second, skirting by.

His warmth and scent linger while I'm flooded with disappointment at the cold reminder. He doesn't kiss.

"How was your day?" he asks, not even a little affected by me. He's calm, cool, and collected. Is this part of his *I don't kiss* stance?

Does it even matter it's *me*, or am I just another girl to him?

Interchangeable.

Replaceable.

Utterly sharable and unremarkable.

My mood plummets. "Busy. You?" I hide my fluster by leading the way to the kitchen. I don't know if he's talked to Walker, but I have no intention of sharing a single intimate detail that happened between us. He kisses me. He doesn't hold back. It's not fair to compare. They're two very different men. They both light me on fire, rife with passion I've never experienced. But outside of that passion, Jess is so different from Walker. How can I not compare?

"Not bad." Jess sets a thermal bag on the island. "After the bakery and working out, I watched Rowdy and Reese's son, Killian, for a bit while they went to their prenatal visit. It was fun." He doesn't seem surprised he enjoyed it. Does he do it often?

Jess babysitting is not something I would have ever expected him to do, much less be happy about. Have I misjudged him, stuck him in a box he doesn't fit into? "How old is he?"

"Two—and not so terrible. He's actually a really sweet kid. They've done a great job with him."

I'm struck dumb by his praise and admiration toward his friends and their child. "How far along is Reese?"

When I met them last Friday, I didn't get into the whole pregnancy discussion with her and Frankie. It seemed too personal to be discussing in a bar when I'm on a first date with *two* of their friends. I'm still a little in awe that I did it, and even more in awe of what happened afterwards and since.

"I think both she and Frankie are six months along, within a few weeks of each other."

"They looked happy and seem to be feeling good. I'm sure it's fun having a friend who's pregnant at the same time. I hope they continue to have healthy pregnancies." I move around the island to grab glasses. "What would you like to drink?" I turn quickly and clarify, "I have water, iced tea, or milk. Mmm, maybe orange juice." I can't remember how much, though.

Within a few steps, he's front and center, his hand on my wrist, stopping my reach for the cabinet. "We have business to handle before we eat."

"Business?" Yep, confirmed. I'm absolutely nothing special to him. Pulling out of his hold, I sidestep him and cross my arms.

He assesses me, not a flicker of emotion across his face except for the tick of his jaw. "Maybe that was a bad choice of words."

You think?

I don't break eye contact. I don't flinch. If he can be cool, so can I. "Why don't you kiss?" *Why don't you kiss me?*

His eyes soften, considering. "I've kissed you." He leans against the counter, crossing his arms, showing off his impressive biceps.

I suppose he has in some manner. Maybe I'm taking this too personally. I should have asked Walker about it, but I got sidetracked by his lusty gaze, heated kisses, and my overwhelming need to be filled by him while he kisses the heck out of me. *He's* not afraid to kiss me. And I love kissing.

I shrug off my doubt in Jess, deciding it's not a hill I'm willing to die on—at least not tonight. "What *business?*" I cringe at the word.

He opens the black felt drawstring sack sitting next to the bag of food. I didn't even notice it before. I move to the opposite side, with the island comfortably between us.

He presents a black box, sliding it to me. "Open it."

It's about half the size of a shoebox. It feels ominous, important. Like if I touch it, I've agreed to whatever's inside. Given our *relationship* is of a sexual nature, I'm fairly certain it's some sort of sex toy. "Opening it doesn't mean I agree to whatever it represents."

His humored smirk surprises me. He's more of a scowler. "Of course not." He easily skirts the island, coming to stand beside me. "I may not always ask for permission, but you are always in control of what happens between us. In this case, we will discuss it fully before proceeding." He quirks a brow. "*If* you agree."

"I think I'd rather eat." I step back, not feeling any kind of warm fuzzy from him or the box. I'm not in an open frame of mind, and interacting with Jess requires open-mindedness.

That little voice in my head is telling me to shut this down. I take another step back.

He won't even kiss me on the mouth. He'll stick his tongue in my coochie and French kiss me there, but my mouth is off-limits. His intimacy barometer is off-kilter. Whatever's in that box must be a doozie for *Mr. I Don't Ask for Permission* to want to discuss it beforehand.

"Berklyn." He stops mere inches from pressing his body to mine, tipping my chin. "What are you afraid of?" His green eyes, nearly the same shade as mine, search the depths of mine like the answers are scrolling there in an endless loop.

"What if I don't want to proceed? Is that it?" Will he be done with me?

Is this the line that marks my expiration—denotes it's time to replace me with a new, more receptive model?

This morning he was deep inside me, taking me against my front door.

Tomorrow, could it be someone else?

Was it someone else *yesterday*?

The thought has a shiver ripping along my spine and sadness pricking the back of my eyes.

"You're thinking too hard about this, Berk." He runs his thumb across my bottom lip. "You don't even know what's in the box, yet you're terrified of it."

"I'm terrified of you. Of what…"

"Me?" He steps back and slides his hands in his pockets. "I don't know how else to convince you that you're in control of what happens here."

"Like I'm in control of you kissing me?" The words fly out of my mouth defensively, wanting him off-kilter as much as I am, wanting him to admit I'm nothing special, just another hole to fill.

I'm granted the scowl I've been expecting. "Is that a deal breaker for you?"

"I…" *Is it?* "Maybe." I focus on the box. "No," I sigh. "But if I don't want what's in this box… Is that a deal breaker for you?"

He moves in behind me, gripping my hips, pressing forward till I'm sandwiched between him and the island. "No. It's a means to progress our play to the next level. If you so choose." He reaches around me and opens the box. "And if you decide you don't want ass play, then there's no reason we can't keep playing like we did this weekend."

"So, you're not done with me?" Gah, I sound so needy. I hate myself a little right now.

Why do I want him so badly? Walker wants me. *He* kisses me. I don't need them both to be exactly the same, do the same things, but—

Jess presses his lips to my neck, pushing my tank top and bra strap down, baring my shoulder. He makes a path for his open-mouth kisses along my shoulder, pressing his impressive length into me, grinding slowly. "Does it *feel* like I'm done with you?"

I arch into him, aching in needful places, fighting a moan, and manage a breathy, "No."

He kneads the flesh of my waist while alternately gripping each breast with his other hand, teasing my nipples hard. "When I was fucking you this morning, did it *feel* like I was done with you?"

"No," I sigh, grasping the counter, fighting the urge to turn in his arms and claim his mouth as mine. The mouth he holds back from me. The one intimacy he's not willing to share—with me. He wants my ass; he wants, wants, wants, and gets it all, but what is he giving?

Pleasure. He's giving me pleasure. The kind he's comfortable with. I sigh and give in to this broody man who wants me in some way I don't understand yet can't get enough of.

He pops the button of my cutoffs and slowly unzips them, sliding his hand to my warm center. "Fuck, I've missed your pussy, Berks. Couldn't stop thinking about you all day. I've been inconveniently hard thinking about tonight. Fantasizing about you coming on my cock with this butt plug in your ass."

"Yes," slips from my lonely and underappreciated mouth before I can consider what that means. What he's asking without actually asking.

"I'm nowhere near done with you, baby."

CHAPTER 20

BERKLYN

MORNING CAME EARLY. ON A LIQUIDY STRETCH, I snag my phone from the charger on my nightstand. Thoughts of being off today sit in the back of my brain. Once a month, we get an off-schedule day off. It's management's way of keeping employees happy, along with shorter shifts and semi-guaranteed lunch breaks. That *guarantee* fluctuates due to trauma emergencies that require all hands on deck. It's not that way in most emergency departments, though it is a growing trend to improve job satisfaction with a better work-life balance in an effort to keep the doctors and nurses they have and draw in new ones.

Shortages are everywhere. Hospitals need all the advantages they can get. And I'm happy to be the recipient of the growing trend of not working us to death. We even get bonuses primarily slotted to help pay off our student loans. In the end, it is up to the doctor how it's used. But if we use it to pay off our loans, it's not taxed as a bonus, and they handle the direct payment to the designated financial institution. I set mine up when I first started working as a first-year. The bonuses have been so great, my loan balance has already been reduced by half.

Once my school debt is paid off, I'm going to designate the rest toward retirement and mortgage savings, both of which qualify for lower taxes as an incentive to build our personal wealth instead of blowing it on frivolous things. A well-established employee who benefits from financial stability is a happy employee—in their opinion. I can't say I disagree in the least.

I squeal when I see my schedule does, in fact, show me off today. I could roll over and go back to sleep, or I could get up, have a lazy morning and then do something fun this afternoon. I could even reach out to Walker and see if he wants to hang out today, if he's available, instead of waiting until tonight.

Thinking of that, as much as I enjoyed ass play with Jess last night and the fact that Walker is only coming over tonight to continue *training* me, I'm not sure I want to welcome that into my day off—at least not all of it. Maybe not any of it.

Jess working me into a frenzy before slipping the smallest well-lubed butt plug in the set into my rear entrance was… Enjoyable and unexpected. He didn't fuck me as he claimed to want. In fact, he didn't even stay for dinner. After the deed was done and I came on his hand, he kissed me on the forehead with instructions to remove the plug in three hours and that Walker would see me tonight to introduce my ass to the next size up.

He said he wasn't done with me, and yet it was all business—to *him*.

He couldn't even eat with me. He said he was bringing dinner. Did I misunderstand? There was plenty of food. Did he change his mind? Was I too forward that I turned him off? By the bulge in his jeans when he made for the door and left without a backwards glance, he was turned on. But as soon as the plug was in place and I came, he was out.

I was a transaction. That's all it was.

With that sad realization, I put my phone back on the charger, roll over and go back to sleep.

I only managed to sleep for a few more hours. Despite my endless stream of yawns as I sip my coffee, I do feel more rested and maybe not as doom-and-gloom about seeing Walker tonight. Though cancelling is still an option.

Jess said what happens between us is up to me.

If I'm in charge, then why do I feel like I have no control over him? He's sand slipping through my fingers. I catch a little now and again, but most of it falls beyond my grasp.

Why do I care? It's not like I'm going to marry the guy. This is a temporary situation. Unlike my mom, I've never considered having two partners. Never dreamed I'd be equally attracted to two men at the same time. Walker. Walker is easy like a Sunday morning. He's fun, peaceful, accepting. I don't feel like I'm missing something or have to try to be more than I am for him to see me. He sees me as I am and likes me. I think—I hope.

But here I am equally turned on and yearning for time with Jess *and* Walker. They are so different in nearly every way, except when it comes to our off-the-charts chemistry. That is equal and abundant on my part. I swear Jess feels it too, but he's fighting it tooth and nail—or I'm totally reading him wrong.

Unwilling to sit here all day and dwell on the state of my triangular love life, I throw caution to the wind and text Reese and Frankie. Maybe they're free to hang out for a mani-pedi afternoon. I ask them to invite Taylor too. I didn't get her number on Friday. She was busy singing on stage with her husband, but she seems really nice and a part of Reese and Frankie's close-knit group. I don't want to alienate her. I know what that feels like. Hello, Jess.

Sadly, I don't have many friends. I have work friends, but as the name implies, they're at work. Plus, it would be nice to have friends who aren't in the medical field, though Frankie is a physical therapist. It feels different since we don't work together.

I kinda doubt they'll be able to meet up. They do all work. And it's short notice—

I'm shocked when I get responses so quickly.

Frankie: *I'd love to meet up!*

Reese: *Yes! I need some me time!*

Frankie: *Taylor's in. I called our nail place. We have 10a appointments. AND it's 15% off on Tuesdays!!! We have to grab lunch after. I'm feeling a margarita in my future—a virgin one, of course.*

Me: *Yay! Send me the address, and I'll see y'all there. I'm down for margaritas and chips and salsa!*

Reese: *Ooooh, salsa. Yes, please!*

Frankie: *Taylor's in. I'm adding her to the chat.*

A moment later, I get a notification of a phone number being added to the group text. I assume it's Taylor. I add her to my contacts.

Taylor: *What'd I miss?*

Taylor: *Oh, I don't care. Send me the when/where, and I'm there!*

Taylor: *Thanks for including me!*

Thanks for including me. I feel that deep in my heart. I make a mental note to remember to always include her. Even though I've hardly spent any time with Taylor, I still feel she's a kindred spirit.

It's nice to be included. To be *wanted*.

I'm not above admitting I might be a tad sensitive on the topic of inclusion—despite two very masculine reasons to believe otherwise.

JESS

I don't know what I was thinking, running off on Berklyn last night. I had every intention of staying for dinner. I'd brought enough food for us, plus Walker, in case he decided to show before his shift at Mel's.

He didn't.

I didn't fully show up either.

Leery, on edge and worried I'd push her too hard, too fast, I knew I couldn't fuck her. I lose all sense of self when I'm inside that sweet body. I'm a complete monster, drilling into her until she comes all over my cock. Which I said I wanted. And fuck if I didn't.

But after she came and that butt plug was in place, I ran. I booked it out of there. I didn't look back until I was at the door. I chanced a glance over my shoulder, catching the devastation of my hurried exit. Her arms wrapped around herself, she stared at the counter, where I left her, unmoving, unwavering, with a single tear running down her cheek.

I did that.

And I wasn't even trying to be an ass. I was trying to protect her from me, from my raging erection that threatened to nail her to the floor of her kitchen or any hard surface.

But I ran for me too. She wasn't taking my bullshit. She didn't call me on it, but I saw the desolation in her eyes when she asked why I don't kiss her.

I don't kiss her because… I can't.

She's temporary. She'll never be mine. And I'm not giving a piece of myself to a temporary fixture in my life.

I can't lose myself in her. I was too undone, too itchy, barely holding on, and despite the need to rail her, I couldn't trust that I could leave afterwards. I might just wrap her up and keep her. And I can't.

So, I ran.

CHAPTER 21

BERKLYN

MY STOMACH HURTS FROM LAUGHING SO MUCH. I don't think I've ever enjoyed myself more than I have with this group of women. I got the rundown on how all of them met their husbands and their connections to each other over mani-pedis. The ladies working on our toes and hands got an earful too. I'm blown away by each of their heartbreaking stories, layered with self-deprecating humor, and a love that is enviable.

Two things struck me the deepest. One, Rowdy—whose real name is Cameron—and Taylor are the secret love children of Captain Jimmy Durant and their mom. None of them knew until after she died. Cap didn't even know. And Cap is now married to Reese and Gabriel's mom. Two, they all love Jess—and Walker, but that's not surprising. Walker is a great, easygoing guy. The surprising thing is Jess. How Taylor talks about him being so supportive and caring. I had to ask her twice to be sure she was talking about *my* Jess—the baker—and not another friend who happens to be named Jess too.

"Why are you so surprised?" Taylor asks over Mexican food and margaritas.

"Because he's not like that with me." I can barely meet their stares. "He's—"

"An asshole?" Frankie offers up.

My head pops up, catching the understanding in her remarkable gray eyes. "Yeah."

She nods. "Gabriel was the biggest ass to me for five years. Turns out he loved me all that time. He was just too stubborn to admit it, thinking he wasn't worthy of being loved."

Dang, that's raw. What a rough childhood to make so many believe they are unlovable. I fight with that a little too, but not for the same reasons Gabriel did. My parents are great—maybe too great. I fear I'll never find anyone who could love me like they love each other. But Gabriel being an ass to Frankie isn't the same as Jess and me. We don't have years of pent-up history. We only have six months if you count the time from when we met and them asking me out.

"And you were with Austin," Reese interjects not too softly and maybe in defense of her brother.

"Don't remind me." Frankie rolls her eyes. "Seems like a lifetime ago."

"Another life," Reese proposes.

"Yeah." Frankie's smile fades as she sips her frozen margarita. "A completely different life." Her gaze locks on me. "It was always supposed to be Gabriel. All the heartache to get there was worth it because *he's* worth it."

My throat tightens as her eyes water.

She blinks up at the ceiling, fanning her face. "Damn hormones."

I want to say something to fill the silence, but I have no words or hormones to blame for my emotions. I'm in awe of their love, their commitment, and their honesty in sharing such personal details with practically a stranger.

"Okay, no more margaritas for you." Reese laughs.

"It's virgin," Taylor reminds us. Both Frankie and Reese are drinking for two, which means non-alcoholic beverages for them.

I sip my real frozen treat. "Good thing I'm not pregnant then."

Taylor clinks her glass with mine. "Same!" She sips from her straw and sets it down, dropping a truth I have a hard time believing, "Jess likes you."

"They both do," Frankie adds.

"Maybe Walker," I admit. "But not Jess. It's just physical with him." He likes my body, though even *that* is hard to trust.

"I don't believe that." Taylor squeezes my arm. "I think he's just protecting himself."

Could be. It doesn't really matter. The longer I sit here and listen to the loving way they talk about their men and their close relationships with each other, it's painfully obvious I don't belong here, and my relationship with Walker and Jess is shallower than I realized. I never should have opened this door of friendship with these women. They've invited me in, but I can't stay. This is a world I was never truly supposed to be a part of—I'm the odd woman out. I can't add much to the conversation. I don't fit in anywhere.

"Oh, no. Are you okay?" Reese grips my hand.

It's my turn to blink away my stupid tears. "I'm sorry. It's—"

"You don't need to apologize. We understand." Frankie is so certain, but she's wrong. She has no idea how much my situation differs from theirs.

I bob my head but remain silent. I can't say what's really in my heart. Walker and Jess belong to them all more than me. I'm just a visitor with a day pass. I have no right to criticize their friends or offer up details Jess and Walker wouldn't want shared—besides, these women know more about *my* dates than I do.

I'm so stupid. I don't know what I was thinking in reaching out to them. Inserting myself into Jess and Walker's world without invite—without the okay from them.

I clear my throat and wave to a passing waitress, asking for our check. It's time I make a graceful exit—or as graceful as possible, given I've already stepped over an invisible line.

"It's getting late. Even though I'm off, I still have paperwork I need to deal with before the end of the day." I hate lying.

I'd never want to disparage their friendship with Walker and Jess, and the longer I sit here, the more likely I am to pour my heart out to them, talking about things I have no business sharing.

Business. Jess' words hit me hard. A reminder of what can never be.

I'm not in control of shit, except my ability to leave this restaurant before I ruin our day with my stupid mouth. If I haven't already.

Deciding I can't wait, I drop enough cash to cover my bill and then some and stand. "Ladies, it was great spending the afternoon with you. Thanks for letting me…" Dammit. My emotions swell. I can't get another word out without letting my tears out too. Instead, I turn and flee before I make an even bigger fool of myself.

Once in my car, it's a free-for-all. I can't hold the floodgates back as I rip out of the parking lot, praying they don't come after me. I've embarrassed myself enough.

I'll text an apology to them later. Maybe tomorrow. Maybe another lifetime from now. Another life where I'm lucky enough to have friends like them.

Sob after sob fills the silence in my car as I race home. The depth of my emotions pulsing through my blood are too much. They're downright overwhelming. I'd barely admitted to having a crush on Jess and Walker, feeling elated when they would come to see me in the ER, even though it meant one of them was hurt. I was proud to be able to patch them up, honored in some silly way that they *chose* me.

When in reality, their dicks did the choosing. Not their minds or their hearts. Just the muscle between their legs that thought I'd be up for a good-time. I'd be good for sharing. *Temporarily.* And they were right—mostly. I thought I was okay with that too.

Apparently, I'm as blind to my own feelings as Gabriel was to his for Frankie. He thought he only wanted the physical. Jess only wants me for sex. Walker could maybe be more, but he already said he wouldn't fight for me.

I'm not worth fighting for.

I'm not worth loving.

I'm only good for sharing.

Temporarily.

I'm really beginning to hate that word.

A situation I'm obviously not made for.

In the heat of it, it was fun. No, not fun. It was elation. A joining of cataclysmic proportions. It rocked me to my core, physically, mentally, emotionally.

I'll never be the same.

They've ruined sex for me. Who could possibly live up to the grandeur of their skills? The sounds, the emotions, the full-body ecstasy they pulled from me was otherworldly.

Earth-shattering.

Life-affirming.

Life-altering.

I'm forever *altered*—by them.

CHAPTER 22

WALKER

I'VE JUST FINISHED WORKING OUT AND AM HEADING to the shower when my phone pings with a text. Given I'm supposed to see Doc tonight, I don't want to miss a chance to chat with her even if only through text.

Her message has my heart stopping, summersaulting, then tripping over itself in an effort to find a steady beat.

Dr. Berklyn Fortier: *I can't make it tonight.*

Me: *Is everything okay?*

Dr. Berklyn Fortier: *I can't do this. I'm sorry. Please tell Jess.*

Panic sets in. She's not just canceling tonight. She's canceling *everything*. She's dumping me—*us*.

Me: *What happened? Let me come over and talk about this.*

Dr. Berklyn Fortier: *There's nothing to talk about. I truly am sorry. I just can't.*

Me: *Stop apologizing. Tell me what's wrong. Give me a chance to fix this.*

My message shows as read, but there's no response. I wait, pacing the locker room, and check my phone every few seconds. No jumping dots. No nothing.

Me: *Doc?*

Nothing.

Me: *Come on. Don't do this.*

Me: *It was going so well.*

At least I thought it was.

I call her. It goes straight to voicemail. I end the call and speed-dial Jess.

He answers on the first ring, "Hey."

"What the fuck happened last night?" I jump right in, not even giving him the benefit of the doubt. He did something.

"Nothing, I'm fine."

"Jesus—with Doc, Jess. What the fuck happened?" I resume pacing, wondering where the fuck he is. I wouldn't mind sparring with him right about now.

"Why are you asking?" Calm. He's so fucking calm.

My anger, my unease surges. "Because she fucking canceled on me through text and basically told us to fuck off! Now she's not answering texts or calls. She turned her phone off," I grate, blaming him. He did something. I know it. "What the fuck did you do?"

"We played. I left." His calm is teetering. I can picture the clench in his jaw.

"Be more specific. How did you play?"

"I got her hot, inserted the smallest butt plug, made her come. Then

I left." He's all about the facts. Not an ounce of emotions. But I'm not fooled. He's rattled.

"How was dinner?"

"There was no point staying once I'd done what I set out to do."

"Wow. Can you stop being an emotionless asshole for one second? This is me. What. The. Fuck. Happened? You went over there for dinner, not to just *play and accomplish a task*."

"I ran," he softly admits the truth.

"Fuck." I tug on my hair and take a calming breath that marginally works. "Well, *she's* running now. You happy?"

"Not even a little." More truth. The remorse in his tone eases my anger. At least he realizes there's no happiness without her—not the kind the three of us were capable of achieving together.

"I'm going to see if I can track her down. You need to apologize." I nearly hang up before adding, "And whatever the fuck you do, don't be a grumpy asshole."

Easier said than done when it comes to him with her.

I end the call.

Doc, please. Don't shut me out.

JESS

As much as I'm angered and hurt she didn't reach out to me directly, I'm not surprised. I knew I was fucking it up last night. I didn't do anything to stop it then or make an effort to smooth things this morning.

Before I consider what to do about Berklyn, Walker sends me a screenshot of his texts with her. His last text, *It was going so well*, has my chest constricting. For him, it probably was, not so much for me.

I know Berklyn. She wouldn't want to come between us. If I fuck it up for me, I fuck it up for him too.

I shoot off a text to her, not expecting a reply.

> **Me**: *Please don't punish Walker because of my fuck up. If you still want to see him, you have my blessing.*

When no response comes, I palm my phone and clock out of the bakery. It's been a long-ass day. Much longer than usual. We had a large catering order that more than doubled our baking for the day. Thankfully, it's done. I really need to talk to Cher about hiring another baker and probably putting in another double oven. Today, the ovens could barely keep up with the demand. If I had another baker, the prep would have been faster, but we would have still been backed up waiting on oven space. We may have to consider opening a whole other location just for catering gigs if we keep growing like we are. We could even expand to the store next door, if Cap agrees to give us the space. And, of course, if the current occupant vacates.

In my car, I answer a call from Taylor. "Hey, Taytay. What's up?"

"I had an interesting lunch today." Her words sound happy enough, but her tone has me worried.

"What's wrong? Who do I need to hurt?"

She laughs. "I don't need you protecting me anymore. I have Landry now."

"What happened at lunch today?" I want to move this discussion along. Not because I don't love Taylor like a sister, but because I need to figure out my next move with Berklyn. I can't let her slip away this easily despite my gut saying let it ride, let her go.

"Frankie, Reese, and I had lunch with your girl."

"My girl?" As much as I deny it, the words do crazy things to my head and heart.

"Don't play dumb. You know who I mean."

"How did you three end up having lunch with Berklyn?" Didn't she have to work? She didn't mention being off today. Though, I didn't really give her the space to talk about her plans for today or any other day. I'm such a jackass.

"She texted us this morning. We went for mani-pedis and then lunch. And margaritas," she adds. "It was fun. I like her."

"Yeah, she's great." Better than great.

"So why does she think you don't like her?"

Because I've given her little reason to believe otherwise. "She said that?"

"I told her you liked her—"

"Why would you do that?" Taytay's sticking her nose where it doesn't belong, about things she doesn't understand.

"Because it's true. I saw the way you look at her, Jess. Don't forget I know you," she insists.

She only knows part of me. "What did Berklyn say to that?" I'm not in the mood to debate my feelings for Berks. I need to know what happened. Were the girls the reason Berklyn cancelled on us?

"She said you don't like her. It's just physical. Is that true?"

"It's not *not* true."

"Jess," she sighs like a disappointed mom.

"So that's it?" Berklyn called our friends and spent the afternoon talking about us? As irritated as I should be, I'm really not. I like the idea of her becoming a part of our chosen family. Though it'll be damn inconvenient to see her around my friends and not be able to have her.

"She didn't really want to talk about it. I got the impression she felt her time with you and Walker was fleeting."

Temporary. Isn't that what I said, what I believed, at least for me?

"She said that?" Her feeling that way guts me. It's not untrue. I treated her like a temp—a stand-in. But hearing my friend tell me how it came across and how Berk took it hurts deeply.

"No. She didn't say much of anything. When we pushed, she ended up making an excuse about work and left. She was crying, Jess. Whatever you have going on with her is breaking her heart—her spirit. You need to make it right."

I groan, swiping my hand across my face. "Some things can't be fixed, Tay. Some things are best left alone to die and wither away."

"Is that what you want? You want her to die and wither away?"

Fuck. "I didn't say that." Not her, never her.

"Sounds like it to me."

"Then you're hearing things."

"You want what's between you to die and wither away," she clarifies. The smarty-pants.

"There's nothing between us. She's right. It's just sex." The words scrape up my throat like razorblades, bleeding my distaste down my throat, across my lips. Shame fills me, but, despite it, I can't believe otherwise.

"A girl doesn't get brokenhearted over just sex unless she wants more and can't have it."

"I don't have more to give, Tay. It's as simple as that."

"I think you're scared."

"I think you're nosy."

She laughs. "You're probably right. I want you to be happy. If she makes you happy, makes your eyes light up like I saw on Friday night, you need to do everything—anything—you can to lock that shit down."

"And Walker?" Can't forget about him.

"It's not like you've never shared women before." I cringe at her words. We've never discussed it. The guys know, but I've never known if their significant others knew too. Apparently, they do. We've never hidden our kink, but we don't talk about it openly. It's no one's business except ours.

"She's different," I admit.

"Yeah, Jess. She is. So, treat her different. Don't make her feel like she doesn't mean more than any other woman you've had in your bed. Shared or not. She's special. We all see it. When will you?"

Taytay, I saw it the moment I first laid eyes on her.

"I hear you." It's all the confirmation she's going to get.

"I'm here if you need to talk. Love you, Jess. Don't let her slip through your fingers." She hangs up before I can rebut her claim or return my love for her.

Why can I tell Taylor I love her but not even consider loving Berklyn?

It's not the same love.

What I could feel for Berklyn is... *Life-altering.*

Those fucking words again, hammering against my caged heart.

CHAPTER 23

BERKLYN

FOR THE NEXT TWO WEEKS I AVOID ALL PHONE calls and texts from Walker. I only received one text from Jess the night I cancelled on them—cancelled everything. His gracious offer for me to feel free to pursue things with Walker with his *blessing*.

I want to punch the guy in his smug *blessing*!

But Walker? Poor Walker. He's too sweet, stuck in the middle of a-hole Jess and fraidy-cat me. I can't—won't come between them.

Jess gives his blessing.

F Jess and his blessing. What a douchecanoe!

God forbid, he might actually want to fight to keep me for himself. He would never. And I'm not sure I'd want him to anyway. But could I be with Walker and not think about Jess? They're roommates and best friends. No matter what they say, I'd be a tear in the fabric of their friendship.

I could never be with one without thinking how amazing it was when also with the other. I guess I'm the problem, then. So it's good I've removed myself from the equation.

I've heard from the hospital staff that Walker has come in nearly every day to see me. I haven't been there. I took the standing offer with my local fire department to ride along with their EMTs. It's good experience for both of us and gives me a chance to work in the field with limited resources and challenging environments. It's also not bad hanging out at the firehouse between calls. It's a welcome distraction. They're harmless, fun and entertaining, but nothing and no one I'd seriously consider pursuing or even hooking up with.

I've had enough of hook-ups.

With Walker, I got a sip of what forever could taste like—maybe. He, probably more than Jess, will be the one that got away. Though, Walker never said he wanted *more*. He said he wanted to *share* me with Jess.

Walker didn't run from me. He ran toward me.

Jess ran away.

I ran faster.

Maybe I even got a head start.

"Here, Doc." Cooper tosses me a bag of Bugles. "Thought you might like a snack."

I laugh at his choice. "I can't believe you have these." We were just talking about how we used to put them on our fingers as kids. Such a simple pleasure. "Thanks. Any water?" I mean if he's giving me food, I might as well push for a drink chaser.

"Yep, coming right up." He grabs two bottles from the fridge and ambles around to take the last available seat beside me on the couch. We're watching last night's football game. We were on a call and missed it. So, we're watching it today like we haven't already heard the Cowboys won. It's the experience that counts.

We clocked out an hour ago, but I stuck around when he asked if I wanted to stay and watch. It's better than watching TV at home in the dark in case Walker shows up, knocking on my door for the umpteenth time. I can only avoid him for so long, and the longer I do, the worse I feel about it. He didn't do anything wrong. Jess did.

But Walker didn't say he wanted more, and the wives in their group inadvertently pointed out how temporary I was. I've never felt so small and inconsequential. I also didn't realize how lonely I was until I discovered what being worshipped—though for only a short while—felt like.

"Whatcha doing on your day off tomorrow?" Coop asks. He's been great to work with this week. He's their critical care paramedic, highly trained and really good at his job.

"I'm back at the hospital. Back to *real* work," I tease. No more avoiding my life.

"Ooooh, girl, those are fightin' words." Clarence torpedoes his crumpled-up napkin, nailing me in the face.

Coop tosses it back with an apologetic side-eye. "She's just sad she can't hang out with us every day."

True that. "I wouldn't mind, honestly. It's a nice break from being stuck behind windowless beige walls and the smell of antiseptic burning my nose."

"I don't know how you do it," Nathan, the quiet one, chimes in. "I like the action of the unknown. We never know where we're going or what we'll find."

They've made my time here bearable, fun even. I shrug at his comment though. "It's not that different, except I don't go to the trauma. You guys bring it to me."

"You'll miss us." Coop shoulder-checks me, eyes on the TV.

"I will," I admit.

JESS

Keeping my head in the game has never been so frustrating. I've avoided entanglements for this very reason.

No. You avoided them because you don't want to get your heart broken. Again.

Whatever.

Gabriel's frown is going to break his face if he doesn't give it a rest. He's just standing there, glowering from across the room, edging my nerves, amping my uncertainty that I don't know what the fuck I'm doing.

"Mustang!" Jonah catches my eye. "What the fuck?"

"What?!" I sneer right back.

"Do you want to lose your fight?"

What kind of question is that? "Yes. Yes, I do." I chuck my water across the room, sighing as it hits the wall and bounces a few times before rolling to a stop at Gabriel "No Mercy" Stone's feet.

He bends and picks it up, meandering my way like he has nowhere better to be. I know he does. He's got his wife and kids at home, waiting on him, ready to reinforce their place as the light of his life, his reason for being.

Fuck. I rub at the center of my chest. I don't need this. Not today. Not any day, really.

"Feel better?" He hands me my water.

"Not really, no."

He nods, eyes staring holes into my soul. "What do you need?" He's a calm, Zen motherfucker. The rustiness in his voice isn't an indication of any emotions he might be feeling, but his intense gaze conveys he's sensing a lot from me. Too fucking much, I've no doubt.

"Nothing you can give." Nothing I can give me either. I'm fucked, because I've fucked it all up for Walker, for me, for our girl.

Another nod. "I heard the girls had lunch the other day."

That was nearly two weeks ago. I'm surprised it took him this long to bring it up. "Hmm." I've got nothing to say to that, but obviously he does.

"Angel tells me your girl was upset. Left in a hurry. Know anything about that?" The only movement on his face or body is the lift of his left brow. So. Fucking. Calm.

Is this the way I come across to Walker—to Berklyn? "I only know what I heard." Won't lie.

"And what's that?" The gym door opening draws his attention to Walker and Rowdy as they enter, making a beeline for us.

"That she was upset." *Duh.* And she was talking about us to our family. Still not pissed that she felt comfortable enough to meet up. Yet, I'm torn up by how it ended.

"What's going on?" Rowdy stops next to Gabriel, his gaze flicking between us as Walker comes to stand on the other side, like we're having a little circle-of-friends moment.

"Trying to figure out what it'll take to get Jess' head out of his ass." Gabriel crosses his arms, head tilted, eyeing me expectantly, knowingly, pain-in-my-assingly.

Walker chuckles. "Good luck with that."

I glare at him. What the actual fuck? He's supposed to have my back.

He raises his hands. "What? I told you you were fucking it up."

He did. I'm not great at listening. No one in this room would debate that. Not even me—especially not me. I do what I want, consequences be damned.

Welcome to the consequences.

WALKER

Everyone in the room can smell the anger rolling off Jess. But me? I see the hurt and fear glistening across his skin like the sweat he's trying to wipe off with the towel Jonah hands him.

He's not fooling me. He wants Doc as much as I do. He *needs* her more than I do, that's for damn sure.

But my heart can't walk away. I just can't. I need to get her back and somehow make him see he can love her too.

"A little birdy told me Berklyn's been riding with the fifty-seventh," Rowdy throws out from left field.

"What? Fifty-seventh what?" I'm so confused. All I can think is infantry.

"Fire department?" Jess grouses.

"Yeah, House 57. She's been riding with the paramedics or a few weeks. Today's her last day," Rowdy clarifies with a big ole smile on his face like he just gave us the key to her kingdom.

Maybe he did.

It takes me two seconds to punch Jess on the arm and sprint for the door. "I'm getting her back. Tonight! And when I do," I point at him, "you better not fuck it up."

CHAPTER 24

BERKLYN

"PIZZA'S HERE!" COOPER HOLLERS TO THOSE NEAR and far as he checks the delivery app.

It's good timing. We have one minute to halftime.

"I'll get…" Clarence's words trail off as Walker enters the room carrying more pizza than he should be able to.

"Where do you want 'em?" He eyes the guys before his eyes land on me. His gaze softens on a deep inhale, like he can finally breathe.

"Here. Let me." Clarence unloads Walker's arms, turning and letting Cooper take some.

Shocked and finding the air thinner than it was thirty seconds ago, I stand but freeze, stuck in Walker's gaze.

"Hey, Doc." He slowly approaches, stopping intimately close, fingering the end of my ponytail as his other hand reaches for mine, holding it softly. "Been looking for you."

I nod, lost for words, unable to think beyond *he's here*, and the tug on my heart that screams, "He came for us!"

His tender gaze caresses my skin as he asks, "You think we can talk?"

Swallowing through my rising emotions, the most prevalent is relief, with hope coming in as a strong second. I squeeze his hand and squeak, "Yeah, sure."

Genius. I'm genius-level smart—hardly—when I get around my protective guys who put me through the wringer these past weeks for missing them, for missing what we never had but I wanted.

Granted, Jess isn't here, but if feels like Walker is emoting enough sorrow for Jess too. I quickly glance behind him just to be sure Jess isn't holding up the wall, waiting his turn.

He never waits. If he were here, I'd already be in his arms.

"Berklyn?" Cooper stands before us with a Coke and a plate piled high with pepperoni pizza. "You staying?"

"I, ugh—"

"She's coming with me, but we appreciate the offer, man." Walker eyes Coop's pizza. "Looks damn good."

"Hey aren't you one of the Black Ops fighters?" Nathan nearly drools over his plate, equally topped with an assortment of pizza. "Um, Stinger James, right?"

Walker's indulgent smile sways my heart toward him, like it needed any help. He sticks out his hand. "Yeah, but call me Walker."

Nathan shakes Walker's hand, smiling from cheek to cheek. "It's an honor. I'm Nathan." He points across the room and starts introducing everyone. "Y'all this is Walker "Stinger" James, he's a heavyweight contender for the Black Ops MMA."

The room erupts with greetings, handshakes, and pats on the back. Kind and humble, Walker takes it all in stride, pulling me into his side, protective and not letting me forget for a second he came for me. Not these guys.

He came for me.

My heart flutters with hope.

WALKER

I couldn't get her out of the firehouse fast enough. The EMTs she worked with seem like nice guys, but the longer we stayed, the more firemen came wandering in for pizza, and the introductions and fight talk were bordering on endless. I was worried she'd run off before hearing me out.

The pizza smelled so good and enticing that I talked Doc into trying my favorite pizza joint. I text my friend on the way who manages the place. He promised me the secluded booth in the back.

My night, my week, is starting to look up.

I've missed my girl.

I relish the feel of her dainty hand resting comfortably in mine as I drive, making me feel all kinds of forgiven.

It's not long before I'm pulling in and parking. "This place is great. You'll love it."

"I'm sure I will. It smells amazing." She eyes the illuminated flaming sign as we approach, her hand once again in mine.

Inside, Dino is on me, shaking my hand, introducing himself to Doc before the door closes behind us. "I went ahead and ordered your favorites."

"Oh—"

"I can change the orders if you want," he insists.

"Um…" I look to Doc. "Do you like sausage and pepperoni? Do you want veggies too?"

Her smile is indulgent as she turns to Dino. "I'm sure whatever you bring will be perfect."

"Perfecto!" He lights up. "Salads. I'll bring you some salads and bread." He turns to leave.

I grip his arm, stopping his retreat, whispering over his shoulder for only his ears.

He beams. "Absolutely!" He motions to the hostess. "Please see Mr. James and his guest to his table."

Once seated, the hostess fills our water glasses and takes our drink orders. She's barely gone a minute before salads and a basket of hot garlic bread are placed before us.

Surprise colors Doc's cheeks a beautiful pink. "He must really like you."

"He does. He's a fan of the team, not just me." I hold up the basket of bread for her to grab a piece.

She's radiant as she exhales and her shoulders drop. "I'm so hungry." Her gaze locks with mine. "This is great. Thank you."

"Don't thank me, Doc." Her thanks is the last thing I deserve. "We fucked up. I want to talk about it but not here. Just know I'm thankful you're here giving me this chance."

She takes a slice of bread, setting it on the side of her salad plate, and sips her water. I do the same and wait. The wheels are turning behind her green eyes I feared I'd never see again. Feared I'd never be close enough to smell her floral scent, never be anything to her again.

After a bite of salad and bread, she sets down her fork, garnering my focus. "I might have been too hasty. We can talk about it later—I'd prefer we talk about it later—in private." She squeezes my hand under the table. "I've missed you."

Fuck. She has no idea how much her admitting that means to me. I lean in, kiss her cheek and let her know, "Missed you too, Berklyn." More than she'll ever know.

Salads consumed, the surprise I ordered arrives a few minutes before our giant pizzas. It's a good thing we have a large table meant for more than just the two of us.

She squeaks when she sees the fries, her gaze flying to me. "You ordered fries?"

I cup her cheek, holding back the kiss I want, hoping she'll give it to me later after we've talked. "You love 'em, and they make the best. I had to get them for you. But I hope you'll share."

"Of course." She steals one, the first bite making her smile. "So good."

I toss one back and agree. "The perfect crispness on the outside to the light fluffy center. Perfection."

We're practically rolling out of the door by the time we get our leftovers boxed up, our check paid, and her visit to the ladies' room complete. Pizza boxes in one hand with a bag of desserts—on the house—on top, and Doc's hand in mine, we walk to my truck. Situated and food stored, I turn on the engine and ask, a little afraid of her probable no, "Would you come over? I don't think Jess is home yet, but I'd like to leave the food for him—" I throw out in case she'd rather go to her place. I'm hoping bringing her home, she and Jess get a chance to make up too.

"Okay," she cuts me off. "But can we pick up my car from the firehouse first?"

"Done." Yep, my night is looking up.

CHAPTER 25

BERKLYN

THE MOMENT I PULL IN BESIDE WALKER AND PUT my car in park, my heart thunders in my chest. Am I ready for whatever he wants to say? Should I have brought him home to my place to ensure privacy?

Walker's smile has me catching a much-needed breath as he takes my hand, guiding me to his apartment while managing to hold all our leftovers with one hand. He's talented but... "Do you need some help?"

"Maybe when I unlock the door."

I end up unlocking the door instead of holding the pizza boxes and dessert. Not that it matters, but it's funny how he wants to carry the *heavy* stuff. It's pizza. How heavy can it be?

I open the door and stand back, following him inside. He shuts and locks the door. I haven't been back to their place since the Friday and Saturday we all spent together. My skin pricks at the memory. It was a great time, soured a little by what followed, but still, for those remarkable sixteen or so hours, I felt like a queen being worshipped by gods.

Then, being with them separately was amazing. I never thought I'd fall for two guys. They never offered me more, yet I've felt their absence profoundly. I think I've been falling for them little by little over the months they kept asking me out. I don't fully understand why I finally said yes. But I'm glad I did, despite my reservations—despite how it turned out.

Now that I'm back here, I'm tempted to take any scraps I can get— even temporarily. I hate I'm willing to settle—do anything—to stop the ache in the center of my chest. The void that's grown since I walked away a little over two weeks ago.

"Why don't you head to my room? You mentioned wanting a shower. Go ahead. I'll put this stuff away and get us some drinks."

I take him up on his offer, glad I have my bag slung over my shoulder with a change of clothes, even happier to remember I packed comfy clothes, perfect for lounging around in. I feel like I live so much of my life showering other places than my own home, carrying bags of clothes nearly every time I leave the house just because I never know what my day in the ER will bring.

Though we had fairly mundane calls working with the firehouse this week, I still brought extra clothes so I could freshen up and not be in my scrubs if I decided to do something other than head home for the evening. Tonight was a rarity. I didn't shower. But I did throw on a pair of jeans and a blouse when I decided to stay and watch the recorded game.

When Walker showed up, I wished I'd showered, not because I stink—I hope. But because... Well, I like feeling fresh and secure, and at the moment, I don't.

Bathroom full of steam, I step out of the stall to find fresh clothes folded on the bathroom counter. I smile at his thoughtfulness. He

didn't know I have clothes, but maybe I'll wear his and save mine for...
Tomorrow? If I end up staying.

I still at the realization that I *want* to stay—I don't want to *only* talk.
Actually, I'm not even sure I want to talk at all. Sometimes not knowing
where I stand is better. The idea of Walker and-or Jess telling me they no
longer want to see me—in any capacity—is a little more than my delicate
heart can take at the moment. Maybe I'll feel braver once I'm forced to
hear what he has to say. I fear I won't be.

Dressed and teeth brushed, I release my hair from its messy bun and
finger comb it, letting it fall in waves around my shoulders. I'll probably
end up with it back in a bun before the night is out, but for a little while,
it feels good to leave it free and unbound.

As I step out of Walker's ensuite and into his bedroom, he turns from
the dresser, folded clothes in hand. His gaze scrapes me from head to toe
and back, a smirk tipping his lips. "Love you in my clothes." He kisses my
forehead as he passes. "I'll only be a minute. Get comfortable."

I'd only seen his room for a few minutes the Saturday I was here before they drove me home. I hadn't realized how big it is. Both his and Jess'
bedrooms have their own bathrooms and then a half bath off the living
space. It's a great apartment. Can't be cheap. My house isn't much bigger
and I have a third bedroom all squeezed in upstairs. Apartment living has
changed to accommodate roommate-type situations where there's equal
space and no concept of just one master bedroom.

It makes me second-guess owning a house. I wouldn't have the main-
tenance if I rented, and I could potentially have a large bedroom like this
and a way bigger, nicer bathroom. I'm back to fantasizing about that dream
house with the mudroom with a shower, a washer and a dryer.

I sigh as I sit on his bed, leaning against his headboard, and contemplate what I want to say—what there is to talk about. My beef isn't really
with Walker. I don't really have a *beef* with Jess, even. He doesn't want me

for more than F-ing, and I don't think my heart can deal with his desired one-dimensional connection. I can't have more with Walker and one-dimensional with Jess. It might work for a handful of times, but in the end, I'd come to resent Jess for not wanting me back. It would cheapen everything, giving my all and only getting a little back. If the roles were reversed, with Jess wanting me and Walker running, my answer would be the same.

I won't come between their friendship. I'd never forgive myself, and eventually, they'd come to resent me for trying.

Is there an alternative?

I want them both. They *both* don't want me—not in the way I need to be wanted—needed.

Knowing what I must do settles deep in my stomach like a rock. I just got here. I swipe at a tear, fighting back more. Can I walk away again? I have to, right?

Put on your big girl panties.

I can't be what *they* need—they can't be what *I* need.

But maybe we could have tonight.

WALKER

The atmosphere in my room feels off, not the way it felt before I entered the bathroom.

Berklyn looks small sitting on my bed, arms wrapped around her raised knees. "Hey."

"Hey." Her smile doesn't quite reach her eyes.

Has she changed her mind? Does she regret being here?

I kneel on the bed, pressing a kiss to her warm cheek. "You okay?"

"Yeah." Her eyes search mine. "You?"

"You're here. I'm great." No lie. Anywhere she is, I want to be. Especially my bed.

She cups my cheek, leaning in, sighing, "Kiss me."

I'm hesitant, unsure. I can't mess this up. "We need to talk." Don't we?

"Later." She presses her mouth to mine. "I need you," her plea rips at my heart.

Who am I to deny her? We said talk *later*. We never specified when later was.

Yeah, that's a slippery slope. But as her tongue slides against my lips, seeking entrance, I dive head first right over that slippery slope.

She pulls me down to settle over her, wrapping her legs around my ass, killing my resolve to take it slow, to show her I want more than sex.

I want it all with her—with Jess too. But maybe I can love her right, and she'll open her heart to the possibility of fighting for Jess. I think she wants him to fight for her, but sometimes we need the girl to fight for us. Show us what we're missing, what it could be like, that it's not so scary on the other side, especially when tumbling into Doc's warm embrace.

"I need to taste you," I press into her, breaking our kiss. I take her wanton gasp as permission to continue trailing down her body, removing clothing from her, from me as I go.

By the time I settle between her thighs, we're both naked, and she's glistening wet, waiting for my touch, my kiss, my loving. God, she's beautiful. I could stare at her for hours. I could jack off to this view for the rest of my life. But, lucky for me, I have the real deal right in front of me, and I'm not wasting another second.

"Walk," she cries as I run my tongue along her seam, parting her flesh, tasting the rarest and most cherished treat in all of mankind—her.

Gripping her ass, I tilt her to my mouth, diving in, fucking her with my tongue, reaching, flicking. I drink her up while holding her down, growling my approval, my need into her center, eating her like the succulent dessert she is—an endless treasure.

"Doc. Fuck," I groan when she clutches my hair and my hand on her stomach, pressing to keep her on the bed as my fingers replace my tongue and kiss, tongue, and suck her clit like a savored candy—sweet, tangy.

"Walker!" She swivels her hips, fucking my fingers, directing my tongue.

I press into the mattress, resisting the need to slam inside her and feel her come on my cock. I know that heaven.

I'll get there, more than once if I'm a lucky man.

"I'm… I'm… I…" she moans as she comes, her body squeezing and sucking my fingers in and in.

"Damn." Greedy, greedy, beautiful cunt, wanting everything. Thankfully, I'm prepared to give it. I kiss her tenderly, soft licks as she comes down, her body relaxing with tremors shaking her legs when I touch just the right place.

Wiping my face on my sheets, I come up over her, pushing her legs up to rest on my shoulders as I notch my cock at her entrance. "You're amazing, Doc. You know that?"

The tears in her eyes have me pausing, taking a second till she wipes them away and gives me a smile that sucker-punches my heart.

"I think you're the amazing one, Walk." She trails her hands down my chest, sending shivers down my spine as she continues lower till she grips my shaft, urging me forward. "Don't wait. I want to feel you—"

She arches on a gasp as I thrust, filling her, groaning my contentment at being inside her again. Her body is my home, my sanctuary, my safe place.

I have to use everything I can to keep her, to lock her in, to be sure she understands how important she is, how much she is needed, wanted.

Over and over, I ram home, faster, faster until she's screaming my name, clenching around me and coming with a rush of moisture, threatening to take me with her before I'm ready.

I ease her legs to settle around my hips, and lower over her. Still deep inside her beautiful pussy, little quakes squeezing my cock as I ravish her breasts, teasing and nibbling before sucking each tip deep.

When she's calls my name and swivels her hips, pulling me closer, begging me for more, I settle my weight over her, locking our mouths in languid kisses. Wrapped in my arms, I fill her slowly, rubbing my base against her clit in circular thrusts.

Needful hands and full-body tingles ride my desire, pushing me to take her deeper, give her more, and more, and more.

"Oh, fuck!" my girl cries as she comes undone in my arms.

My orgasm pulses through my body, my heartbeat raging in my ears, and with her arms wrapped around me, her legs squeezing my ass, keeping me deep, I lose myself, filling her with my release in throbbing waves, crying, "Doc," into our kiss.

I don't miss her sniffles as I break our kiss. "Berklyn?" Did I hurt her?

"Just hold me," she whispers, keeping me right where I am, deep inside her. "Don't let me go," she pleads.

"Never, Doc. I got you."

When she quiets, I reluctantly extract myself, collecting a warm washcloth to clean us up. Then I slip back in bed, silently wrapping her in my arms, eating up her sighs as she falls asleep.

As my contentment settles around me, I can't help the niggling notion:

Why does this feel like an ending instead of a beginning?

CHAPTER 26

JESS

I ARRIVE HOME FROM MOPING AROUND ROWDY, Gabriel, Landry, Cap and their families for about as long as I can stand it. After Walker ran out of the gym claiming he was going to get Berklyn back, Gabriel turned to me, brow cocked, asking, "What about you?"

"What about me?" I tossed my towel in the hamper and stalked to the showers.

They followed. They can't let a man die happy and heartless and alone.

"What about *you* and Doc?" Rowdy asks.

"There's no me and *anyone*." I strip on the way to the showers, giving them a good look at my taut ass, hoping that will "end" this conversation.

"Jess, man." Gabriel comes about as close as he dares as I slip under the shower.

Jesus, can't a guy get a break? It's not like this locker room hasn't seen some deep discussion. If these walls could talk. But, seriously, I don't need their help with my love life or lack thereof. I fuck. End. Of. Story.

"Don't do this," Gabriel continues. "Don't shut yourself off from what you can have with Berklyn. She's good people. Our women like her. That's saying something. She's a doctor, for fuck's sake." He's selling hard.

"And for some dumbass reason, she likes you," Rowdy adds, taking his place next to Gabriel—*the fucking king of us all.*

Fuck. I scrub my face, fighting to listen instead of lash out. I didn't mean that sarcastic shit. I love Gabriel. I love all these guys. They're my brothers. Brothers I never had growing up. "I hear you."

"But are you listening?" Gabriel backs up as I start to wash my hair, and water splashes near his feet.

"Probably not." I won't lie to them. Give them or me false hope. I'm a lost cause. Berk is better off without me.

"What do you want with her—them?"

I wouldn't mind another night with her, maybe two… Maybe a lifetime.

What. The. Fuck? That's Walker, not me. I'm not built for that. But still, I want…

I slap the wall, grumbling into the cascading water my discontent, "Fuck. Fuck. *Fuck.*"

"Yeah, he's listening." Rowdy gives me a nod. "Don't let her slip away."

"She likes Walker," I growl, the words ripping up my throat, raising my ire.

Gabriel leans against the wall and shrugs. "She likes you both. You two don't mind sharing. I've heard of weirder situations. Maybe this is how you're supposed to find love. Together. Maybe she needs two men to be happy—*you two*, specifically."

I don't miss the surprise on Rowdy's face that quickly morphs into agreement. "He's right. Nothing wrong with it as long as you all know and are honest about what you want—who you want."

I wish I were so easily swayed. But maybe I've been discounting Berk

and Walker's needs more than I realized to talk myself out of mine…
Maybe I do need them both…

The thought echoes in my mind when I arrive home and drop my
bag in my room and head to the kitchen for a drink. But I pause, hearing
moans coming from down the hall.

He did it.

Good for him—good for *them*. He'll be good to her, the best.

My chest hurts, that itch under my skin is back. I ignore my twitching cock that thinks we have a right to go and join them. I don't. I lost
that right when I ran, when I didn't treat her like she deserves, like I really wanted deep down.

Fear. I fucking hate it.

It doesn't matter anyway. She didn't come back to me. She came
back to *him*.

In my room, I slip in my ear buds and turn on some music before
heading back to the kitchen. On the fridge is a note from Walker:

DOC IS HERE.
COME SAY HI WHEN YOU CAN LEAVE YOUR FEAR AT THE DOOR.
~ WALK

P.S. THERE'S PIZZA IF YOU'RE HANGRY

Leave my fear at the door. That the question of the day, isn't it? I never
considered myself fearful. I'm the tough son of the biggest asshole I've ever
met or hope to meet. He took so much from me, and he was proud of it.

Why do I let him have control over my life, even after all these years?
Angry, regretful, defensive—those are the words I would have used to describe my actions—not fear.

Fucking fear.

I crumple up the note and toss it in the trash. I don't want Berk seeing it. I grab the pizza boxes from the fridge and check out what they brought home. Dang, it's two of our favorites from my favorite place—our favorite place. They must have gone for dinner. Dino would have loved to see Walker with our woman. He's always trying to set us up. See us settled. He probably stuffed them full of food considering how much they brought home.

I consider watching TV in the living room but decide to eat in my room. I don't want to make it uncomfortable for them if they come out for a sustenance break from fuckin'. I swipe my face and shut my door, fighting the envy plaguing my gut, but even if I'm wanted, I may not be welcome without a conversation first—an apology.

Kicking off my shoes, I plop on the bed, turn the TV on, and discard my music and earbuds. I can't hear *them* all the way in here. I turn up the volume to be sure and scarf the cold pizza. It's not as good as it is hot out of the brick oven, but little is. It's still damn good, even though I barely taste it for all the crow I'm eating with each bite.

Hours later, I blink awake, staring at a movie I don't remember starting. Glancing at the clock, I see why. I've been a sleep for over two hours. It's after midnight. I clean up my mess and glare down the hall to Walker's room. Is she still there? How many times did he make her come?

Is she happy? Content?

I turn off the lights and double-check the front door is locked. As I brush my teeth, I strip down to my boxer briefs. I hate sleeping in clothes. It's hot and confining.

Is Berk naked? Is she wrapped around Walk like a warm blanket?

Fuck. What if I go in and fuck this up more?

I spit toothpaste in the sink. Rinse my mouth and toothbrush. Drying my hands, I catch sight of my reflection, the desolation in my eyes, making me take a second look.

Why couldn't she come back to me?

Yell at me.

Tell me I'm an idiot, but come back to me all the same.

Make it perfectly clear so I don't have any space for doubt… Fear.

Can I leave my fear at the door?

Before I second-guess my actions, I'm down the hall, silently turning his knob in case I'm faced with the visual of what they are to each other. When silence is all that greets me, I enter and still next to Berk. She's sleeping soundly on her side, facing me, backed up to Walker, who's sleeping on his back.

I suck in a quick breath when her eyes pop open. Blinking a few times, she whispers, "Jess? You okay?" Worry rides her beautiful face.

Again, not really thinking this through, I toss back the covers and sweep her in my arms, holding her close, smelling her natural scent mixed with Walker's. "Not even a little bit," I admit. There's no hiding the remorse in my tone.

Surprisingly, she snuggles in close, wrapping her arms around my neck, naked as the day she was born. "What can I do?"

"Sleep with me. You can be mad at me, but do it in my bed. Let me hold you." Truth—Every. Damn. Word.

Walker sits up, rubbing his eyes. "Jess?"

"You coming?" I ask in invitation, stalking to the door, not stopping to confirm if he heard me or even follows. I do hope he follows—I'm not trying to steal our girl from him, but maybe I'm trying to steal a moment.

In the sanctuary of my room, I lie down with her the middle of my bed against my chest, pleading, "Don't hate me," into her hair. My heart thuds in my chest, impatiently racing for forgiveness I don't deserve— and haven't asked for.

She nuzzles into my neck, tenderly pressing a kiss into my undeserving skin, whispering, "I don't hate you."

Heat spreads from the warm of her lips as Walker climbs in bed, saddling up behind her. I hold my breath, waiting for him to steal her from my embrace, tell me I'm too late in some cosmic joke of toxic jealousy, but he doesn't. He simply drapes an arm over her hip, his head hitting the pillow beside her, his eyes already closed, and is out like the dead.

Always been envious at how well he sleeps.

My attention flares back to the amazing woman in my arms, breathing into my chest one slow exhale at a time. I take a fortifying breath, syncing up with hers, and start to relax for the first time in what feels like forever, but has, in fact, been since the last time she slept in my bed, in my arms, with our cum deep inside her.

I concentrate on the sound of them breathing, Walker's heavier than hers. Both rattle the bindings around my heart. Gabriel's words play in my head. *Maybe this is how you're supposed to find love.*

On a groan I didn't mean to voice, Berk's hand caresses my jaw, working its way into my hair as we lock eyes in the near darkness. An urge I don't remember feeling since I was a lovesick teenager seeps into my thoughts from the deep recesses of my bones.

"I want to kiss you." The admission is raw and tight with emotions I don't have any business feeling, a want so foreign, it's like it doesn't belong to me. Yet with every fiber of my being—this is me.

"Are you asking?" She pulls back, her gaze catching the moonlight through the open curtains, the green hue vibrant like the woman they belong to.

I rise above her, cupping her cheek, our lips nearly touching. "Do you need me to?"

She smiles. "No. You never have to ask to kiss me, Jess."

God. My name on her lips, draped with understanding and dusted with want, is all the answer I need and more than I expect.

With more tenderness than I've ever shown, our lips join, moving slowly, reverently. Uncertainty and inexperience have me wanting to pull back, but she sucks my bottom lip and flicks her tongue, making me ache for more, for everything.

On a growl, I slide my hand into her hair, adjust my angel and penetrate the heat of her mouth, devouring the taste of her, letting instinct take over. She grips the back of my head and shoulder, holding me tight, the bite of her nails spurring me on. Her moans feed my soul, make me forget why I don't kiss, why I've avoided this vulnerable intimacy not just with her but with every woman before her—except one.

Hours, days, weeks, centuries pass with Berk locked in my arms, our bodies entwined, wanting more, as she kisses every fear out of me, eating me up like Sunday dinner. And I do the same. We don't take it further. Our hunger spikes and calms us, only coming up for air occasionally, but one glance and I'm back for more.

Kissing has never been like this, not even as a stupid lovesick teen.

CHAPTER 27

BERKLYN

ON A MUMBLED MOAN, I OPEN MY EYES TO FIND myself in Jess' bed with Walker asleep beside me and…"Ohmygod." I grip the hair of the man spearing my insides with his tongue, his hands tight on my thighs, spreading me wide. "Jess," I gasp and writhe as fingers replace his tongue and his heated gaze shoots to mine.

"Morning, Berk," he rasps before licking my clit, not breaking eye contact until my head falls to the pillow on a stifled moan.

It's early, barely dawn, yet the man between my thighs is full of exuberance as he eats me like I'm the best part of his day. My heart leaps at the thought. Then falls when I remember: I can't be.

He's kissed me, but that was only late-night jealousy and claiming to get us to this point. Sex, or nearly…"Ooh," I bury my head in the pillow, away from Walker. I don't want to wake him. He's sleeping so soundly while I'm dying at his side.

Clenching, begging, reaching, clawing at Jess' shoulder and hair, I come on a silent cry that has him holding me down, forcing me to take the onslaught of his mouth on my clit as wave after wave of explosive tingles rack my body over and over again.

He hovers over me, his mouth glistening with my desire. His gaze heated, he moves closer. I lift, preparing for more of his amazing kisses. But that's not what I get. He frowns, pulling back, and without a word, he disappears into the bathroom, shutting the door behind him. Maybe to wash his face, maybe to shower. Whatever it is, he appears to be done with me

As bliss recedes, reality seeps in. He changed his mind. He doesn't want to kiss me. He'll never want more than sex. He'll never want *me*. With shaky limbs, I roll to my side. With little grace, I leap from the bed and dash for Walker's room, searching for my bag of clothes. "Where is it?"

"Where is what?"

I screech and turn, finding Jess standing in the doorway, naked, his cock bobbing against his abs, hard and ready. I swallow and cover myself with my arm and hands as best I can. "Look away!"

He frowns, stepping into the room. "Berk. I've seen you naked—"

"Please." I frantically look for something to cover myself with that's not a piece of furniture.

Jess throws me a shirt from the floor. "What's going on?"

I hold it in front of me, covering myself. "Nothing." Just a mortified woman here, freaking out. "I just need to leave." *Run. Run. Run. I never should have come.* I didn't intend on staying the night in his bed. But then he kissed me—

"Leave?" His angry face has me frantic.

"Can you turn around and let me get dressed, please?" I plead, hating the desperation in my voice. I just want his eyes off me.

"Berklyn." His scowl deepens, forcing his brows to nearly touch. "I was just between your thighs, tongue-deep in your pussy that tastes like you and Walker. You think I don't like what I see?"

I flinch at the rawness of his words. "It doesn't matter." I can't be what he wants.

"The fuck it doesn't. You're being ridiculous," he barks, steam practically coming out of his nostrils as his hands fist at his sides.

Ridiculous? Am I? I shake my head. I can't. "I have to go." I pull on the t-shirt he tossed me, spotting my bag by the door. I skirt around him, barely avoiding his half-hearted attempt to stop me, and swipe my bag off the floor. Finding my keys in the outer pocket, I make a dash for the door, shoes be damned.

I ignore his entreating words asking me to *wait* and *stop*.

Run. Run. Run.

I make it home in record time, dash into my house, shower, change, and back out the door, heading to the hospital. I have work. I can't sit around and mope about the man who doesn't want more with me, or the one who quite possibly does.

I can't have both.

So, I can't have either.

WALKER

A loud thud has me jerking upright in bed. Rubbing my eyes, I blink into the morning light of Jess' bedroom. It's empty. A crash of something breaking sounds from beyond his door. I assume it came from the kitchen or living room. Throwing off the covers, I race out of his room, sliding to a halt at the sight of our living room destroyed.

"What the fuck?!"

Couches are overturned, flatscreen is face down on the floor, coffee and end tables demolished. How the hell did I sleep through all of this?

Jess freezes with a dining room chair over his head, ready to be airborne. He's naked, sweat coating his skin, his dick swinging in the breeze, making my eyes flash to his.

"I'll repeat myself. What. The. Fuck?"

"She's gone." He sets the chair down, his chest heaving. "I kissed her, and she fucking left." There's no missing the outpouring of rage in every word.

I about face, return to his room, grab two pairs of joggers out of his drawer, needing a moment to slow my roll before I make things worse.

I toss him a pair. "Put those on. I can't talk to you with your monster cock hanging out."

He motions to me, brow raised. Yeah, mine's not much better. Plus, I have morning wood that's quickly deflating from the rude awakening.

After pulling on the borrowed shorts I've no doubt I'll hear about wearing commando, I pick my way to the kitchen, avoiding broken glass and splinters of wood. After pouring two glasses of OJ, I slide one across the breakfast bar to him. "Tell me what happened."

"After y'all came to my bed last night—"

"You mean after you stole her from my bed—"

"Yeah," he shrugs, "that. You fell asleep like the dead. I held her. Told her I wanted to kiss her. She asked if I was asking. And I said *do you need me to?*"

He's cute how he's relaying their complete conversation.

I lean against the counter and hide my smug smile behind my glass, sipping my juice, completely intrigued.

"I kissed her—"

Wow. That's a big step for him. "How was it?"

167

His eyes bug. He bites his lip and looks down. Never seen Jess flustered. "It was… Good."

I know that's a lie. I've kissed Doc enough to know kissing her is spectacular. "Just good?"

He shakes his head, pushing debris out of his way before he picks up a functioning barstool and sits. His gaze lifts to mine, both shoulders rise and then fall. "Don't know what you want me to say. I tried. I gave her something I haven't given any woman in a long time, and she threw it back in my face."

I pull out the fixings for scrambled eggs and toast. If we're going to get serious, we need food. "But she was fine last night? What happened this morning?"

Was she fine though? I had the distinct feeling she was telling me goodbye with every touch and kiss. Her tears. She was fucking crying before she fell asleep in my bed, in my arms.

"She was perfect. Slept in my arms all night. I woke her up with my mouth on her pussy. What chick doesn't love that?"

True. He does excel at it, based on the women I've seen him with. He uses oral to compensate for not kissing them on the mouth. But it sounds like Doc got the whole package last night and this morning. "Did you fuck?" Did she cry?

His returning scowl isn't an answer. He could dislike the question. It's not a denial of them fucking. But one thing is for sure: he finally let her in, and she hurt him by disappearing this morning.

"No," he sighs into his glass. "She came, I went to the bathroom to wash my face and brush my teeth, thinking she might not want to kiss me with *her* all over my face and mouth."

Wow. I'm kinda surprised by his thoughtfulness. But then again, I've never seen him kiss a woman. He may not know some find it hot tasting themselves on your tongue as you fuck 'em.

"She was gone when I glanced out the bathroom door. I found her in your room searching for her clothes in a panic." He downs the rest of his orange juice.

"Why was she panicking?"

"I have no idea, but she freaked out about me seeing her naked."

"What? We've seen her naked more than once. We've been deep inside her—together," I clarify, as if that makes it even more okay to see her in the buff.

"She kept asking me to turn around, look away. I got pissed." His voice rises. "She's fucking perfect. Why wouldn't I want to see her naked?" He comes around the corner, rinsing his glass. "She pulled on one of your t-shirts, grabbed her bag and ran. She didn't even get her shoes."

"She left here practically naked?" That seems out of character for Doc—and *him* for letting her.

"Yeah, she didn't want *me* to see her naked, but she's fine with the rest of the world seeing her ass as she dashed out of here like it was on fire."

"But you let her go?" He didn't chase her? I would have totally chased after her, made her stop and listen to reason.

"I was naked too. A naked MMA fighter chasing a frazzled, half-dressed woman into the parking lot for anyone to see didn't seem like a smart choice. Plus, she wasn't in the headspace to hear anything I had to say. She was too upset."

"She cried last night. I kinda felt like she was saying goodbye. Like she was giving me one last fuck."

"What? Why would she agree to come back just to run off?"

"We're missing something." I'm sure of it. Women are complex. Doc is no different. "We never did talk like she and I said we would. We ended up—"

"Fucking. Yeah, I heard."

I can't hide my smirk. "You should have joined us."

He shakes his head. "I didn't want to intrude."

That's not like him. He likes to take charge. Maybe he didn't want to take over. He kissed her. Does that mean he's changed his mind about wanting more than sex?

I pour the eggs into the skillet and watch them puff up before I start to run the spatula through them, getting a weird satisfaction from the peeling sound the eggs make as they're scraped from the pan. Best. Sound. Ever.

Well, besides the sounds of Doc coming undone for me—for us.

"I think you need to worry about your fight. Let me worry about Doc." I motion to the toaster, prompting him to push the handles down. "We'll figure it out."

He doesn't seem hopeful. I don't blame him. He was making a big gesture, only Doc didn't see it. Or she did, and it scared her. Either is a possibility. "Don't act rejected and throw your shields up again. We won't know what's really going on in that head of hers until we see her again, get it from her directly, and see where we go from there once all the cards are on the table."

His frown lessens slightly, which has my shoulders relaxing.

"After breakfast, we need to clean this place up."

He pulls down plates and refills our glasses. "Yeah, sorry about the mess."

"You're paying for the new TV," I clarify just in case he thinks there's any doubt. Though if he needs me to, I'll pitch in.

We're a team. And now that we're on the same page, hopefully we'll get her back.

CHAPTER 28

BERKLYN

M Y PHONE HAS BEEN SILENT. NOT A SINGLE PHONE call or text, not even from my mom or dads. It's a sad state of my life. I could be dead, and no one besides the hospital would even miss me, would even *know* I was gone.

Out of sight. Out of mind.

Was I being stupid, insecure, childish? Jess not reaching out to me is understandable. In his eyes, I ran out on him. I was outlandish, unreasonable. The anger on his face, thrumming through his body, haunts me.

Walker not calling or texting hurts. He's the peacemaker. He soothes ruffled feathers and hurt egos.

You're the one that left. Why would they reach out? My inner goddess is not helping.

I incise my patient's boil on their back, thankful I have a mask and full-face protection as the skin splits and begins to ooze with pus. My stomach churns, threatening to expel my lunch from the putrid smell. I take a deep breath through my mouth and let it out slowly, calming my traitorous body for its revolt. I'm not normally squeamish. In fact, when it's not covering me, I usually find the gross stuff fascinating. Not today.

Needing a minute, I call over a first-year to finish the job and step away. My skill isn't really needed. The nurses brought the patient to my attention because I'm not bothered by the icky stuff. In fact, most nurses could do the debridement. It's the first-year's lucky day.

"Are you alright?" Nadine asks, peeking around the curtain to see how the resident is doing.

"Yeah, I'm thinking the tuna for lunch wasn't such a great idea."

She scrunches her face, lip curling. "Cafeteria tuna is *never* a good idea. Are you looking to get botulism?"

I chuckle and rub my tummy. "It's not *that* bad." And, of course, *no*. No one *wants* botulism.

She grips my elbow, urging me down the hall. "You look green. Go sit in the lounge. I'll bring you a Sprite and saltines."

I actually end up lying on the stale couch, trying not to think about whose butt sat where my head now lies. The queasiness eases the longer I'm horizontal. Even when Nadine brings me the soda and crackers, I just close my eyes and drift, my mind taking me back to Walker. He was so tender and loving. And then Jess and the shock of him admitting he wanted to kiss me, and then the press of his lips to mine, gentle and then not so gentle.

He didn't take it further despite my desire to feel his hardness moving inside me as his tongue tangled with mine. If all he wants is physical, then why didn't he go there? Why spend hours kissing me to simply fall asleep in each other's arms?

All questions I'll probably never know the answer to.

By the time a soft tap on my shoulder wakes me, I've slept through the rest of my shift. Nadine just smiles and eyes the watered-down drink and uneaten crackers. "I guess you were tired too." She pops a hip.

Guilt flares as I sit up. "I didn't mean to fall asleep." Certainly not for the rest of my shift. I yawn and do a mental status check on my stomach. No more nausea, thank the heavens.

"Don't worry about it. You've worked plenty over the years to cover for a little nap. Plus, we weren't that busy today. Must be the new moon. Everyone's calm."

I toss my cup and store the crackers in my pocket. I may need them on my way home. "Thanks for watching out for me." Nadine might miss me if I were dead.

That's one.

"Don't mention it." She motions to the front of the ER. "That guy is here to see you."

My heart leaps as if it knows who's here. "Who?" I try to hold back my hope that it's Jess or Walker come to fight for me.

"He didn't say, and I can't remember which one is which."

"Dark hair or dirty-blond?" I can't say "big" as both of them are god-like in size.

Her smile is knowing as if she can read my mind. "Dirty-blond with golden eyes."

Pitter patter goes my heart. "Walker."

"Whatever his name is, Dreamboat is here for you." She winks and slips out the door.

Dreamboat. It's a pretty accurate statement.

WALKER

Doc in scrubs just does something to me. Maybe because I know how smart she is and how hard she worked to become a doctor. It's not an easy process, never mind career. It takes time and dedication, but it also takes serious brain power. She's beautiful and brilliant, and though I love her in her cutoff shorts and a t-shirt or a dress, I particularly like her in scrubs. I'm partial to the green ones she's wearing today. They show off her eyes.

I frown as my gorgeous girl nears, looking tired. Maybe she was as worked up as Jess was this morning, and it's carried over to her day.

"What are you—"

"Can we talk?" I kiss her on the cheek, cutting off her canned *why are you here* spiel. I purposely waited till the end of her shift to show, hoping she'd be more likely to say yes.

"Can we go to that pizza place again?"

That was easier than I anticipated. "You liked it, huh?"

"I did, but I've been dreaming about the fries."

My girl and her fry fetish. I'd never hold out on her. I glance behind her, catching a few staff watching us. "Why don't we drop your car off at your place first?"

"Okay." She checks the time on her watch. "I need to grab my stuff. I'll pull around front in, say, five minutes."

"Sounds good." I resist kissing her again. She's at work, and I don't want to insinuate my place in her life amongst her peers.

Fifteen minutes later, her car is dropped off, and we're on our way to dinner. I text Dino, letting him know we're gracing him with our presence again. He's elated.

After a basket piled high with fries, drinks, salads, and ignored bread basket, I get down to it before the pizzas come and the real eating begins.

"I'm sorry for whatever made you cancel on us in the first place, but also for this morning. Are you okay? What can I do to make things better?"

"You don't owe me an apology." She points a fry at me before giving it a bath in ketchup. "I don't know if there's anything you can do. I think we want different things."

"Which is?" *You wanting Jess and only Jess?* Is on the tip of my tongue. My gut sours at the idea. I know she likes me, but does she like *me* enough?

She shakes her head, her eyes watering as the silence pulses between us. Then her eyes widen as she scans my face, touching my cheek to bring me closer. "Your stiches. They're out!"

I lean in closer, relishing her warm touch, amping up my need to steal a kiss, but I rub my healed cut, sans her stitches, instead. I almost miss her stitches, knowing they were there, in my flesh, because she put them there. They made me feel like I carried a little piece of her. "Yeah, Frankie removed them a few days ago."

"I can't believe I didn't notice last night."

I point to the basket between us. "You were distracted by fried goodness."

Her smile feeds my soul. "Why are you so nice to me?"

"I like you." It's simple enough.

She nods. "By that logic, Jess doesn't like me very much then." It's not a question but a perceived fact. And maybe not fair. He has his moments of niceness—so maybe he likes me a little.

"I can't speak for him, nor do I feel comfortable speaking about him." She looks disappointed. "But…" I tip her chin, holding her gaze. "Fuck it. He likes you a lot. Maybe too much."

She sits back, eyeing the waiter as our extra-large pizza with both pepperoni and sausage is delivered. Once he's confirmed we're good and leaves, her attention returns to me. "I think he likes sex with me."

I chuckle. "What's not to like?" I mean, seriously. Her brows shoot up, and I lean in, whispering, "Doc, being with you has been the best sex of my life. Sharing you," I exhale and shake my head, "mind-blowing. Plain and simple." I slip a slice of hot steamy goodness on her plate. "But," I emphasize by squeezing her hand, "it's not all I like about you or want to do with you."

"What do you want to do with me?" She forks a bite of pizza—the horror—and blows till she's sure it's not too hot.

I gesture around. "Everything. I want everything, Berklyn. Even if it means sharing you with Jess." I tilt my head. "Actually, especially if it means sharing you."

"Wow," she mumbles around her bite.

I wave it off. I'm not willing to go down that road and admit all the forevers I want with her. "You need to figure out your shit with Jess."

"*I* need to figure it out? He *kissed* me and took it back. He doesn't want anything from me but sex." Her voice cracks. "I thought for a minute I could do that, but turns out, I'm not made for casual sex-only kinda deals." She motions between us. "I don't see how any of this will work. I won't—"

"His big match is on the fourteenth," I interject. I can't unfurl the Jess issues for her. They need to work it out. "Come with me. We can celebrate with him afterwards and get you two on the same page. But give him this time to focus on his fight. He's messed up over last night and this morning."

She laughs. "Hardly. He was mad."

"He was." Can't deny it. "He *kissed* you, Berklyn. He *never* kisses women."

"Does he kiss you?" I don't miss the hurt in her eyes, the idea if him being venerable with me and not her.

The thought gets a laugh out of me, but she's not laughing. I lean in, getting close enough to feel her warm breath on my face. "We're not gay, Doc. We like to share women. We don't fuck each other. But we like to fuck the same woman at the same time." I sit back, fold my slice and take a huge bite, a little miffed she doesn't know this, or didn't notice in the moment.

"I'm sorry," she says. "I find it hard to believe he hasn't kissed anyone else. Who makes it through life, having sex and not kissing?"

"Jess." It's all the explanation she going to get. Any further revelations will have to come from him directly.

She grabs another slice, devours a handful of fries, contemplating.

I can't take the silence after a few minutes. "Hang out with me. No sex. Just dinner and friendship. Get to know me. Then, we support Jess at his big fight. We'll figure out the rest from there."

"No sex?" Is she pouting?

I give her my best smirk, inordinately pleased at her disappointed tone. "Oral and a good fingering or hand job isn't off the table." I wiggle my eyebrows, reeling her in. "Come on, say yes."

"Yes." Her smile is free and lights up her eyes that had been looking rather pensive.

"Good. Now eat, so I can finger-fuck you on the car ride home."

CHAPTER 29

JESS

J ONAH, USUALLY THE VOICE OF REASON, CATCHES my eye. "You want to forfeit?"

"What?!" I rear back as if he actually struck me. "No. Why the fuck would you say that?"

Coach frowns at Jonah over his shoulder as he continues wrapping my hands.

The former heavyweight boxer shrugs his massive shoulders. "Just seems like you don't want it. You're a million miles away."

If a glare could melt skin, he'd be in a world of hurt. "I'm right fucking here," I seethe.

"Hmph. You sure? Seems like you're still wallowing in Doc's pussy."

I'm on him in two seconds flat, my forearm pressed into his neck, pinning him to the wall with Coach trying to pull me off. "Don't," I growl. "You don't ever talk about Berklyn like that. You hear me?"

"You said it was *just* sex. Temporary. Why do you care how I or anyone else talks about her?" he pushes, trying to dislodge me.

Fuck. I hate I ever used those words to describe what's between Berk and me. There's no *just* to any part of our connection—sex or otherwise. She may have written me off after I bared my soul to her in the form of a kiss, but she deserves his respect. She deserves *mine*.

With a shove, I release him and step back, pacing away. If he knows what's good for him, he'll get the fuck out of my dressing room.

But like a man with a death wish, he follows me, getting right in my face. "You love her, man. Quit fighting it."

My shoulders lower as my arms fall slack at my sides. It's not possible. How? When?

He cups the back of my head, tugging until our foreheads touch. "You. Fucking. Love. Her. Stop fighting it. Redirect that energy to winning your match. Don't waste another second denying yourself or her—or Walker. He loves her too. Don't ruin what the three of you could have with uncertainty and misguided doubt over a fucked-up past."

Could it be that simple? Just choose Berklyn over my history with one particular woman?

I've given that history too much of my time, energy, and soul.

It's ridiculously simple. The girl from my past isn't worthy of any of that, yet I've given her power over my future as though I need the same protection now. Berk is worthy of everything I can give her and more, yet I'd given her nothing but my body.

But I did give—I kissed her, and what did she do? She ran.

She showed up first…

She proved me right!

Because she got scared? You held back first.

I deserve more!

She deserved more.

I deserve more.

You deserve each other—you deserve love.

"Fuck," I sigh, releasing the weight that's been riding my life since I left home to live with Gran.

I've been looking at Berk with the same tainted lens I looked at all women with since the first. Never even considered she'd be different. Yet she has been. I consciously pursued her—with Walker—for over six months. I've never done that.

I don't do repeats. I've repeated with Berklyn and still want more.

She doesn't have to prove she's different. She just is.

Why haven't I been able to see it until now? Walker tried to tell me. Gabriel and Rowdy, shit, even Taylor, tried to tell me.

Why is it so clear now? Berklyn is like no other. I kissed her, and it felt amazing—fucking fantastic—and the world didn't end. She might have run, but she wasn't reacting to my kiss. She was reacting to what I've shown her over and over again: I didn't want more than sex from her. Even kissing her didn't disprove that point. The average, normal person kisses during sex. It was a huge deal for me, but for her, it was just another level we'd skipped that can lead to sex.

I haven't told her I want more. She's not a mind reader. Fuck I didn't even fully know until this moment. How could she?

"Fuck, Jonah. I lo—"

"Nope," he holds up his hand, "don't fucking tell me first. Tell her. Tell Walker. *They* need to hear it."

Good point.

Jonah releases my neck, stepping back. "Now, who the fuck is standing in your way of getting to your girl tonight?" He taps me on the chest, pushing.

I growl and push back.

"Who?!" he shouts.

"Rip," I growl.

"Who?" Coach comes to stand on the other side of Jonah, donning his menacing face.

"Rip "R.I.P." Prescott!" I seethe.

"Who's taking him out?"

"Me!"

"Who?!"

"Me. Jess "Mustang" Riley. His worst fucking nightmare!"

"Fuck yeah, you are!" We clash fists.

I'm ready. So fucking ready for this and ready to get my girl after I knock RIP the fuck out.

WALKER

Doc looks fucking amazing. I thought I loved her scrubs, but this sparkly number takes the cake, my heart, and the air from my lungs. I can barely keep my eyes off her to concentrate on driving to the arena for Jess' fight.

"Stop. You're making me blush." She shoves my shoulder before looking away.

It's too late. She's been blushing since I picked her up and told her I couldn't wait to get her out of that hot dress and fuck her in nothing but her CFM heels.

"Think you could ride my fingers on the way?" It's not the same, but it might take the edge off. I'll still be hard as fuck, but hearing her—feeling her—come on my fingers would settle me in a way I never felt before her.

She laughs. "I'd need to go to the bathroom first."

My brows shoot up. "Are you considering it?" Hot fuck!

She shrugs, biting her lip, giving me her come-hither eyes. "Maybe. But I really need to go. I had too much iced tea with dinner."

I spot a convenience store up ahead. "I could top off the tank while you do your business." I grimace at the idea. She's too fucking fancy to pee in a souped-up gas station, but it's probably not much better than the arena restrooms.

When I pull up to the pump, putting the truck in park, she asks, "You want anything?"

"What, like, snacks or your pussy?" I take advantage of her shock, leaning over the center console and steal a kiss, holding the back of her head, taking her tongue for a come-fuck-me ride. Before she can break our kiss, I slide my hand up her skirt that is indecently short when she sits, and growl at the heat radiating between her thighs.

"I bet I can make you come before my tank is full." I have about half a tank. If I work her just right and talk real dirty, she'll get there. The idea of her scent on my hand while watching our boy put a world of hurt on his opponent gets me crazy hard.

Doc pulls back, a gasp on her lips before she whispers, "I might tinkle on your seat if you do that."

A full body laugh erupts. That would be something. I'm not sure I find it as distasteful as she's thinking, yet…

"I'd rather make you squirt, baby." One more quick kiss and I release her. "Go. There are better drinks and snacks at the arena. You just take care of you."

BERKLYN

Lips tingling, the ones on my face *and* between my legs, I unbuckle and hop out with Walker's help. He doesn't release my waist until I'm steady on my feet. "You good?"

I tug on my dress, regretting how short it is. "Yeah, thanks."

He pats my butt as I pass. "Berklyn."

I stop short, something in his tone has me needing to see his golden eyes. "Yeah?"

"I'm really glad you decided to come tonight. It'll mean a lot to him." He squeezes my hand. "It means a lot to me."

My heart pitter-patters, thumping away for the sweetest dirty-talking man I know. "It means something to me too." A quick peck on the lips and I'm darting across the empty lanes of pumps to the front doors.

"Hey, pretty lady."

I still, my hand on the door. A flash of something metallic catches in the corner of my eye. I pivot, taking a step back. "Yes?"

A rough-looking guy in a track suit flashes what he might believe is a friendly smile, but I beg to differ. It's creepy. "Don't you look like a pot of gold at the end of a rainbow," he twangs, apparently not from around here, at least not originally.

I assume he's referring to my shimmering gold sequin dress I chose to wear tonight for Walker—*and* Jess—and me. Fight nights are fancy, right? Walker is wearing a suit with no tie. I'd actually prefer his white button-down with no jacket. I like his sleeves rolled up. The arm porn his forearms produce with every twitch of his muscles is on point.

I start to take another step back until he sways, like he's dizzy. "Are you okay? Do you need medical help?" On the verge of stepping toward him to grip his arm, the words "I'm a doctor" freeze on my tongue.

The metallic object I saw a flash of a moment ago turns out to be a gun.

A gun he now has aimed at my face.

"Yeah, Goldilocks, you can give me all of your money." He points the gun at my wrist. "That fancy watch too."

My years of trauma training, learning how to breathe through the panic and doubt, shoving emotions down and focus on the facts, kicks in.

Fact: He has a gun.

Fact: He wants money.

Fact: He wants my watch.

Fact: He has a F-ing gun, and he's weaving.

Through a stuttered breath, I hand over my watch. "I don't have any cash on me." I hold up my arms after he snatches the watch from my grasp. "I'm a doctor. I can help you."

"Bullshit. You ain't no doctor." He stumbles backward before righting himself, gun still pointed at my face, his hand shaking. "I don't need your fucking help anyways. I need money!"

Fact: I'd rather have a steady hand holding me at gunpoint.

Breathe. One. Two. Three. Four.

I motion in the direction of Walker's truck, not taking my eyes of him. "My purse is in the car. I can get you money. I don't have much, but I'll give you what I have. Just put your gun down."

Walker. I can't take this guy toward him. I can't chance Walker getting shot instead of me because I have no doubt Walker will play hero given half the chance. No, not *playing*. He'd *be* a hero.

In a split second, the gun goes off. A piercing pain rips through my shoulder, the *bang* ricocheting in my ears before a second shot rings out. I'm thrown to the side when a large body hits me, wrapping around me before I'm crushed to the pavement. The air whooshes from my lungs, trapped under an enormous weight.

"Berklyn," Walker groans as a third round is fired.

And then another.

CHAPTER 30

JESS

RIP "R.I.P." PRESCOTT ATTEMPTS A CHEST JAB. I SEE it coming. One second, I'm moving to deflect, and the next, I'm nearly taken down by a crushing pain erupting across my chest, stealing my breath, making my eyes water and allowing the asshole to land his punch.

"Fuck," I seethe, having no clue what the fuck happened. It felt like my world was ending, and the motherfucker hadn't even touched me.

Staggering back, clutching my chest, the gripping pain—not from his blow—eases as I suck in air, dodge his next attempt and land an uppercut. He stumbles back, giving me a few extra seconds to recover. The crowd's reaction barely registers as adrenaline surges and anger crushes any dregs of self-doubt and narrows my focus.

This asswipe is going to learn the true meaning of R.I.P.

Fire burning in my gut, I come back swinging, landing hit after hit until the bell sounds.

I sit on the stool in my corner and suck down the streams of water

Jonah squeezes into my mouth, chanting, "You got this." Coach wipes my face, spouting Rip's weak spots, reminding me of my strengths. It all sounds muffled and distant, like Charlie Brown's parents, "Wah wah wah."

Shaking my head, I rub at the ache in my chest that travels up my left shoulder, not from his blow, but the pain that proceeded it. I should tell them. What if something's wrong? Like *really* wrong.

Like heart attack wrong.

The bell sounds, and there's no time.

I bounce on my feet a few times before charging, but since the chest discomfort doesn't worsen, I ignore it. He's not getting the advantage, not if I have anything to say about it. And the hammer of my fists and the snap in my kicks say I have everything to say about it. He's not winning. He's not getting a chance to ring my bell, to make me lose concentration, to make me doubt I'm better than him.

I win this. I get the girl and her other guy. We'll be a family. The three of us.

I. Can. Scrub. The. Floor. With. This. Motherfucker. Starting right now!

Five. Four. Three. Two. One. *Ring.*

Another round in my favor. He's all mine, running on the defensive. I swear I saw him cry after my last roundhouse kick.

This day is mine.

This day is mine.

This day is mother. Fucking. Mine!

More water. More smack talk. More wah wah wah.

Ring. Third round.

My roar echoes off the walls when I come at him, landing hit after hit, kick, swipe, punch, jab. Step after step, he backs up, running scared, trying to dodge and distract with messy form and childish hits. My heart pounds, urging me on, needing to show my girl and Walker that I can fight for us just like I'm fighting this asshole.

He gets lucky and catches me on the chin. I growl my dissent for letting him land a single blow. It's time for lights out. Enough of this crap. I've got a woman to claim and a life to lead that's not all about fighting—at least not this kind.

I'm learning. I understand I need to be all about fighting for Berklyn, not against Walker or bowing out to avoid getting in his way, but *with* him.

Jonah and Coach are screaming at me to *end this*. The crowd is chanting my fight name, "Mustang."

I'm wild.

I cannot be tamed.

The crowd begins the countdown of the final round. There will be no more rounds. The only ringing Rip will be hearing is when I ring *his* bell.

Two steps. A block. A one-two punch. He stumbles, head down. I finish with a shin kick coming back with a right cross, landing squarely on the chin. His unfocused eyes don't see me as he starts to fall.

Lights out, motherfucker!

This day is mine.

BERKLYN

They say you don't feel the pain of a gunshot wound when it happens. Whoever said that was an idiot or has never been shot. I feel it. It's excruciating. Yet, I can't muster an ounce of concern for myself as I work to dislodge Walker. He's not moving, which I pray means he's only unconscious.

Not as gently as I like, but as carefully as we can, myself and the gas station attendant roll Walker off me. I rise to my knees, ignoring my blood-soaked dress and the scrapes, and check his pulse. It's steady but weak. He's losing blood. Fast.

"Do you have bandages and tape? A first aid kit?"

"We've got some stuff." The attendant jumps up. "I'll grab everything we have."

Walker's pallor is concerning. Struggling to rip his shirt open with my lame shoulder, I cringe at the hole in his chest oozing blood. Unsuccessfully, I try to tear pieces of his shirt to use as gauze, but I'm not strong enough. I finger the corner of his shirt into the open wound, stuffing it as far as I can to staunch the flow of blood.

In the distance, sirens whirl in the night air that smells like gasoline and iron. Blood. Walker's blood... Maybe mine. I quickly glance at the guy who tried to rob me, lying face up, eyes open, unseeing, shotgun blast to the chest. The attendant shot him and ran to help me and Walker. The perp was dead before he hit the ground. The smell in the air includes his blood too, though I'd rather ignore that fact.

The attendant pushes through the door, arms loaded, and dumps the contents next to me. "I brought alcohol. Thought you might need it."

"Yes. Good thinking. I need scissors."

He produces a pair from his back pocket. "The ambulance is about five minutes out." The phone in the crook of his neck tells me he's still talking to the 9-1-1 operator. "Police are nearly here."

"Good." I point to the bottle of rubbing alcohol. "Pour some on your hands and mine and then the scissors."

Once done. I cut the rest of Walker's shirt away from the packing in his chest and secure the makeshift bandage with a gauze pad and medical tape. "We need to roll him to his side, toward you so I can check his back." I'm positive he was shot in the back diving for me. Damn hero. I blink away the tears that threaten to steal my vision. I can't break down, not now. I... he—

"Are you a doctor?" His question doesn't stop him from deferring to me, which is good. Walker is a big guy. It would be hard to maneuver him and keep him steady without cooperation.

"I am. I'm an ER doctor at Mercy." I swipe at my brow. The effort to move Walk took its toll. I'm fading.

"Wow, the luck."

I want to laugh. There's nothing lucky about this situation. Walker got shot because of me. The big dummy.

"In case I pass out, you need to pack gauze in the wound, cover it with a bandage and tape the edges. Then keep pressure on it, but not too much."

Fighting to focus, I work to pack the entrance wound as I did his chest, except using gauze instead of pieces of torn shirt. Once I've done all I can with his back, I check his pulse. It's stronger, which means packing the wounds has helped stop the bleeding, allowing blood to circulate instead of pump out of his body with each heartbeat.

When he's on his back again, I lay my head on Walker's chest, careful of his wound, and listen to the steady intake of air and the thump, thump, thump of his heart. A wave of dizziness hits, and I blink back the urge to close my eyes and rest, taking comfort in his body.

He saved me.

Walker. My Walker. The hero.

I push off him, rising to my knees, and sway.

A firm grip on my good shoulder keeps me upright. "You're not looking so good, Doc." He points to my left shoulder. "Maybe we should check out your injury too?"

Maybe he's right. I pull down the sleeve of my dress and groan at the effort. There's not much give but enough to see the entrance wound. "Can you check my back? How bad is it?"

While he stands to check, I whimper as I pack gauze into the entrance wound just below my clavicle.

"I don't see a hole back here."

No exit wound. Not good. I sway when I dig in a little too deep.

Did the bullet hit bone and ricochet?

My vision narrows.

Then darkness.

Then... Nothing.

CHAPTER 31

JESS

"THEY NEVER SHOWED?" AFTER BEING announced the winner, I was rushed out of the arena for photos and interviews. I didn't get a chance to even look for Walker and Berklyn before finishing up and showering.

Now I'm dressed and ready to leave, ready to celebrate with my family by choice, and that includes Walker and Berklyn, though she has no idea.

Jonah checks his phone. "No one's seen them. Their seats were empty."

Fuck. I scrub my face. I guess they changed their minds or got distracted by each other on their way to support me. Disheartened, I shuffle out the door to the car with my guys all around me.

If they didn't want to show, I'm not going call and beg. It's too late now. But, still, Walker was excited to share this night with me. *I* wanted him here. I wanted *them* here.

He said he'd bring her. He always keeps his word. If he'd changed his mind, he would have texted me at least.

I check my phone again. Nothing. I should call. What if they're avoiding me?

I manage to stave off calling Walker until I slip into the backseat of Gabriel's SUV.

There's no answer.

I try again.

Voicemail.

Knee bouncing, there's no reason to panic. They could be having sex, and she'd be pissed if he stopped to answer his phone. I'd be pissed.

But still…

I call Berklyn.

It rings and rings, then voicemail.

The vision of them fucking twists my gut. Good for them. But still. What the fuck about me? Us?

Two more tries to Walker. On the fourth and final attempt, he answers.

"Jess?" Only it's not Walker. It's a woman's voice I don't recognize.

"Who is this?" The back of my neck tingles. This is a bad sign. If he were home sexing up Berklyn, a stranger wouldn't be answering his phone.

"My name is Nadine. I work with Dr. Berklyn Fortier. We've met. You probably wouldn't remember," she nervously prattles on.

"Why do you have Walker's phone?" Wait. She *works* with Berklyn! "Where are you?"

"I'm here at Mercy. You're listed as Walker James' emergency contact. Jess, I'm sorry to be the one to tell you—"

"Wait! What?!" I come off the seat, tapping Gabriel. "Get to Mercy Hospital. Now!"

"—Mr. James and Dr. Fortier were shot—"

All I see is red.

BERKLYN

I come to in a panic. It's not slow and gentle. It's jarring, painful, and anxiety-riddled. Looking around, I recognize my ER, the medical staff working on me. I know *he* must be close. "Walker!"

"Dr. Fortier, you must remain calm. You've lost a lot of blood." Dr. Zimmer attempts to restrain me.

"Where is he?" I force his hands off and stumble to my feet, gripping the bedrail they hadn't raised. Amateurs. My world sways before my eyes, and a friendly face grips my arm, holding me up. "Nadine, where is Walker? Tell me he's okay."

Please, God, let Walker survive. I did what I could, but—

"He's stable. He's in surgery. Where you're heading as soon as an OR opens."

"I'm fine." A wave of nausea begs to differ with my self-diagnosis. I bend forward, leaning against the bed. "Emesis bag. Stat!"

The trash can is shoved under my chin. "It was closer," Nadine apologizes.

I don't respond as I heave the contents of my stomach, making a sickening splash in the large bin. The pain in my shoulder nearly takes me down.

"Sit." A chair touches the back of my knees.

I drop, boneless and barely able to stay upright, thankful I no longer have to pretend standing wasn't zapping every ounce of my strength. Leaning over the trash can, my forehead resting on my right hand of my uninjured shoulder, I vomit again and again, until there is nothing left but dry heaves and exhaustion.

A cool cloth is laid across the back of my neck, and Nadine's face comes into view as she squats. "If you're done, do you think you can get back in bed?" She dabs at my face and mouth, cleaning me up.

She's good people.

"I'm not sure if I can." I hate admitting that.

Doctors make horrible patients. I dislike reinforcing that stereotype, but my stubbornness was preening. Now I'm paying for it.

"It's okay. We got you." She nods to the orderly and another nurse whose name escapes me. "Let's get her back in bed."

The ER beds should not be called beds. They're glorified gurneys, the mattress barely any thicker. But I roll to my side, my injured shoulder up, curling into myself. So tired. "Nadine?"

"Yeah, honey?"

"If you find my phone, call Jess. He needs to know about Walker." He'll want his family here. I try to say more. Tell her to use Walker's phone. But everything feels floaty, far, far away.

"I already spoke to him. He's on his way."

Good. She's such a good nurse. That's goo…

"Her stats are dropping—"

"Why is there blood—"

"Call surgery. We're coming up. She can't wait—"

"Where is that blood coming from?"

JESS

Pacing the waiting room, I avoid talking to anyone unless they're the hospital staff providing an update on Walker or Jess. Both of my people are in surgery. *Both.* The thought is enough to bring me to my knees and pray. I'm not a kneeler, but I'm not above praying. Near crushing worry claws at my chest, compounded by the running diatribe in my head. Listing all my failures on repeat is probably not the best way to stay positive, but it's the only way I know to keep from smashing my fist through the wall on each turn as I stride back and forth, occupying my brain and ignoring my emotions.

I could lose them.

I could lose them *both*.

How the hell do the fates let *both* of them get shot? One is bad enough.

Is this a sign for me to back the fuck off? Or a sign for me to get my head on straight, be here for them, and forget about my past, my fears, my inadequacies?

Seems like they may actually need my *all* just when I realized I want to give it to them. But is that me justifying selfishness, or leaning into real love?

I'm leaning toward the latter. I'm *praying* it's the latter.

I'm in too deep to walk away.

But if that's what they want… Could I do it?

Could I watch them ride off into the sunset together without me?

Maybe they weren't on their way to me…

I suck in a breath and collapse into the nearest chair, my head in my hands, when the answer hits home: I'd give them up if that's what they want.

I'd walk away *for* them.

I'll throw them a fucking party, God. Just let them survive. This isn't about me at all. They're too amazing and important to lose. Please. Please. Please.

CHAPTER 32

BERKLYN

WARMTH FLITTERS THROUGH MY UNCONSCIOUS state. A tender touch calls to me. My cheek is the recipient of a caress that has me aching to wake up to see the owner of such gentleness. My body's numb except where each tender stroke lands.

My cheek.

My lips.

My hand.

Up my arm.

Across my forehead.

A press of a kiss to my lips. One. Two. Three times.

I groan in frustration, my eyes not obeying my command to open.

"It's okay, Berklyn. Take it slow. There's no rush, but I'd sure love to see your green eyes smiling at me, taking me in, forgiving me with each blink, each gaze, each brush of your lips against mine." His voice is hoarse, but I could never mistake him for anyone other than Jess. He's here. Relief floods my chest.

"Jess! Walk-er?" I manage through my dry, scratchy throat.

"He's out of surgery, still in recovery. I hope they'll let me see him soon. They said surgery went well." He softly caresses my cheek and along my lips. "Can you open your eyes?"

I'm trying. What he said a moment ago hits me. "Forgive?" I blink away the fog and smile as Jess' ruggedly handsome face comes into view. God, I've missed that face. I feared I may never see him again.

"Yeah, I'm hoping eventually you'll forgive me for being an ass, for being afraid of this thing between us." This time it's his mouth that touches mine. Soft, tender, intimate, leaving me wanting more—if I were in any state to want more or even feel my face, except where he's touched.

I don't know how to respond to that while feeling drunk from his kiss alone—or the pain meds, too. So instead, I ask, "What happened? How long have you been here? Where is here?"

His lips tip, but he doesn't let his smile free. "You and Walker were shot. Do you remember?"

I nod. How could I forget that? "He saved me."

His jaw clenches. "He did. Got shot in the process."

I flinch at the reminder and groan from the pain.

"I didn't mean it like that. I just mean… Fuck, Berk, you *both* got shot." His voice breaks, and he closes his eyes. "I'm thankful he was there. I just wish saving you meant neither of you were injured."

"Me too. I didn't want him to try—"

"No. He did the right thing. I just wish it were me instead of the two of you." His eyes water, and it breaks my heart.

I cup his cheek, barely able to hold my arm up. "No, that wouldn't be any better."

He leans into my touch, holding my hand to his face. "I was so fucking scared I'd lose you and him." He swipes at my tears leaking out of the corner of my eyes. "Don't cry, baby. You're alive. Walker is alive. I'm going to take care of y'all. Don't worry."

My chin wobbles. I've no words.

He kisses me one more time before getting back to my questions. "I arrived right before you went into surgery." He laces our fingers. "Do you remember seeing me?"

I frown at that. "No. I remember getting sick, and Nadine needed help getting me back in bed." Did I pass out?

"You were bleeding. *A lot.*" The worry in his eyes and the bow of his brow conveys how much that scared him.

"I'm okay. I'm here. I'm glad you're here, but you need to go be with Walker. I don't want him to wake up alone." I look around. "Can you find the call button?"

He holds up the control lying next to my leg. "You okay?"

"Yeah, I'd like to see him too, if I can."

His scowl deepens. "You need to stay here. I'll check on Walker and come back. I don't want you to be alone either."

That's not realistic. One of us will have to be alone. "Walker needs you."

"And you don't?"

"I didn't say that. But I won't choose my comfort over his. Plus, this is my hospital. I know most of these people. I'll never truly be alone." It's a lie. I know my ER staff. This is surgery. I only know these people in passing or by reputation.

He pushes the call button for the nurse. "I won't leave you." *For long* goes unsaid.

I'm thankful as I don't really want him to go. I want to be selfish and keep him at my side. But sweet Walker would sacrifice for me. He *did* sacrifice to save my life. He took a bullet for me. Giving him Jess is the least I can do.

Pressing his forehead to mine, Jess whispers across my heated skin, "I want this. The three of us." Then he's gone, replaced seconds later by the nurse.

His *I won't leave you* and *I want this* linger long after I can no longer feel his presence. Does he mean it? Does his declaration mean what I hope it means? I'm afraid to believe, to hope. But if today's events don't prompt me to believe in more, believe in hope and belief itself, then when will I? I was shot. Walker was shot. And we're still here.

My heart thumpity-thumps at the possibilities as hope blooms.

JESS

I have to tell her, but I don't know how. I don't even know how I feel about it. I found out by mistake and begged her nurse friend to let me tell Berklyn. She agreed as Berk's friend, but I only have hours before it's medically necessary to follow up, or worse, Berklyn discovers it herself. Right now, she's still a little out of it from surgery and blood loss. As soon as I see Walker, ensure he's okay, I'll be back at her side.

But before that, I make a call.

Cap answers on the first ring. "Hey, Jess. How are they?"

The hospital wouldn't allow everyone back. I told them I was Walker's brother and Berklyn's fiancé. It was her nurse friend Nadine's suggestion. She said it would be better if I was her husband, but given most in the ER would have doubted that turn of events, this was the next best thing.

Saying I was her fiancé didn't bother me a bit. In fact, I rather like the notion.

"Berklyn is awake. Surgery went well. I just stepped away to check on Walker. He's out of surgery and in recovery too."

"That's good. You need anything, son?"

"Actually, I do. I need them to be in the same hospital room. We need to be together. Do you think you can use your sizable connections to make that happen?" I want to say "with three beds," but I don't want to push it. I'll sleep on a chair or the floor, or, even better, with Berk.

"On it. I'll call you when I have news. But consider it done." Before he hangs up, he adds, "I'm proud of you, Jess. This is a good thing. It's time you had your own family."

Family. He has no idea.

"But I'm still a part of yours, right?" I'm teasing, but I wouldn't mind the confirmation. Cap has amassed an amazing family. Some related by blood, all related by loyalty, strength, and love.

"You never have to ask. When you're ready, we'll all be there supporting Walker and Berklyn—and you. You can count on it."

"Thanks, Cap." I hang up with a sense of rightness and make my way to the nurses' station in the middle of the surgical recovery area.

Normally, I'd growl that someone take me to Walker. But I'm going with *honey gets you more bees* approach, or whatever the fuck the saying is. Why would anyone want more bees?

"Can I help you?" A friendly male nurse smiles at me.

"I'm here for my fiancée and brother. I just saw her, and I'd like to see my brother now. Walker James. He just got out of surgery."

His eyebrows shoot up. "You're Dr. Fortier's fiancé?"

On one hand, I'm happy the lie is sticking. On the other, he doesn't have to look so surprised. I know I might not be a typical doctor's significant other, but I damn well intend to be hers.

"I am." I cross my arms over my chest, knowing it makes me look bigger, tougher, meaner. My sugary sweetness has all dried up. Screw the bees and their honey addiction.

"Well," he clears his throat, "we're happy she's doing so well. Let me check on Mr. James." He types on the computer. "Yep, there he is. Let me take you to him."

I follow Mr. Nurse and end up catching Walker just as he opens his eyes. His nurse pats his arm, saying, "I'll check on you in a bit. You're doing good. Just push the call button if you need anything." She gives me a smile as she passes through the open curtain, closing it behind her.

Walker's stare is intense. He blinks a few times as I move closer, gripping his hand he barely raises in greeting. "You had me scared. All of us."

"I'm okay," he rasps.

I offer him a sip of the water sitting on the table beside his bed. He takes a few short draws on the straw.

"Where's Doc?"

"She's just around the corner. She's doing okay. She hasn't been awake long, just got out of surgery too."

He immediately relaxes. "I'm sorry about your fight. Did you win?"

"It's okay. Though I wish you'd been there instead of here." I try for humor, but it falls flat. "But, yeah, I won."

"That's great." His gaze is steady, assessing. "What aren't you saying?"

He knows me too well. I always think I'm so tough, carrying everything close to the chest. No one can hurt me if they don't know my shit. *He* knows my shit, at least most of it, and he would never hurt me. But this, I don't want to tell him. I don't want to give him hope and then steal it away.

I shake my head. "It can wait. You just got out of surgery. Cap is working on getting you and Berklyn into the same room so we can all be together." *You want that, don't you?* What if he changed his mind? What if he no longer wants to share her?

"Good. I was going to make a stink about not being with her. I really need to see her. Be sure she's okay."

"She is." I tell him our little lie about me being his brother and me being Berklyn's fiancé. He's not mad. I don't think I'd take the news nearly as calmly as he is. Maybe it's the meds.

"Jess," he squeezes my hand, garnering my eyes, "whatever it is, you need to tell me. Let me share the burden. We'll figure it out together." He's so sure. I've always envied his certainty. He might not always be confident in himself, but he's always confident in what he knows to be right.

"Before I tell you, I need you to know, I want this. The three of us. I want it. Not just sex. I want it all. I'm in—all in. If you still want me there." I hate being vulnerable, but if I can't be with him and Berk, then who?

His smile is reassuring. "I still want us. She wants us. But we need to make it official. Ensure we're all on the same page." He squeezes my hand. "What changed your mind?"

He's being nice instead of asking when I got my head out of my ass. "Everyone's being so supportive of the idea. It was pissing me off at first, felt like everyone was in my face, in my business. But then it hit me, that's what family does, right? They support you and call you on your shit."

"Yeah, they do. They've got us," he assures.

I lean down till my forehead touches his. "You're my family, Walk. My true family. I want us. I want Berk with us."

"You had me at *I want this.*" He grips the back of my head, pulling back till our eyes lock. "Tell me what's wrong?"

"Berklyn is pregnant."

CHAPTER 33

WALKER

"IT MIGHT NOT BE OURS," THE IDIOT BEFORE ME balks. He knows better. He hesitated in telling me because he knows it's either his or mine.

"It's ours. You know it. Stop deflecting. It's a sign. We're supposed to be together." I'm ecstatic about this news.

Jess closes his eyes, taking a deep breath. "Then what does it mean that she's bleeding? They think she's miscarrying."

No. That can't happen. Poor Doc. "You need to go be with her."

"She doesn't know. I was supposed to tell her, but she woke up worried about you and insisted I be here when you woke up."

"Fuck that. Go!" I point at the curtain. "Come back when you have news. I'll get them to wheel me to her. I need to see her sooner rather than later." I grip his arm. "Don't you dare tell her you don't think the baby is ours. You know there's no chance of that. She's ours. Has been from the start. This just proves it."

I see the uncertainty in his eyes.

"Go before I make a stink and force my way to her."

"I hate you," he grumbles.

I chuckle. Pain rips at my chest. On a moan, I still. That hurts like a bitch. No more laughing. "No you don't."

"We need to talk about what happened, but for now, I'm glad you're okay." He gives me a curt nod and stalks off.

I'll take him all grumpy as long as he's going to Berklyn and taking care of our girl while I'm laid up—while she's out of commission too. There's no one more protective than Jess. He gives Gabriel's protective streak a run for its money.

Jess won't let anything happen to her, and if she does lose this baby— my heart hurts at the possibility—he and I will be there for her, and when she's ready, we'll be more than happy to put another inside her.

The thought of her round with our child occupies my mind as I start to drift off. If I can't be with her, I might as well rest and build up my strength for when I can.

BERKLYN

While Jess was gone, they moved me to a room. I expected to be in recovery for another hour or so. Hospitals are notorious for taking their time in getting patients admitted from the ER or unplanned surgeries. It's a juggling game to assign a patient to the correct floor based on their needs. There are only so many beds, so many nurses, and all the other staff who keep the wheels churning. Being an employee doesn't make me immune to the red tape bureaucratic process. It just makes me more aware.

I, however, was not anticipating being moved to a VIP suite. I've never seen one. I've only heard of them. I didn't believe the rumors about how nice they are until laying my eyes on one—basically, a hotel suite with hospital beds.

I look at the orderly kindly pushing me into the room with two nurses in tow. "This has to be a mistake." I can't afford this. Though… Ohmygod, there are three beds, a couch, and a recliner. Did Jess arrange this?

"It's not a mistake, Dr. Fortier. You and Mr. James will be staying here together. Your fiancé should be up shortly after his visit with his brother." The tall nurse points to her nametag. "I'm Polly. I'll be one of your nurses."

"Hi, Polly. Please call me Berklyn." I doubt Walker will want to be called Mr. James either.

Wait? *Fiancé? Brother?* What the what?

I don't question her. I'm too busy getting situated in my new larger and way more comfortable bed. This is nice. A girl could get used to this.

The other nurse introduces herself, but the drowsies are setting in as I blink and fight to stay awake.

"Rest." Polly pats my hand. "Your body needs it. I'll be sure Mr. Riley finds you."

For a minute, I don't know who Mr. Riley is, then I remember it's Jess' last name. Since he's my fiancé, I suppose I'll be Mrs. Berklyn Riley—Dr. Riley.

Hmm, I close my eyes and let that sink in. My fiancé. I could get used to that. I like Dr. Berklyn Riley-James even better.

A soft click has me blinking my daydream away as Jess approaches the bed.

"I'm sorry. I didn't mean to wake you." The rough grate in his voice lures me in. I want to sink into his hold and forget this day ever happened.

"Mmmit'sokay." The grogginess is harder to push away this time. It's like I've been drugged, or maybe I'm more aware of it the further I'm away from surgery and anesthesia. My shoulder aches, but it's not bad.

Pain killers. I glance at my IV pump, noting the bag of normal saline and a smaller bag of morphine. That's why I'm sleepy and not really hurting.

"Walker?" I mumble.

Jess carefully sits on the edge of my bed, placing his hand on the other side of me, leaning closer. "He's good. They're getting ready to move him up here."

"Did you do this?" I motion around the room.

He fingers the tips of my hair lying across my pillow before catching my eyes. "I asked Cap to call in a few favors. He has contacts everywhere. I wanted us to be together. Thought you might want Walker close. He's about ready to break down walls to get to you."

That notion does funny things to my heart. "I do want us together. I want to be sure he's okay." I can't wait to see how he is for myself. What damage was done.

"He's good, Berk." He eyes my shoulder. "Are you hurting?"

"No," I motion to the IV pump, "I'm good. Meds have kicked in."

"Are *you* okay?" He gently brushes my cheek with his fingers. "I mean, I know you're hurt, but what happened… Are you okay? Do you need anything?"

"I haven't… I think it'll take time to come to terms with what happened. Walker risking his life for me. I wish…"

"What? That he hadn't sacrificed to save you?"

I glance out the window. Do I wish that? "I wish he wasn't hurt." Tears threaten at the thought of losing him, the hole in his chest and back. What if I'd been too hurt to help him?

"Hey." Jess tips my face back to him. "He did exactly what I would have done. What either of us would do again. You need to get comfortable with that if you want this thing between us. We're protective assholes. We'll gladly take a bullet for you every day that ends in Y."

"So, every day then?" That's a lot to take in. It's heavy and light. He really wants me after everything? I'm not temporary?

His smile is perfect, gentle, endearing, understanding, and oh so handsome. "Yeah, baby. Every. Damn. Day." He presses his warm lips to mine. "And then some."

"I hate the idea of you all getting hurt for me. I guess I'll learn to live with it." My heart skips at the thought. "Are you not mad at me anymore?"

"Naw." He runs his nose along mine. "You just proved life is too short to take another breath without you in it. I don't want to waste any more time." He tweaks my chin. "You think you can stand to be around me?"

God, can I. He and Walker have been my running fantasy since they first asked me out, maybe from the first time we met when I was patching up Jess. Everything feels light and fluffy. Maybe it's the meds. "You have no idea how much I want that. I want us, the three of—"

The door opens behind him, we both turn our attention to the bed as it slowly enters the room. A sleepy-eyed Walker comes into view, his smile spreading as he takes us in. "Hey, roomies."

I'd laugh if I didn't know it would hurt. "Hey, yourself." Tears threaten as Jess squeezes my hand before moving toward Walker, helping the orderly turn his bed so they can move him from the ER bed to the plush one in here.

Once he's situated in the larger bed that Jess moved to abut mine, Walker reaches across, looking for my hand but stops when he realizes it's nowhere to be found with my arm in a sling. "You okay, Doc?" He frowns, glancing at the orderly as he leaves before returning his focus to me. "I was so scared. I thought I lost you."

"Me? You were the one bleeding in *my* arms. I had to staunch the flow of blood with your shirt! What were you thinking running toward a man with a gun?!" My voice quivers as the memory of him tackling me and taking a bullet so I could live eats at my stomach lining, making me cramp up. I wince from the pain.

"Doc?"

"Berklyn, what's wrong?" Jess forces the beds apart to stand between us, looking at my body as if he can see the damage with x-ray vision.

I want to roll to my side, but my body hurts too badly, and I'm too weak to even attempt it. "Cramping," I bite through the discomfort. "Is that where the bullet ricocheted? My abdomen?"

"Did you tell her?" Walker questions Jess.

"Not yet."

"Tell me what?" I feel, not for the first time, cramping like I'm on my period.

"Berklyn." Jess holds my face between his hands, his eyes sad and telling. Whatever he's about to say is not good. "Based on your blood-work, you're pregnant."

"What?!" I rear back and regret the sudden movement immediately. Crying out in pain, I close my eyes and whisper, "That's not possible."

"We haven't been using protection," Walker interjects.

A baby. The three of us produced a baby. God how big would their baby be? "You're upset?" I look at Jess' worried brow as I can spot Walker's smile a mile away. I'm pretty sure I know how he's feeling.

Jess moves in, pressing his lips to mine. "I'm shocked, but I'm not upset about the baby." He kisses me again, whispering, "I'm amazed."

Relief floods me as I turn to Walker. "And you?"

His returning smile is crooked, a little drunk.

Do I look drunk? I feel a little high.

"I'm ecstatic. It's a sign we're all supposed to be together." He grips Jess' arm. "As soon as I'm able, I want to kiss her too."

I catch Jess' chin. "What are you worried about?"

His eyes soften and melt my heart. "You're bleeding."

MUSTANG

His words are sobering.

"I have an IUD. It wouldn't be healthy for the pregnancy." Then it hits me. I'm hurting, cramping, and the period feel. "I'm losing the baby?"

The flow of tears can't be stopped. After today's events, finding out I'm carrying one of their babies—and now losing it—is too much for my big girl panties.

CHAPTER 34

JESS

IT'S BEEN A LITTLE OVER TWO WEEKS SINCE I brought Berklyn home to our apartment. It didn't take as much convincing to let me take care of her as I thought it would. She was released before Walker, which was frustrating and hard. I wanted to take care of both of them, and my time was stretched thin trying to be both places at once.

In the end, Berklyn was my focus, which Walker agreed. The guys at Black Ops took turns hanging out with Walker in the hospital, being his advocate, his strength when he was having a bad day. His injury, far graver than Berk's, required his hospital stay be a few more days than hers. His recovery will be longer too. I still saw him every day and ensured that he either saw Berklyn in person or over video chat. That connection was needed by both of them, which I fully supported.

Thankfully, he's home now. Has been for a few days.

It may seem like a quick turn of events, a change of heart, but truly, it was always going to be the three of us. I fought it. Berklyn fought it. Walker was the only one who always had the balls and heart to believe we could be more than temporary. That I was worthy of more than only a few stolen nights with Berklyn. That the three of us have something special, and there was no reason for either of us to give her up just so she could be with the other.

She wouldn't have stood for it anyway. She wanted us both. If she couldn't have Walker *and* me, she'd walk away. She *did* walk away. That morning, after a night of glorious, life-altering kisses, she ran. Because she couldn't choose—wouldn't. And I was an idiot tied up in knots over her rejecting me after sharing my soul with her through kisses. Fucking kisses. She didn't know. I didn't tell her. None of us are mind readers. An important note for our future.

"Jess!"

I drop the pan in the sink and rush to the bedroom, finding her standing between the bathroom and bedroom in only one of my t-shirts.

"What's wrong?" I move into her space. "Whatever it is, we'll deal with it together."

She smiles and softly chuckles, filling the space between us with her lightness. I take it in and grip her hand as she says, "You're so sure."

"I am." I glance over my shoulder at Walker, working to sit up in bed. His recovery is going well, but he's still sore and tender, which, of course, he would be. He had a hole through his body where the bullet traveled. The bullet meant for Berklyn, that in all likelihood would've killed her. He saved her. I'll never stop being thankful for that. "You need help?"

"No," he grates, punching out air and flopping back down. "Maybe."

"You okay?" I ask Berklyn before helping Walker.

She waves me off. "Yeah, I'm fine."

I still need to know why she called my name, but before I push, Walker needs me. "You want to sit up or go to the bathroom?"

"Both." Frustration mars his brow.

"Hey, don't be so hard on yourself. You're getting better every day. Getting up on your own will probably be the hardest because you're using your core, which pulls on your chest muscles. You know this." I offer him a hand to grip and put my arm around his back as he begins to rise.

"You want a sponge bath?" Berklyn follows as I help him to the bathroom. She stops at the door as he tugs his gym shorts down to pee, not an ounce of embarrassment to be had.

"Don't get me hard while I'm trying to pee, Doc," he growls, holding his dick down so he doesn't make a mess.

She backs away.

"I'd like to fuck you in the shower." His gaze flies over my shoulder, a smirk ghosting his lips. Him teasing about sex is a good sign. It's been too long since we've played. I've kissed her, but kept it PG until she's further along in her healing.

She crosses her arms, making my shirt rise up her thighs, perking up her tits.

I'll never tire of seeing her in my clothes. My dick starts to get ideas I know I can't—shouldn't—follow up on.

"I don't think that's in the cards for either of us for a while." Disappointment saddens her eyes that were bright a moment ago. "Besides, we've got a doctor's appointment to get to."

"What appointment?" I turn, trusting Walker can wash his hands without assistance. Once he's up, he's usually good.

"Dr. Murtaugh." She disappears into my—our—closet.

I'm close behind. "The baby doctor?" I groan when I find her naked, not even any panties on. "What the fuck?"

She winks over her shoulder, fully aware of how much I love the sight of her body. I don't know what happened. Getting shot squelched her self-consciousness. She's proudly naked, not even worried over her surgery scar on her left shoulder. It's pink but healing nicely. It'll be a scar she'll wear with pride. I'll make damn sure of it. But for the moment, I grip her hips, grinding my growing hardness against her. "You're teasing the beast, Berk."

She grabs my hands on her hips and places them on her breasts. "My hormones are going crazy. I need you."

"Turn around," Walker rasps from behind us at the threshold of the closet.

I pivot, gently bring Berklyn with me, placing her front and center between the two of us. "Our girl needs us." I eye Walker.

Is he up for this? He gives a slight nod, his shorts tenting from his arousal.

I kiss across her good shoulder, squeezing and teasing her breast. "How long do we have before we need to leave?"

"An hour at the most. Maybe forty-five minutes." She presses her ass into me, reaching out for Walker. As he steps closer, she gently lowers her head, asking, "Will it hurt if you kiss me?"

His smile is slight but true. "I don't give a fuck if it does, but, no, I'm fine." He closes the distance, parting her lips and kissing her with a ravenous hunger that transforms into slow, sultry kisses that have me growling my approval as I strip out of my clothes and run the tip of my cock between her folds from behind.

She's still healing. Walker's gaze lands on me, his brow cocked, lip-locked with our girl. I nod, confirming I'll be gentle, fucking her for the both of us.

He takes over playing with her tits as I sink my fingers into her soaked heat. "Fuck, baby, so fucking wet."

She moans and swivels her hips. "I need you inside me, Jess," she says into their kiss as her hand slips inside his shorts. "Tell me if I hurt you," she whispers to Walker.

"Doc, you could never hurt me." He shoves his shorts off, letting them drop to the floor. The sight of her jerking his cock is more than I can take.

"Slow," I growl as I remove my fingers, grip her hip, bend my knees, and slide home, taking her from behind, holding her tight against me with one hand on her stomach and the other cupping her between her legs, rubbing her clit against my hand as I slowly slide in and out of her sweet-as-hell pussy.

Though we don't have much time, it's not a race. It's slow, sensual, a joining of three souls, coming together, intimately sharing our bodies, hearts, healing us from the inside out.

Walker grips my ass, helping me thrust a little deeper but not harder, not faster, fucking her hand as I fuck her pussy. Her kisses become frantic, needy cries of pleasure and pleas for more. I can't fuck her harder. I can't jostle either of them. The only more I can give is my heart. So, I lay it out for her.

"The first time I saw you, Berklyn, you were standing at the nurses' station in the ER. I was a bloody mess. You looked up, did a double take on a gasp and came toward me. Your hand on my chest stole my breath and nearly knocked me over. I knew then I had to have you."

"Jess," she cries, her body trembling on the edge of release.

Walker growls into their kiss, demanding she kiss him harder, feed him her pleasure.

"I was coming for you the night of my fight—the night I nearly lost both of you. I'd already decided I wanted this, whatever *this* entails. I want it all with you—the three of us. I fell for you that first night in the ER, and I've been falling every day since. I love you, Berklyn. We both do. Marry us, be ours, and let us be yours."

"Fuck!" Walker moans on the edge. "I love you, Doc. Be ours. Say yes."

Our girl starts to shake, a moan erupting from her soul as she comes on my cock, pulling me with her, filling her up with everything I have. "Yes!" she cries. "Yes!"

"Fuck. Fuck. Fuck!" Walker comes, the warmth falling between us coating their stomachs, her hand on him, and my hand on her pussy, christening us a triad in whatever form that looks like. It's our world to mold, cherish, protect.

She said yes. I don't know how it'll happen, but somehow, I'll marry her—*we'll* marry her.

CHAPTER 35

BERKLYN

WEAK-KNEED FROM MY ORGASM, JESS CARRIES ME to the shower, where the three of us clean up and then dress for our appointment. In the hospital, immediately after finding out I'm pregnant, I had the IUD removed. It can be a dangerous procedure to an already rocky pregnancy, but it would be even riskier to leave it in if the pregnancy progressed. Other than the heartbeat, I didn't want to know any other details of the pregnancy. I wasn't ready to invest my heart in something that seemed uncertain.

I never even stopped to consider if I wanted this pregnancy or not. I was instantaneously saddened by the prospect of losing it, which really means I did want it. I was just scared to fall.

Then I stopped bleeding after a few days in the hospital. I called an OBGYN friend at Mercy. He'll do a sonogram today to see where we are. If I'm still pregnant. Is the baby healthy? Am I out of the woods? Did me getting shot and undergoing surgery put our baby in danger?

So many questions that living in denial will not answer. Maybe denial is too strong. More like fear of confirming I really did miscarry, or fear that, even if I am still pregnant, it's not viable. I took a pregnancy test today, just to confirm. The positive result is not a guarantee. The pregnancy hormones could still be in my system even though it would have been an early-term miscarriage.

But I'm hopeful. Hope is my new black. I wear it every day. I feel pregnant. My breasts are tender. My hormones are making me horny and emotional. Though, admittedly, it could be my big alpha males who are making me unnaturally horny. Today, we'll find out for sure. I'm far enough that the heartbeat should be detectable.

Either way, I have on my big girl panties. Ready to know the truth, ready to handle it with my men beside me.

From the backseat of Jess' Charger, I glance at Walker in the passenger seat. He looks exhausted and a little pale, and it's just mid-morning. Maybe our earlier shenanigans were too much. It was hot, but not worth jeopardizing his recovery. My shoulder aches perhaps a little more, but Jess went easy, gentler than he's ever been. And his words... Oh my God, his words, they were melt-my-heart perfection.

I could picture marrying Walker. That was easy, because he's easy— we just fit. But, honestly, I held back those type of thoughts because I never dreamt I'd find love with Jess, and I wanted *both*.

With Jess, I pictured great sex, but him giving me his heart without even knowing how I feel means everything. His vulnerability, the tenderness he's shown me since the shooting has soothed my misgivings about him wanting more with me. I'm no longer temporary.

I'm his fiancée. I dreamed I'd be his for real. Now it's true. Now, they're *both* my fiancé. I refuse to think of the legality of it right now. I choose to bask in the glory that they both want me—equally—and not just for sex but for *everything*.

Riding the elevator to the doctor's office, I gently lean on Walker as he holds me close with Jess holding my hand. The guys met Dr. Murtaugh in the hospital. He's the one who removed my IUD. Seeing him today shouldn't be an issue for them. I hope. It'll probably depend on if he does an internal sonogram. I'm not sure how they'll deal with a giant wand being stuck up my—

"We're here." Jess grip on me tightens as we exit the elevator. "Are you nervous?"

I nearly trip at the worry in his voice. "I wasn't until now."

Walker chuckles. "Ignore him. *He's* nervous."

Jess shrugs. "I just want you to be okay, healthy. Hopefully that means the baby is too."

"They'll both be fine," Walker assures. "They survived being shot. Our baby and girl are tough."

I love his confidence. I feel like superwoman when he looks at me. When, really, I'm just the woman a superhero fell in love with. I'll take his endless confidence in me and pray I don't let him down.

"Yeah they are." Jess kisses my temple. "Love you no matter what news we get today."

Thumpity-thump beats my heart.

"Ditto," Walker chimes in and kisses my other temple.

They're like bookends. The sexiest about-to-be-dads bookends. "I love you both."

WALKER

"Two," I repeat on the drive home. "Two!" I look to Jess to see if he's panicking.

He's not. Asshole. He's supposed to be in this with me.

He's also the one driving, so maybe it's good he's the calm one right now. "Two," I whisper to Berklyn as I hold her in the back of Jess' car on the ride home. I needed to be close to her and our *two* babies.

Twins. We're having twins.

She snuggles into my side, my hand on her already growing abdomen at nearly nine weeks along. She's careful of my chest wound, and I'm careful of her shoulder. We're a mess. A pregnant, soon-to-be-parents-of-twins mess.

I'm in shock. They seem to be handling it with ease.

Jess stops to pick up our favorite pizzas. Dino comes out to greet us and personally deliver our pizzas and a basket of fries to the passenger seat, where he smiles at me with Berk in my arms. I wonder how he'll feel when he realizes Jess and I are both hers. Will he accept us and still give us all the free extras he does now?

Twins. Lord, help us.

JESS

Food devoured, I'm ravenous for our girl. The taste from this morning wasn't enough. Especially not when I know it's a possibility that we *both* could have knocked her up. She's pregnant with two babies. There are two placentas, two sacs, two umbilical cords. Dr. Murtaugh said it's possible she could be pregnant with superfecundation twins, where two eggs were released and fertilized at the same time. Paternity isn't a question with only one source of sperm, but we both fucked her at the same time, so we could have both gotten her pregnant.

He said it's rare.

So is our love.

I want us both to be inside her again, but she's still healing. Walker is still healing, but I can do my best to make this good for them. The DVP will have to come later, after they're healed, and hopefully DP, but probably not while she's pregnant.

"Lie back, let Walker play with your gorgeous tits." I assist with a hand on her good shoulder, propping a pillow under her as she lies across Walker at an angle to avoid putting pressure on his chest near his wound.

He's naked on my bed below her. She's naked on top, her back to his front. "Spread those beautiful legs, Berklyn. Show me where you need me."

Her legs fall open, no hint of shyness to be seen. Damn, pregnancy does a body good. Her pussy is pink and glistening with arousal. I give my cock a hard tug and grunt at the pleasure and the idea of sinking into her heat. But not yet.

I check in with Walker to confirm he's okay, I get a small nod as he shifts a little to capture a kiss while teasing her nipples. I've never been much of a voyeur—that's more Walker's bag—but I have to admit it's hot watching her grind her hips in response to his touch, her needy pussy clenching around nothing but air.

Running my fingers to her opening, I spread her moisture before slowly inserting two fingers and circling her clit. Scooting closer, kneeling between her legs, I grind my cock against her inner thigh, fighting the urge to sink home.

I have every intention of licking her to orgasm, but Walker's groans and possessive touches and her needful cries tell me they need more. They need each other.

Keeping my fingers pumping inside her, I lean over, nuzzling her neck, kissing up her jaw. She breaks their kiss and grips the back of my neck, sighing, "Jess."

I steal her mouth, needing to taste her in some form and groan when a big hand lands on my back, urging me to stay right where I am, groaning, "Fuck our girl. I want to watch."

Oh, he'll watch all right. But he's going to feel it too. I break our kiss, ignore Berk's protest when I remove my fingers and catch his eyes. "Not this time." I pat Berk's thigh. "Can you lift your hips a second?" I sit back, palming my cock and nod to Walker. "Slip inside her."

I don't have to ask twice or give any further direction. He eagerly grabs his cock from under her ass and slaps her pussy with it a few times, making her gasp. "You ready for me, Doc?"

She bites her lip, watching him as she swivels her hips. "Please, Walker. I need you." She reaches for me as he enters her, biting back a moan.

The sight of his cock coated in her sweet juices as he slowly slides in and out of her with a slow grind of his hips has me tugging harder on my cock and rubbing my swollen crown over her clit.

"Jess." She arches, her hand landing on mine, circling my shaft. "I need you both. This is how you got me pregnant."

"Fuck," Walker and I both exclaim and lock eyes.

We can't, right? "I don't—"

"Can you take us—"

"Yes, you can," she answers Walk's unfinished question. "Go easy. But hurry," she squeezes her tits, "I'm so close. I might come as soon as you enter me." She tugs at my cock. "Fill me. I love you. Love me, Jess."

Fuck. How can I say no to that?

"Jess," Walker encourages.

Fuck. *He's* supposed to be the voice of reason.

I'm the one who loses my head when I'm inside her or so close to the promised land. "I don't want to hurt you or our babies," I choke on the last word.

We fucking got her pregnant when she was on birth control, more than likely the first time together. It's like it was destiny telling us to get the fuck on with it. There's no waiting for fears and uncertainties. She's ours. Always has been. Always will be.

Lubed up, I groan, "Fuck," as Walker stills and I run the head of my cock along the base of his shaft to her entrance, pushing, pushing as they both moan and she beseeches with her eyes and needy cries, watching where we're about to be joined—the three of us.

Walker's hand lands on my ass, urging me forward with a firm, "Now," as he rubs her clit, making her hungrier for us.

I growl, liking his assertive side, but scowl at him, reaffirming I'm the one in charge here. This fuck is mine to give.

As I push through, dipping inside her tight heat, her pussy walls clench, and she cries out, coming on a long moan that has Walker and me stilling, groaning and cussing through her tight grip on our cocks.

"Fuck, Doc. You feel so good coming on our cocks." He raises a brow, waiting for me to move.

One hand on her breast and the other on her hip, I push in all the way and then pull out to the tip before sinking back in. Over and over again. Walker takes her mouth, fucking her with his tongue like he would with his cock if he wasn't injured. Soon as he can move without making old man sounds, he can lead again.

Braced on one arm, I lean down, taking her nipple in my mouth, and fuck her like she's the only woman for me, which, of course, she is. I grind and thrust, taking her, filling her full of our cocks as he stays still, letting my cock rub against his inside her, bringing us a level of pleasure monogamy will never know.

We aren't gay. I'll never fuck him, but this level of intimacy is high on my list of sacred favorites I'd only want to share with him and her. Forever.

I've never been one for norms.

I fight *and* bake for a living.

MUSTANG

Why should I expect my love life to be any different?

God granted me a best friend who's better than a brother. He's my other half, if there's such a thing. He's light to my dark. Then He gave us a woman who loves us equally, our kink, our hearts, our souls, our way. Now, He's blessed us with twins.

My mangled heart doesn't feel so mangled anymore. Our girl healed it, helped it grow, set it free to love the way we each deserve. Fully, compassionately, loyally, passionately and with every fiber of our being—it's the three of us, soon to be five.

Life is good.

Life is better than good.

It's fucking amazing.

THE END

EPILOGUE

JESS

T'S LATE WHEN WE PULL UP TO THE REAR ENTRANCE of Sugarplums Bakery. Putting the car in park, I catch Berk's inquisitive gaze as I undo her seatbelt and then mine. "I wanna show you something."

"Does it include baked goods?" Her smile is bright and hopeful.

How can I deny her? "I think I can manage that. If you're up to it, I need to start a few doughs now so I can come in later tomorrow."

I left Waker at home, or so she thinks. He's working on a surprise with a little help from a few of the guys. I'm keeping Berklyn occupied, which is no great hardship.

Inside, I turn off the alarm. Cher and Cap are in on the surprise and know I'm bringing Berklyn here to work but also to discuss our future—and a bit of the past.

I lock the door behind us, guiding her through the kitchen to the front. "Everything is put away, but this is the front of Sugarplums."

She releases my hand and walks to the front door, looking out before turning and eyeing the empty display cases and décor. "I love the name, and it's so cute in here." She takes a deep breath. "And smells heavenly. It smells like you." Her eyes light up at the realization. "I thought it was a bodywash or something."

I laugh at the hazard of the job, smelling like baked goods. "You should smell it when bread and cinnamon rolls are fresh out of the oven."

Her eyes light up. "Did I tell you how much I loved your cinnamon rolls?"

"No, but if you play your cards right, maybe I'll make you some." I catch her hand and pull her to the back, down the hall, pointing out the stock room, restroom, and coming to a stop in Cher's office. "I have a chance to become a partner in the business." I don't know why those words have my stomach fluttering.

Berklyn steps into me, resting her palms on my chest, her open gaze assessing. "I think that's a great idea. Your kitchen skills are amazing."

I swipe my thumb along her cheek. "I rather think I excel in other places besides the kitchen."

Her blush is inviting. "I hear your fighting skills are impressive too."

Is she teasing me? "Berk," I grumble her name like it pains me, but she's not fooling me.

She averts her gaze, steps away and shrugs. "Your bedroom skills are... Alright."

I snatch her wrist before she can put more space between us. "Just alright?" I growl.

Her squeak when I squeeze her ass, bringing her chest-to-chest, has me releasing the chuckle working its way up my chest. It's hard to pretend to be upset when she's so darn cute.

"Yeah, I mean... I've had better."

Oh, no she didn't.

I release my hold, dropping my hands to my side. "Really?" I cock a brow and relish her uncertainty and the way she bites her bottom lip. The lip I can't wait to nip and suck when I catch her. "Challenge accepted. You better run, Spitfire."

Her mouth falls open nearly as wide as her eyes, screeching, "What?!" Then she takes off, disappearing through the office door.

My smile can't be helped, because, damn, how could I ever think I could live without this—without her—in my life?

BERKLYN

Oh, shoot! I shouldn't have teased the grump. I race down the hall, catching the door frame in the kitchen to swing right but freeze when I reach the other side of the kitchen with the ovens behind me and the stainless-steel workbenches between me and Jess, who rounds the corner a second later.

"Where you gonna go, baby?"

"Nowhere," I sigh on a deep exhale. Who am I kidding? I couldn't outrun him even if I was really trying. He's playing, and it's amazing to witness the heat in his eyes and the smirk on his lips. He set a trap, and I willingly walked right into it. But he needs to know… "I'm done running." I hold out my arms, lift my chin. "I'm right here if you want me."

"Berk." His evil grin fades as he stalks closer. He cups my cheek seconds before he's in my space, tilting my face to his. "Did I not make it clear? I've always wanted you. I always will. I want this." He presses his glorious mouth to mine before pulling back. "I want our babies." He cups my growing stomach. "I want Walker and you in my life, in our bed, in our own version of what happily ever after looks like. You got me?"

Jesus on a cracker, my heart's pitter-patter is threatening my ability to breathe as his sincerity squelches any doubts I may have still held on to as a souvenir. I don't need a memento. I have the real deal. "Yeah, Jess," I cup his cheek in the same manner as he is mine, "I got you."

He presses his forehead to mine, his heavy breath cascading along my face, joining mine. "I love you, Berklyn. I will die to keep you safe. Do anything to earn the love in your eyes every day of our lives."

How'd I get so lucky? "I love you too." I wrap my arms around him, going for a hug. He steals a kiss as he returns my embrace.

Needy and full of promises, he groans into our kiss as he breathlessly breaks our connection. "I really do need to do a little work. You think you can keep me company while I do it?"

"Can you do it naked?" I'm teasing, but he is delicious eye candy. It's a perk.

He laughs and smacks my butt. "Can you?"

I step to move to the other side of the workbench, giving him room to do his thing. "I'm not the one with the hot bod—"

"Don't finish that sentence." In a second, he wraps around me from behind, turning my chin to lock on his fierce stare. "Your body is a work of art, Berklyn. I don't want to hear you disparage it again. You're growing our babies. There's a miracle," his hand rubs over my belly, "happening right here."

His gaze softens. "Don't confuse the fact that Walker and I work hard on our bodies to stay in top shape for our fights to mean we want or expect you to do the same. The only hard body I want in our bed is mine or Walker's. What you think is *extra* is the sexy flesh I grip as I fuck you, the succulent curves I can't get enough of, and the feminine sway that makes my dick hard."

Ohmyholyjesusonacraker. I melt against his chest, closing my eyes, and take his words to heart. He loves my body. I'm learning to do the same. I'm nearly twelve weeks prego, but it's not all baby. It's fries too. I'm working to be perfectly fine with that. In the meantime, he can grope my extra anytime he wants.

How did I ever think this man didn't care, had a heart of stone? His passion burns my insides, aching to have him fill me again and again. "You sure you can't work naked?"

He chuckles and kisses my nose. "It's unsanitary." He releases me, and I reluctantly sit on a stool facing him. "But," he leans in close, "doesn't mean I'm not going to fuck you when we're done, or that I can't bake naked at home."

My smile nearly hurts it's so big. "I'm getting sweets and sex. Two of my favorite S's. I can't wait."

JESS

I move her to sit beside me as I work, preferring her close, and it's also safer than being in the path of flour and slapping dough as I knead it. My attention slides to her, catching her admiring my arms as I fold and *thwap* the dough on the counter. I may or may not have added a little flex to up the ante. The first few times she flinched, startled and in pain. Her shoulder.

She was shot, dipshit.

It's easy to forget she's still healing when her wound isn't visible and she so rarely complains of discomfort.

"I'm sorry," I apologize and warn her the next few times. Eventually, she waves me off and stops responding to the jolt of the maneuver.

Both she and Walker are doing well with their recoveries. She no longer requires a sling. He's able to get out of bed on his own, though he groans from the effort. The muscles will take a while to heal completely.

They've started physical therapy. It seems to be going well. They go together, but prefer I don't linger to watch.

I drive them as often as my schedule allows. Cher has been understanding and has agreed to hire an additional baker to ensure the day-to-day baking tasks continue to run smoothly, allowing us more flexibility and the ability to focus on more business-type tasks over being tied to the kitchen. Though we love to get our hands dirty, and I don't see that changing anytime soon.

"I learned to bake from my grandmother. My mom's mother." I keep my eyes on the dough I split up into bowls to rise. "I never knew my mom. She died giving birth to me."

"Oh, Jess." Berk's hand lands on my forearm. "I'm so sorry."

I shrug it off, knowing I should miss her, yet I don't have any reference of what it's like to have a mom in my life. "It's okay. It's hard to miss what I never had."

That doesn't seem to ease her concern. I doubt the next part will make it any better.

"I lived with my dad. I was the only kid. I didn't get to see my maternal grandmother often. But she wrote to me. Sent me money, continued to check in over the years. I got to spend time with her over the summer a few times. Until I got older and decided I'd rather hang with my friends than spend time with an old lady."

Berklyn's brows rise in disapproval.

"I know." I feel the same. I'm *still* ashamed of all the years I missed with Gran. "I was an ungrateful punk. Didn't think about much beyond having a good time and being with my friends and girlfriend."

"Girlfriend*s*?" She stresses the plural.

"No. I only ever had the one."

"What was her name?"

"Gina." I cringe at the memory. "She was my first for most things." And not in the way she's assuming.

"How old were you?"

"Fifteen. Thought I was a man. I was big for my age. Physically, I matured quickly. I was thick with muscles like my dad, leaner though. He had a gut, but he was never hurting for female attention. I hated how my lady teachers looked at him. Like he hung the moon. I knew he was an asshole drunk who fucked anything in a skirt."

"No."

I nod, continuing before I lose my way in baring my soul. "I came out of my room one night to get a drink of water, thinking Gina had already left."

"No—"

"Yeah, I found her riding my pops with her tongue down his throat."

"Jess." She's up and pressing into my chest. I forget about the dough, welcoming her embrace.

"Apparently, it wasn't the first time. He got an evil thrill out of telling me how often she left my bed to come to his, where he'd fuck her like a *real* man before sending her back to me for cuddles." I hate the catch in my words.

Her sniffles have me tipping her chin to swipe at her tears. "That was the last night I kissed anyone until you, Berk." My forehead presses to her shoulder. Her grip on my waist tightens.

"I'm so sorry," she whispers, burying her head in my shoulder, wrapping her arms around me, squeezing like she can wipe the memory free.

I wish she could.

"I left that night, stayed with a friend and caught the first bus the next morning for Gran's. I'd been saving the money she sent me over the years. It was enough for bus fare, food, and to live on for a while in case she wasn't there."

"Was she?"

"She met me at the bus depot. I never asked her how she knew. I think one of her friends who still lived in town told her. It was a small town. Everyone knew our business. Not like it was hard to know. I wasn't all that quiet when I left that night. My dad yelling down the road that I wasn't man enough to fuck her, so he did, and he put a baby in her."

Berklyn rears back, her fierce gaze catching mine. "Wait. What? How do you know it wasn't..." Realization dawns. "You didn't have sex with her?"

"Nope. We did lots of other stuff, but I wanted to wait, make it special. I thought she was saving herself for me. Apparently, she'd lost her V-card before we even met. As a bonus, my dad knocked her up. I'm not even sure she didn't plan it."

"That's F-ed up!"

Damn, she's so cute. Rarely cusses, unless Walker and I are fucking her, then her tongue gets looser as she gets hotter.

"What happened to them? Did he get arrested? She was a minor."

I run my fingers through her hair, cupping the back of her head, loving her eyes on me. I want to keep them there, always on me. "I have no idea. I never heard from or saw them again. Avoided trying to hear anything. They're dead to me."

Her watery gaze skates across my face to land on my mouth. She runs her fingers along my bottom lip. "She broke a sacred thing. She broke your trust. Took your innocence and trampled all over it." My girl leans in, pressing her head to my chest. "It feels insufficient. But I'm so sorry, Jess. No one deserves that."

"No. They don't. I never wanted to feel that vulnerable again. That's why I pushed every sexual encounter into a singular box—a sex-only box." I sit on the stool and bring her between my legs. "From the first moment I saw you in the ER, I wanted to kiss you, Berk. I wanted to devour you and be devoured *by* you." I hold her hand, kissing her knuckles. "I'm sorry

I hurt you. I didn't know any other way to be. How to have sex without losing myself, giving a part of my heart, my soul, I didn't have to give."

"It's okay. You've already apologized, and I've already forgiven you, but if you need to hear it every day, I'll tell you." She presses her lips to mine, breathing into our kiss, "I love you, Jess "Mustang" Riley. I promise, my kisses are only yours—and Walker's." She smirks on a teasing eye roll on the Walker part. It's a given. Her acceptance of us gets my dick hard.

"I need to fuck you."

The catch in her breath has me pulling her on my lap and straddling me, teasing the skirt of her flowy dress up her thighs, revealing her white lace panties. She swivels her hips, rubbing her pussy against my ridged cock. "Yes, please."

In one motion, I lift her dress up over her head. Her bra follows. Her tits, full and taut, beg for my mouth. I don't make them wait. Swiveling on the stool, I gently lay her over the clean edge of the cool table. She gasps, arching off, then settles as I tease each breast with my tongue, licking and sucking.

"Jess." She grips my hair, trying to guide my movements.

Only, I don't budge until I'm ready, eating up her cries of frustration with my mouth and letting my fingers do the nipple teasing. "So greedy, baby."

"I ache for you. Don't make me wait."

Reaching between us, I free my cock, pull my t-shirt off, slide her panties to the side, and surge forward, filling her in one long stroke. "Fuck, Berklyn. You feel so good." Always. So. Fucking. Good.

"Yes." She wraps her legs around my waist, her heels stabbing my ass as I flex into her deep and swivel. "Oh, god, right there."

I chuckle into our kiss. "Love when you let me know how good it feels."

"Gooood… So dang good, Jess," she pants. "Please don't stop."

"Not stopping, Berk. Ever." She never needs to worry about that.

I fuck her good, across the worktop where the dough is rising uncovered a few feet away. But I could give a flying fuck. My girl is finally mine, even after revealing my painful past. I can't wait to show her our surprise. The idea has my hips moving faster, pinning her to the table, relishing her cries of ecstasy, and driving home my point by kissing her like there's no tomorrow.

She knows everything and is still smiling up at me, clenching around me.

There's definitely no one else for me besides her.

Forever my girl, the mother of our children—my best friend and me.

How did we get so lucky?

The fates finally came through for me.

I prayed for a miracle I never thought I'd get.

He gave me her, Walker, and two miracle babies growing inside our girl.

She was right, our connection is mind-blowing, life-affirming, life-*altering*.

WALKER

Jess texted they were on their way. We made a mad dash to finish up. Then I shoved everyone out the door, telling them we'll see them for the party on Saturday.

Love, love, lots of love, all the thanks. Now, get the fuck out.

I take the quickest shower of my life, happy I thought of everything we need to bring for our sleepover, including soap, shampoo, conditioner, towels, and most of her toiletries I thought she'd want. Plus, a few scraps of clothes, not that she'll need any. I don't intend on letting her out of our bed for long.

I'm finally feeling better, like I can move my arms and take a full breath without feeling like my chest is going to split open. I'm lucky the bullet didn't hit any vital organs. It nicked a few ribs, grazed a lung and missed my heart. The physical therapy has unquestionably helped. It's hell while I'm doing it, but improvement from before starting and after is vast. It helps that Doc is there doing her own therapy, giving me something sexy to look at as she works through her own challenges and inspires me to work that much harder.

Speaking of hard, I toss on a t-shirt and shorts, sans boxer briefs. I don't plan on being clothed for long. I hope Jess understands, I won't be watching much tonight. I need to be inside our girl with me on top for the first time since the shooting. I love her riding my cock, but I love the driving force behind my thrusts when I'm in control.

I open the door when I spot the headlights pulling into the drive-way. Crossing my arms, I smile that I don't feel any discomfort—or barely any. Okay, maybe a little but not enough to mention or stop me from loving on our woman.

"Walker?" Doc's smile is uncertain as she takes in the front of the house and my position at the open front door.

"Hey, Doc." I motion to the box in her arms. "Whatcha got there?"

"Cinnamon rolls." Her full-blown smile has me stepping forward, offering her my hand as she ascends the stairs with Jess on her heels.

My eyes fly to him. He only shrugs. He knows they're my favorite. Maybe they're Doc's too. "Oh, yeah, did you have one?"

She hands me the box. "I did. Jess had a few bites too." She's proud she tempted him to break his no-sugar rule. "You've been holding out on me."

I take her hand and shove the box in Jess' chest. He's had her to himself long enough. "A guy can't give up all his secrets right away, Doc. We had to work our way up to sharing *the* cinnamon rolls from Sugarplums." Though, I know Jess could make them at home with his eyes closed. She probably knows that now too.

Her laugh frees the little bit of nerves still clinging to my spine. "We've got a surprise for you," I add in case she doesn't already know.

"I've gathered." Her gaze follows Jess as he heads for the kitchen. "Where are we? Whose house is this?" She looks around the empty space like we're trespassing.

Jess comes back, his hands in his pockets, unusually sheepish.

Balls up, man. Don't chicken out now.

He frowns at me before pressing a kiss to Doc's forehead. "Have an open mind," he whispers across her skin.

"Okay?" Her gaze darts between us. "One of you tell me what's going on, please."

I pull her to me, pressing my mouth to hers, forgetting for a moment I can do this anytime I want. She loves me. She loves both of us.

Jess clears his throat, pressing into our sides. "Surprise, remember?"

"Fuck," I hiss as I break our kiss. "Sorry. I missed you is all."

She grips the back of my head, keeping me from pulling way. "I missed you too. How about you tell me what's going on, and maybe I'll suck you both off right here?"

Hard dick alert!

"This house is ours," I blurt before all the blood rushes from my brain to my cock and I lose the ability to talk good. *Fuck.* It's already happening.

"If you like it," Jess adds.

"Yes, of course. If you like it. It's ours."

She's a doe in headlights as she gapes at us, her green eyes bouncing between us. "Ours?"

"Yeah, let us show you." I wave over my head. "That's the living room, eat-in kitchen, den." I point down the hall as we start for the stairs. "Guest bedroom, office, garage, gym, laundry, mudroom are that way."

"Mudroom," she sighs.

Jess sweeps her into his arms as we climb the stairs. She's not moving fast enough as we pick up our pace. "Three rooms here, plus master, another laundry room, game or playroom, and a…" He sets her down just inside a room I've been working on for days.

Her eyes widen, if that's even possible. "It's… What did you guys do?"

I tug on her fingers, guiding her in farther. "It's a nursery. We did it in neutrals since we don't know the sex of our babies."

Jess comes up beside her. "We can change it. We just wanted you to see what it could be—"

"If you like it," I trip over his words. "We're not pressuring—"

"Guys," she cries, tears streaming down her face.

I step into her. "You don't like it."

"We can change—" Jess starts.

"No!" She grips our shirts. "I can't believe you did this."

God, does she hate it?

"It's perfect." She swipes at her tears, pulling away, wandering the room, stopping before the two white cribs, the changing table, dressers, wall art, and a double rocker, big enough for two of us to sit and hold our babies. "I can't believe—"

"Believe it." Jess cups her jaw, and I move in next to him.

"We want you happy and settled before the babies get here. We know with twins it can be tough near the end, so we didn't want to waste a second." I'm praying this pregnancy is as easy as possible. She's a doctor. She'll rock this pregnancy. I pray.

"How did this happen so fast?" She keeps scanning the room, stopping when she spots a poem about twins on the wall, about asking for an angel and receiving two instead. Her tears fall free again. "How?"

"It's Cap's—the house. He'll happily rent it to us till we're sure. Then sell it to us for a steal. He takes care of family, and you're a part of that family now." Jess pulls her into his chest.

More tears.

"If you don't stop crying, I'm going to join you." No joke. My girl is sensitive. I'm feeling her angst, her joy, her gratitude, and it's overwhelming.

She reaches for me, pinning me with her watery gaze. "Maybe a dick or two in my mouth will help?" She smiles.

I bust a gut laughing. She's beautiful and buoyant. A trooper who knows how to lighten the mood and make my dick hard all in one fell swoop.

Jess picks her up. "There's no cock sucking in here."

Smart. I follow. "Yeah, I don't want to get hard every time I walk in our kid's room from the sense memory."

Our girl rolls her eyes and snuggles into Jess' chest, her gaze on me following closely. "I love you both, and as soon as we're done. I want a real tour of this place."

"Deal." I kiss her cheek seconds before Jess sets her down before his—our—massive bed.

The guys and I moved it in today—well, them more than me. Besides the nursery, the couch and a TV in the den, it's the only furniture in the house. If she doesn't want to stay here, then we're stuck with the normal king in my room or the queen at her place.

She takes a second to scan the room. From the gleam in her eyes, she likes what she sees. It's an impressive place. Her smile conveys she can't wait to explore. But before I can tell her she's free to, she says, "Get naked. Now."

BERKLYN

The sight of my guys standing before me in nothing but their heated gazes, dicks hard as stone, bobbing for attention, and their hands fisted at their sides, has me dropping unceremoniously to my knees in antici-pation. They're beautiful in any state of dress, but naked and hard for me is by far my favorite.

Before I can touch them, Jess frowns, grabs a pillow off the bed and stalks to me, kneeling. "I'm not sure how I feel about this with you pregnant."

Jess lifts me so Walker can set the pillow on the floor where my knees were before, and gently sets me down on the soft cushion.

"Better?" I ask Jess, not fully understanding·his concern, other than for my knees.

His furrowed brow doesn't ease. "It's hot, thinking of you choking on my cock, but you're breathing for three. Is it safe?"

Walker runs his finger through my hair as I lean into Jess, giving him a tender kiss for his concern. "The babies get their oxygen from the um-bilical cord. Me gasping a little while pleasing you won't hurt our babies." As long as he's not planning on suddenly choking me out, which is not on our list of turn-ons. They can save choking for the octagon.

He cups my cheek, preventing me from leaning back. "You sure?"

Dang, his protectiveness over me and our littles is such an aphrodi-siac. "I'm sure." I reach between his parted legs and grip his cock as I press my mouth to his, running my tongue along his lips until he opens on a groan. His grip on my face is sure as he takes over, sucking my tongue, nipping at my lips before plunging in for more.

"Fuck, that's hot," Walker groans beside me, standing close enough to poke my eye out if I'm not careful, as he strokes his cock.

Not breaking my kiss with Jess, I knock Walker's hand away and start pumping his impressive length, moaning as I find their tips moist with precum. Our kiss grows hotter, needier, as I grip them firmly enough to make them growl.

My eyes prickle as I consider it's me making them hard, making them heady with desire, taking them closer and closer to the edge, and we've barely even started.

Jess breaks our kiss to undress me as Walker steps back, watching with his cock in hand, his eyes never straying. Once I'm naked, Walker kneels at my side, capturing my mouth as Jess stands in front of me, his cock close enough to lick.

It's hard to concentrate on one while trying to include the other, but I do the best I can—and it's not an issue anyways. My men firmly have the reins. While I'm kissing Walker, I reach for Jess, and he takes over directing me—his hand snaking into my hair moments before he tightens his grip and pulls me away from Walker's mouth, murmuring, "Suck."

The heat in his eyes hardens my nipples. I grip his base, run my tongue over his swollen head, sucking lightly before pulling him into my mouth as far as I can. His groan of approval has me working extra hard to please him. I'm not very experienced. I've done a few blowjobs, but it had been years before that first night we were all together. Walker didn't complain. So maybe—

"Hey." Walker cups my jaw, gently urging me off Jess' velvety hard length. "You don't have to perform for us. If you need to stop, take a breath, rest, you do it. Whatever you need."

"Okay." His tenderness only makes me want to please them more.

I grip Walker's shaft, adjust my position so I can reach them both, urging them closer with me between them, their cocks nearly touching, right in my face. Holding them secure tip to tip, I run my tongue along the underside of one to the other, stopping in the middle to lick both tips before wrapping my lips around the sides of their cock heads as far as I can, my tongue pressed to the bottoms, and suck like they're dream pops.

"Fuck," Jess moans.

"So fucking hot, Doc." Walker caresses my cheek, letting his hand move over my head and down the back, petting.

Jess' grip tightens on the back of my head as I release Walker and grip Jess to take him deep.

I take turns, sucking on one while using my hand on the other, getting them close, then backing off, the entire time envisioning them inside me, fucking me together, filling me to the brim. I'm so wet, my thighs are slick with need.

On a frustrated groan of, "Stop," Walker extricates from my mouth with a pop. "I can't take any more, and I'm not coming anywhere else except inside your pussy."

"Let's move to the bed." Jess lifts me so easily, which is good as my legs are stiff from kneeling.

When he lays me down in the middle of the bed, I sigh on a stretch.

"Sore?" Jess' concerned gaze travels my legs as they start to massage my thighs to my knees and back.

"A little... Stiff."

That gets a growl from Jess as his massage turns to more intimate touches between my legs. Walker hovers over me, braced on his arms to kiss me silly, plundering with his tongue as Jess enters me with his fingers. All I can do is breathe through the onslaught and moan my approval, growing wetter and more desperate by the second.

"I need inside you, Doc." Walker kisses along my jaw to lick and suck each nipple. I try to move to straddle him, but he stops me with a gentle hand on my uninjured shoulder. "Not this time. I'm on top." His honey eyes meet mine. "Okay?"

"You sure?" I don't want him to hurt himself trying too soon.

He nods. "I'm sure." He grips my breasts, squeezing and twisting my nipples, making me flex my pelvis, urging him forward.

JESS

If he's going to fuck her, he needs to get on with it before I push him to the floor, sink into her warm heat and ride her till she's coming on my cock. She's so wet, ready to take us. I'm torn between fucking her, tasting her, drinking her up, or letting him go first.

I must have growled my impatience as Walker catches my eye and nods, tapping my hand as he moves between her thighs. Reluctantly, I slip out of her, sucking her pleasure off my fingers as he lifts her thighs to rest over his and guides his cock to her entrance.

"Walker!" she cries as he slams home on a growl that has my cock twitching against my abdomen, weeping for her, so fucking ready to be right where he is, her walls wrapped around me, squeezing, making me insane.

If she wasn't already pregnant, I'd be working to get her so as soon as she'd let me. Now that we're here, I can't get the idea out of my head. The fates had plans for us. I pray everything goes by the books, no troubles, nothing but sex day and night.

I lean in, taking her mouth, and knead her breasts as he fucks her, making her cry and moan into our kiss, which makes me hotter and needier for her, eating up every gasp, moan, and plea.

"Fuck, Doc!" Walker roars. "You're gonna make me come if you keep gripping me like that." He rubs her clit, his eyes boring into the two of us and my hand on her breast.

I take over rubbing her clit as I suck her nipples.

"Fuck, yes. Just like that." He thrusts, gripping her ankles, her legs spread wide, shoving his cock into her harder and harder.

The whole fucking bed is rocking. Good thing it's extra sturdy besides being extra large.

"Walker! Ohmygod," she mewls, head thrown back, stiffening, crying her release into the sex-laden room of our new home.

"Doc," Walker barks as he comes in short jerky thrusts, making our girl moan and reach for him, pulling him down to lie over her, kissing him tenderly as his ass spasms, pumping his cum inside her.

I move to the side, giving them a moment, the space to be what they both need in their afterglow. Berk grips my hand, keeping me from moving far.

Walker kisses her shoulder before falling to the opposite side, mumbling, "Love you. Love you both," and closing his eyes.

"Love you." Berklyn leans over, kissing his chest before turning to me, her fiery eyes locking on my achingly hard cock. "How do you want me?"

Any way you'll have me is on the tip of my tongue. But I grip her ass and bring her over me, straddling my lap, my hard length hugged by her pussy lips. I grip the back of her neck, bringing her mouth to mine. "Ride my cock," I grouse before locking my mouth and hers, notching my cock to her entrance and thrusting inside.

On a groan, I fight the urge to throw my head back and growl my consent, mindlessly pistoning into her heaven, hard and frenzied, until I fill her so full, it's dripping around my shaft and balls.

Instead, I kiss her harder, deeper, not letting up until she cries out my name with my thumb on her clit, bathing me in her release, coating my cock in a rush of moisture that has me clenching my jaw, holding off, rubbing her sensitized nub until her trembling wanes.

I kiss her shoulder as her head rests on my chest before gently rolling her to her stomach with her knees bent to protect the babies. I run my mouth up her back, rumbling, "Not done, baby, not near done."

She sighs and writhes below me, turning to kiss my arm, planted beside her.

It's such a tender move, I look up, catching Walker's watchful gaze, not missing his hardening cock. I silently question what he wants. He moves closer, pulling her to straddle his lap like she did me with his cock nestled between them.

Kneeling behind her ass between their spread legs, I grip her ass cheeks, running my cock through her moisture before pushing inside. I fit my front to her back, kissing from her shoulder to her neck, whispering, "You think you can make Walk come again?"

She rises up just enough to look at a smirking Walker and me over her shoulder. "I can sure try."

He chuckles, grabbing her breasts. "There's no try, Doc. Jess fucking you on top of me is a sure way to make me come."

I rise to my knees, pulling her with me so her back is resting against my chest as I thrust, gripping her breast and fingering her clit. "Stroke his cock, Berk. See if you can make him come all over himself before I come inside you."

"Fucker," Walker chuckles. His hands traverse her body, urging her to move with me as she takes him in her hand. After a few strokes, he pushes my hand away from her clit. "Hold my cock against your pussy. Let my shaft rub your needy clit."

She does as he says, and he groans at how wet she is against his shaft and how sexy she is, taking me, making love to us. His words turn me on as much as it does the two of them. Walker's a sweet guy, but he loves his dirty talk.

I love how it makes her pussy clench around my cock.

"Oh, God," our girl moans, pushing into my thrust over and over.

I give up trying to kiss her. It's too much. The three of us, living my deepest, darkest fantasies, giving us her heart, her body. It's sensory overload, and I'm about to explode.

I grip one hip and tease the opposite breast, fuck her harder, deeper, lost in their sounds of ecstasy, their pleas to make them come.

"I'm almost there," Walker moans, his eyes never leaving us.

"Fuck. Fuck. Fuck," I groan as my balls tighten and I ride the wave higher and higher.

"I'm…" she cries.

"Fuck!" he moans.

"Yes!" I growl as we come as one, pumping into her, on to her as she squeezes me and comes on my cock, stealing my breath and feeding my soul.

BERKLYN

This place is amazing. Walker passed out after his second round. I was thrumming with exhilaration and dying to see the house.

Every amazing room investigated, Jess plops me on the kitchen island and feeds me sliced ham, cheese, apples, and crackers. A little midnight snack from the stocked fridge.

They went all out, ensuring we had what we needed for a few days, even if I decided I don't want to live here.

But I do. I can't hide my smile.

Jess brushes my cheek, his amused green eyes eating me up as he stands between my legs. "What do you think?" He presses his mouth to mine. One taste of his apple-flavored tongue and I'm desperate for more.

"I love it. When can we move in?" I'm not even thinking about having to sell my place or concerned that we might be moving fast. We're having babies together. The moving-too-fast train has already left the station.

His smile is heartbreakingly sexy. I run my fingers over his lips. "You need to do that more."

He laughs. "What? Smile?"

"Yeah." I press my smile to his. "It looks good on you."

He runs his nose along my neck. "You know what else looks good on me?" His hands caress up my thighs, pushing his t-shirt up to my bare ass, squeezing and kneading.

"What?" I gasp as he thumbs my clit.

"You." He sucks my bottom lip, releasing it with a pop, sending a shiver down my spine. "You look good on me."

A heated kiss and a few quick maneuvers later, we're naked, and he's sliding into me as he pulls me off the counter. I wrap my legs around him, and he grips my ass, holding me up as he fills me deeply and slowly. He's in no hurry. His strength is intoxicating, making me feel petite and girlie, like he could carry me all day through this pregnancy, and it'd be no hardship.

"Fuck, Berks." He sighs into our kiss, and my back hits the fridge as his pace increases. "I'm gonna love you every day for the rest of our lives."

I shudder a gasp, my insides fluttering, squeezing his cock, so close to the edge. Just a little more. "Right there," I moan when he hits the spot.

His chuckle dies when our mouths crash, tangling for position as he fucks me in our new kitchen.

"Walker would love to watch this," I sigh into our kiss.

He chuckles again. "We'll give him a show over breakfast."

"Yes." The thought nearly sends me sailing, making me desperate for him, for Walker, for what they give me together and apart. I'm selfish. I want it all—with them.

"I love you," he whispers, his eyes so full of wonder, mine prick with tears, my emotions rising to meet his.

"I love you, Jess. I can't wait to have forever with you and Walker."

"Forever."

"And ever."

"And ever—hey! Y'all are eating and didn't invite me?" Walker strides in, his hard dick swaying with each step.

My eyes widen. Is he really upset?

He snags an apple, crunching a bite as he comes to stand beside us and plants a kiss on my shoulder. "You think you can take us both, Doc?"

My body trembles at the idea.

"Fuck," Jess growls. "She's squeezing my cock at the idea of it." He pulls me from the fridge, pivoting so my back is to Walker, who grips my hips and kisses my jaw as his cock rims my already occupied opening.

"Breathe for us, Doc."

WANT MORE JESS, WALKER, AND BERKLYN?

Thank you for reading Jess, Walker, and Berklyn's why-chose love story.
Do you want to attend their engagement party, see what the future
holds for them? Then scan the QR code below to access bonus content
for them as well as further reading recommendations.

If you have any questions or concerns,
please feel free to reach out to me: dana@dmckdavis.com

ADDITIONAL BOOKS BY

D.M. DAVIS

UNTIL YOU SERIES

Book 1—*Until You Set Me Free*
Book 2—*Until You Are Mine*
Book 3—*Until You Say I Do*
Book 4—*Until You Believe*
Book 5—*Until You Forgive*
Book 6—*Until You Save Me*

FINDING GRACE SERIES

Book 1—*The Road to Redemption*

BLACK OPS MMA SERIES

Book 1—*No Mercy*
Book 2—*Rowdy*
Book 3—*Captain*
Book 4—*COWBOY*
Book 5—*MUSTANG*

ASHFORD FAMILY SERIES

WILD Duet
Book 1—WILDFLOWER
Book—WILDFIRE

STANDALONES

Warm Me Softly
Doctor Heartbreak
Vegas Storm

www.dmckdavis.com

AUTHOR'S NOTE

This has been a hard year for me with my mom being sick. I'm grateful for your patience, waiting for MUSTANG to come to fruition. It's hard to believe this is the last book in the Black Ops MMA series. I have a feeling a novella or two will be in their future. And don't forget, there will be a second-generation spinoff series with the Black Ops offspring. Join my newsletter to stay in the know. Thank you for loving this series and for taking this journey with me.

Thank you to my husband and kids for their endless support and understanding through this trying time as I figured out how to be more present for my mom in all the ways she's needed, though at times it took me away from them.

Thank you to my author friends, Divas, and my PA Ashley Blank for your support and sticking with me. You feed my soul and lift me up. I am eternally grateful for you.

Thank you to my editors Tamara and Krista for *still* being my editors despite my long dry spell. They make my words shine and my stories coherent.

And to the readers and bloggers, if you're reading this right now, thank you from the bottom of my heart.

Keep reading. I'll keep writing.

I'm blessed to be on this journey. Thank you for taking it with me.
XOXO, Dana

ABOUT THE AUTHOR

D.M. Davis is a Contemporary and New Adult Romance Author.

She is a Texas native, wife, and mother. Her background is Project Management, technical writing, and application development. D.M. has been a lifelong reader and wrote poetry in her early life, but has found her true passion in writing about love and the intricate relationships between men and women.

She writes of broken hearts and second chances, of dreamers looking for more than they have and daring to reach for it.

D.M. believes it is never too late to make a change in your own life, to become the person you always wanted to be, but were afraid you were not worth the effort.

You are worth it. Take a chance on you. You never know what's possible if you don't try. Believe in yourself as you believe in others, and see what life has to offer.

Please visit her website, dmckdavis.com, for more details, and keep in touch by signing up for her newsletter, and joining her on Facebook, Reader Group, Instagram, Twitter, and TikTok.

STALK ME

Visit www.dmckdavis.com for more details about my books.

Keep in touch by signing up for my Newsletter.

Connect on social media:
Facebook: www.facebook.com/dmdavisauthor
Instagram: www.instagram.com/dmdavisauthor
Twitter: twitter.com/dmdavisauthor
Reader's Group: www.facebook.com/groups/dmdavisreadergroup
TikTok: www.tiktok.com/@dmdavisauthor

Follow me:
BookBub: www.bookbub.com/authors/d-m-davis
Goodreads: www.goodreads.com/dmckdavis

Printed in Great Britain
by Amazon

31859144R00152